Death of A Supermodel

A Fashion Avenue Mystery

Christine DeMaio-Rice

Cover art: Flip City Books
with grateful assistance from The Cover Counts

Interior formatting by Heather Adkins
cyberwitchpress.com

CHAPTER 1.

"Why are your fists clenched?" Ruby asked.

Laura barely heard her over the grinding music. Experimental thumpy beats under what sounded like a stack of automobiles being crushed was *du jour* for the New York Fall shows, and though she'd fought it, her sister had demanded a trend, any trend and every trend, not be missed on their first season's show. The noise didn't seem to bother the attendees or the models, but Laura wanted to bore her own ears out with an awl.

"Where's Thomasina?" Laura hissed.

Ruby shrugged. She looked pale and drawn, still gorgeous, of course, with her curly blond locks that contrasted so well with Laura's blondish, brownish, curly-ish mop, but sick—no, hung-over, and she stayed that way the rest of the day, which placed most of the responsibility for the show's last minute details on Laura.

Dymphna Bastille presented herself in the Westchester Shift, a magenta wool crepe dress with a hemline that landed somewhere between public acceptance and private business. Laura took out a hankie and held it under Dymphna's chin. The model responded by rolling her eyes. Laura felt like a rhino looking up at a giraffe.

Dymphna spit her gum into the hankie, adding a little extra lipstick-stained string at the end with a barely discernible smile that was about as good as it got with any of these women. Laura pushed her into the runway's blinding lights.

"Does she seem eighteen to you?" Laura asked, watching the fabric drape over the model's perfect little butt.

Ruby waved off the suggestion. "Mermaid's contract says—"

"What if they're lying?"

"Then this whole industry's in trouble."

Laura tried not to care, but she did. She'd signed a deal with the CFDA: no models under eighteen and none with a BMI under seventeen. She'd already seen the BMI thing slipping through the cracks when Thomasina had shown up for Monday's weigh-in at sixteen and a half, claiming she'd had a stomach virus. The dress swam on her at the fitting, and Laura had spent half the night altering it. The waist shouldn't fit anyone who hadn't had their liver, spleen, and large intestine removed, but it fit Thomasina. She looked like a wire hanger in that dress. Laura looked at the rack. The gown was ready with its eight matte gunmetal buckles at the bodice and hematite beads from waist to ankle. She scanned the rest of the back room. Giraffes flitting, flirting, and preening. Monty had a girl in the chair getting sprayed with some kind of aerosol epoxy. No Thomasina.

Beside her, Rowena Churchill—no relation—shook her arms and cracked her neck, prepping for her walk down the runway like a batter stepping up to the plate. She wore a maxi dress of the same wool crepe as Dymphna's, with a chain mail belt slung low on the hips. The garment would retail at fifteen hundred dollars no matter how hard the Carnegie sisters tried to get the price below a thousand.

"How old are you, Rowena?" Laura asked as she shifted the belt buckle half an inch to the left.

"Eighteen."

"Have you seen Thomasina?"

"No."

Without another word, Rowena hurled herself onto the runway, her walk matching the aggressive lights and music. Laura imagined her eating the audience on the walk to the end of the runway and spitting them out on the way back. She had superstar written all over her. In two seasons, she was going to be unaffordable.

Ruby nudged her with an elbow. "Penelope's here."

Laura scanned the audience, placing the faces she knew. Pierre Sevion, their agent, sat in the front row, looking at who was there instead of the runway. Ivanah Schmiller, wife of their startup investor, sat close by. Her husband, Bob, was nowhere to be seen. Jeremy St. James, Laura's ex-boss, who still brought a shock of heat to her throat, was three rows back, probably having given up his seat in the front row for someone else. His arms were folded, and his brown eyes focused on the clothes in front of him. The tilt of his straight shoulders leaned into Pierre, who was speaking into Jeremy's ear.

"I see her," Laura said.

Penelope Sidewinder, former model, top reviewer for *WWD*, and famed reformer of all things giraffe, sat with a notebook in her lap, pursing her thin beige lips tightly, the rest of her expression obscured by her tiny frameless glasses. A reporter from the *Post* photographed her instead of the model on the runway. She ignored him quite pointedly. The New York *Post* was well beneath her.

She was the architect of the new weight and age requirements for giraffes, bringing the whole industry to heel with a PR campaign funded by her ample savings account and SuperPAC-sized capital from MAAB—Models Against Anorexia and Bulimia—after Juanita June's collapse during a *Vogue* shoot. Laura feared she would look too closely at

5

Dymphna's age and, God forbid, Thomasina's weight, without giving the clothes enough attention to review them.

On the runway, Rowena glanced at the fashion reviewer and swung her head away to look at some other wildly important person in the back row. Heather Dahl presented herself to Ruby for approval, stubbing her cigarette beneath her borrowed Blahnik.

"Do you think she'll review us?" Ruby asked as she popped up Heather's collar before pushing the model onto the runway.

"If she does, we won't have to worry about buying fabric. We'll use the review as collateral on a loan."

The music changed, and the lights went dark. Laura approved another giraffe and sent her out, but her mind was on Ruby, who leaned like a drunk on a Saturday night.

"Are you going to be sick again?" Laura asked as she primped the giraffe with a last name like alphabet soup, checking the buckles on the woman's shoes.

"No," Ruby said, but she coughed a little.

"Please do not puke on the clothes. It's our only sample set."

"I won't," Ruby said, looking as though she really wanted to puke on the Italian calfskin jacket crossing her path.

"What did you eat this morning?"

"A Momlette." A Momlette contained onions, potatoes, egg whites, no salt, white pepper, cream, and a little flour because Mom didn't know how to make anything without flour.

Ruby ran out of the room. She'd spent the previous night at a party while Laura hemmed and pressed. Making contacts, she said. More like making hay. Laura had no idea who Ruby was seeing, but her sister had been scarce enough over the previous weeks to really piss Laura off. Ruby always cited her lack of skills and general fatigue, but the upshot was that fifty-hour weeks were not going to cut it. Fifty-hour weeks in their position weren't going to put the show on the runway. That was work/life balance, also known as luxury living.

Laura glanced into the audience and noticed that Jeremy

was gone. A second later, the salty smell of his skin tingled her nose, and she felt him behind her.

"That was the last group," he whispered. "Where's the Hudson?"

Laura glanced back. The Hudson was still on the rack in all its shimmery last-dress-of-the-show glory.

"You have to keep on these women," he added.

She looked at his coffee eyes and unshaven cheeks, and knew it was no small thing for him to come up to Central Park to see her show. His own show was in three days, and he was undoubtedly working the same hours she'd been. His dark hair was mussed and needed to be cut, not that it wasn't perfect, but it looked the way it usually did the days before a show. She missed those weeks from seasons past, the two of them quietly pinning garments and scoring patterns while the rest of the city slept. She used to bathe in the smell of him, the sound of his voice, the tilt of his neck, until it all changed, and she had demanded an apology from him for counterfeiting his own work. It took two months, and he did, grudgingly stating that though his side business never impacted her directly, it did indirectly because he was using her patterns to lie to people. Then she'd admitted that he was recreating his own work, and that he paid for the patterns with her salary, and they called a truce.

The giraffes brushed by, coming in from the finale like a bus unloading. But there was no finale. Laura scanned the girls. They were all the same, but different in enough small ways that the Hudson wouldn't fit them. Any one of them could have been fit for that goddamn dress, but Ruby had insisted on Thomasina, her new best freaking friend. The lights flickered, and the music changed.

Which girl? She cast an eye on Rowena, and her mind ticked off measurements and shapes. Close. Close enough by a quarter inch in the bust and an irrelevant bicep shape from working out with free-weights.

She grabbed Rowena and pulled her to the back of the line.

"Send them out!" she shouted, and Jeremy herded the girls out for the final walk.

Rowena, understanding what was happening as if she'd read Laura's mind, hurled herself into the dress as if wrestling it into submission. The eight pewter buckles of the bodice clicked as she stepped in. Laura pulled them tight, flattening the model into a tube only slightly wider than a drinking straw.

"Your shoes," Laura said.

Rowena wore a pair of high-heeled elf shoes that added the right note of whimsy to the wool crepe dress. But with the Hudson gown, they were wrong, wrong, wrong. Laura checked under the rack for the hematite platforms that went with the gown, but they weren't there. She glanced at the exit. The last girl was on her way out, and Jeremy looked back, making a *hurry up* motion with his hand.

She checked Rowena's feet. They were a nine-and-a-half anyway. Rowena would never fit into those shoes even if Laura could find them.

"Take them off," Laura said.

Rowena kicked off her shoes, but that made the dress three inches too long, and the gunmetal beads dragged on the floor.

"Shoot," Laura hissed.

"Don't worry," Rowena said and bolted to the exit. She plowed through two rows of sashaying stick-figures like a barrel rolling down a hill, holding up the front of her dress and whipping the fabric around so it took the light and stayed out of the way of her bare feet, which now looked intended. Laura decided Rowena was one giraffe who needed to be a rock star as soon as possible.

Laura was so delighted, she forgot that, as the designers, she and Ruby were supposed to follow the last model out. Jeremy, on the other hand, hadn't forgotten and pushed her onto the runway.

"No!" she said like her life was on the line, because she was suddenly sure that if she went out there, she would die of stage fright.

"I'll pull you right out there, kicking and screaming."

"Ruby's in the bathroom. We have to skip it this time."

"Ruby already had her moment on the runway." He wrapped his arm around her waist and pushed her out.

It was bright, which she knew from the run-throughs. But her eyes hurt as her pupils contracted, and when she looked back, all she could see was Jeremy's pale blue sweater. She turned, trying to shield her eyes with her hand, but the lights were everywhere. She didn't dare look at the faces in the front row—buyers, critics, and ladies rich enough to use Fashion Week as a shopping spree. Laura nodded and wondered if they were disappointed at what they saw. Mousy little her.

At the same time, she felt relief. The show was done. All she had to do was bask in the warm glow of it and clean up the mess. It was over, and all the fighting, worrying, and scraping for every last yard of fabric was done. This was her moment, not to absorb admiration, but to relax before the impending crisis of the fabric orders.

But even the happy moment and grinding music weren't enough to cover the scream from the back room.

That put a damper on things. The music continued because it was on a loop, but the murmuring and some sympathy screaming went on even as Laura hightailed it to the back room. What had been a hive of activity four minutes before was an empty space in a tent with the litter of cigarette butts, seven-hundred-dollar shoes, and wooden hangers all over the floor.

Ruby stood in the middle of the space with her feet together and her hands balled into fists, screaming.

"What?" Laura barked, feeling the presence of models, businesspeople, and whoever else barreling into her.

Ruby pointed to the back of the back, where the bathrooms were. Laura bolted past rows of empty racks and piles of clothes she'd spent months working on. The crowd followed like rats scurrying behind a guy with a flute.

Ruby didn't join them; she seemingly had already seen enough of whatever there was to see back there and felt no need to see it again. Fine. Laura would kill the spider, trap the rat, or whatever had to be done, and the whole incident would be the talk of the town. Maybe it would overshadow Dymphna Bastille's age. Or lack of it.

The bathrooms were the most luxurious port-a-potties money could buy. They were trucked in, attached to the tents, and cleaned four times a day, which Laura knew because the fee was a line item on her books. The white tiles and granite sinks were spotless but for a sprinkling of face powder and a streak of purple eye shadow on the mirror.

As she turned her head, she saw that Ruby's shrieking wasn't over a rat or a spider, but over her new best friend, the model with the body to launch a thousand high-end lines.

Thomasina Wente was sprawled on the floor in a pool of foul-smelling vomit.

CHAPTER 2.

Not again was the first thing that went through her mind. *Please, God, if you're out there at all, not again. Not another body. Not another series of interviews at the precinct. Not this again.*

She picked up a hematite platform at her feet, then dropped it. The cops would want it exactly where it was.

"Overdose," came a voice from behind her. Rowena had gotten in the door first, despite the fact that she wore a gown meant for an Oscar acceptance.

"Out!" Laura cried. "Unless you're a paramedic. Out, out, out!"

"Pee!" Rowena shoved herself and the gown into the stall next to Thomasina and clicked the door.

Laura had no idea whether Thomasina was dead or not and wasn't qualified to make that determination. She poked her cellphone and realized her hands were shaking. "I can't dial," she said.

"Ruby was calling," Rowena said.

Laura put away her phone and rubbed her eyes. She heard the toilet flush, and the door to the stall door opened with a clack. Rowena gathered her skirts and stepped out. She leaned over Thomasina. "This is bad."

"Just wait for the paramedics," Laura said. "Trust me. The police want everything where it is. If you spit when you talk, you'll mess up their scene."

Rowena stepped back, holding the skirt of her gown above the floor, and leaned against the back wall, still as an oak.

"Do you think she's dead?" Laura asked.

Rowena shrugged.

Apparently, Thomasina was as popular with the other giraffes as she was with Laura. "When the cops start asking questions, you shouldn't be so flip about it."

Rowena cracked her gum, and Laura resisted the urge to hold a hankie under her chin. "I'm not flip."

Laura's conversations with Rowena usually warranted little more than yes and no answers, or short statements about one's ability to walk in a tight skirt. She never spent much time talking to giraffes; she didn't have the space in her schedule. Ruby was the one who extracted gossip and news. Ruby was the one who'd brought Thomasina back into the fold after the model knocked her off a runway. Ruby not only tolerated, but embraced Thomasina's haughty affectation.

And Ruby was the one who tapped on the door. "Can I come in?"

"No," Rowena snapped.

Laura felt trapped in the tiny room with a dead giraffe and a rock star model wearing a matte metallic ball gown. "Do you have a show after this?" Laura asked.

"Yes."

"You ever string more than four words together?"

Rowena cracked her gum. "Sometimes."

Laura tried not to stare too hard at Thomasina. Lying down, her arms and legs looked even more like chicken bones. Laura tried to determine if Thomasina was breathing by watching her chest. There was no movement that she could detect.

"Lancaster's tomorrow?" Rowena asked.

There was a huge rooftop shoot at the Lancaster Glass building with Chase Charmain at the crack of dawn, before the tent shows started at ten o'clock. Thomasina had bent over backward to get it into her schedule for Ruby. Damn. The photos had a chance to get into *Black Book*, and there was her model, sprawled on the bathroom floor like a fistful of jackstraws. Getting a last minute replacement during fashion week who could fit into clothes fit specifically for Thomasina would be impossible. Except that she was stuck in the bathroom with someone who might be just the one.

"Maybe you can do it?" Laura asked timidly.

"I'll be tired."

"Yeah, never mind."

They paused. Rowena looked in the mirror, and Laura stared into the middle distance, thinking of every model she knew or had known. Ruby might be able to do it. She was certainly gorgeous enough, if three inches shorter than Thomasina, but she was loath to ask her sister to cross from designing into modeling again. She simply didn't have the temperament.

Rowena piped up. "If I skip a party tonight, I guess I can make it."

"Are you sure?"

Rowena shrugged, staring at Laura with heavy brown eyes, as if she meant to squeeze eight hours of sleep into three because she was that powerful and her dreams were that big.

"Call is at six thirty," Laura said, "and if Thomasina makes it, you'll be getting up for nothing."

"Good."

They were interrupted by a perfunctory knock, followed by the door opening and a parade of competent people pushing through the entry.

"Carnegie," Detective Cangemi said, "shoulda known."

Paramedics descended on Thomasina. From their reaction,

Laura surmised that the woman still had life in her as they pressed, pushed, and shouted for things.

Cangemi gently led Rowena and Laura out of the room.

"What were you thinking?" Cangemi asked after Laura described what had happened and how she'd contaminated the scene. "Of all people to know better." He'd moved everyone who had seen the body to a corner of the back room. He'd rolled full garment racks around an area with two folding chairs, so they couldn't be seen, but there was no sound protection, and they spoke quietly. The tent would be closed down for the rest of the day, which would disrupt just about everyone but the cops.

"It was a borrowed shoe, and I was just thinking I had to return it or I was going to have to pay for it."

"You don't buy your own shoes?"

She rolled her eyes. "We rent them. They're like eight hundred dollars a pair."

"I thought you were a big, successful designer now."

"I don't even know how I'm paying my rent next month."

"Did you touch anything else?"

"I don't think so."

"How have you been?"

Laura sighed. She hadn't seen him since a week after she'd discovered André, Jeremy's VP of sales, had killed his backer, Gracie Pomerantz, over a counterfeiting ring. They had a follow-up lunch to tie up some loose ends, and she agreed never to try to chase killers all over town again. He'd solved the case, and she'd only succeeded in nearly getting herself killed.

"In the last six months or since Thomasina dropped dead in a luxury port-a-potty?"

"We don't know if she's dead yet," he said.

"You're a monumental hairsplitter."

"I think the last time I saw Thomasina Wente was on a runway with her elbow in your sister's ribs. How did she end up doing your show?"

Such a straightforward question, yet fraught with side

meanings. *What happened that killed her at your show? How pissed were you? Tell me a good story because I'm looking for the cracks in it.*

"Ruby doesn't like conflict. So when Thomasina went down the runway crying, and then apologized in like three magazines and took out that full-page ad in *Women's Wear*, Ruby finally picked up the phone for her. Then they became best friends, like…" Laura crossed her index and middle fingers and held them up. "And then she started showing up at the office late at night to pick Ruby up for whatever, and trying on the clothes, so then she became like, my sister's muse or something."

"How do you feel about her?" he asked.

"In general, I don't trust people who didn't make their money honestly. But Ruby likes her, so she kind of grew on me. And she's a professional, even when she's bitchy. And she knows her way around a garment. A lot of these girls act like we're imposing on them. She never did."

Cangemi made a note. She leaned forward to see what he was writing, and he glanced up at her without moving the book because he must have known she couldn't read it. Either the words were in shorthand or his handwriting was so bad it was unreadable.

"How is it going with the blond guy?" he asked. "I let him interview me. Didn't like it."

Stu had pitched the tale of Gracie Pomerantz's murder to the *New Yorker* and, much to his surprise, had been offered a feature. He'd just been happy to get in the room; getting paid to write the article was a dream come true. Then the interviews started. Every conversation with him became an interrogation. Every question was loaded. He was much more fun when he was a bike messenger.

"It's fine," she said, because Stu was none of his business.

"And the company? How is it going?"

He seemed genuinely interested and warm, and Laura needed a friend after the show, the stress of prepping for it, then the episode with Thomasina. "We got a backer through our agent, Pierre Sevion, and that was okay, but it was only enough to pay for everything up to the show, which is today. After that, there was supposed to be matching backing from somewhere. I don't know where, Pierre wouldn't say. But if we get favorable reviews from a major, or any kind of celebrity placement, which is when they wear our stuff to an event and mention it, we get some vague amount of matching dollars that might, and I'm saying *might*, cover our production. Except in order to get the review and the placement, we had to go all out whole hog on the show, and that means the fabric is super expensive, and the matching backing may not cover it. And here's the other thing. Without that matching money, we have to crawl back to the initial investor, Bob Schmiller, whose wife is Ivanah Schmiller, who according to Ruby, has been telling everyone she wants more say in the line."

"Ivanah Schmiller, the interior designer?"

"Decorator. She's a decorator. And yes. If you like vomiting animal skin prints on crushed velvet and chrome, she's an interior decorator. Can you imagine what she'd do to my line? We're built on simplicity and solid workmanship, and she's about rhinestone zipper pulls. So here we are, and Penelope Sidewinder, the most important reviewer in the land, is in the front row, looking at a bunch of models from the dregs of the headshot book who can't be a day over fourteen. Nice, right? Please, shoot me in the face."

He smirked. "How many hours a week you put in here?"

"That's the same thing you asked me the first time we met."

"You look even more tired."

"It's worth it. Having my own line is worth every bit of it." She was determined to believe that, even though her problems hadn't ended, but begun with, Sartorial Sandwich. And it wasn't just her line, but Ruby's, too. Even if she was putting in fewer hours, Laura had to admit she was of equal value. The time spent clubbing and glad-handing might look like hell on a financial spreadsheet, but the general goodwill and chit-chatty publicity had created enough buzz to earn them a two-thirds full tent and a little discount with Mermaid, the modeling agency.

"Maybe you can tell me something." He leaned forward. "What's this all about, these shows? This stuff, it's all summery-looking, and we're headed into the coldest part of the year. Who's buying?"

"Well, if you want something in the stores in March, you have to have it in the warehouse in mid-February. And if you want it in the warehouse in mid-February, you need a month to pack and ship it, so you have to start making it in early December, in which case you need to..." She paused, counting on her fingers as she was wont to do whenever she had to wrap her mind around the calendar. "... order fabric in something like October because it has to be spun and dyed and shipped and so... what is it now?"

"Second week of September."

"Right. So now is when everyone shows the stores what they're going to make. We do one of everything and present it at a show, and then the buyers come to the showroom and look at it and negotiate quantities and prices. Then we make stuff to send to the stores, and you do that whole thing I just did, but frontwards."

"Sounds like a great way to go nuts."

"I'm sure your job is easier." As usual when talking to him, she felt as though she had revealed everything, and he'd revealed nothing. "How have you been?"

He lifted his pant leg to show her his socks. The elastic clung to his leg. The last time they'd met, one sock drooped at the top edge.

"Your girlfriend stopped rolling them into balls, I see," she said.

"She just stopped doing my laundry."

"Ah, sorry. Wasn't over the management of the socks, was it?"

"She says if I'm gonna answer the phone at two in the morning, I can do my own chores."

"I want to ask you something else, but it's really personal."

He grinned. "This should be interesting."

"Do you have a first name?"

Cangemi looked as though he was about to answer when a woman in head-to-toe Italian black tailoring strode up in bootie black heels and pushed a rack out of the way—Roquelle Rik, owner of Mermaid Modeling. She had turned straightforward hostility into her own personal brand, and it sold like hotcakes. Her attention was a wall of will, making Laura shift in her seat.

"What happened to Thomasina," Roquelle said as if stating a fact. Laura had learned the woman never spoke in a question, even when she asked one.

Cangemi broke in to ask, "Who are you?"

"All these models are mine. I'm responsible for them. So—" She let the sentence hang off a cliff as if that was exactly where it belonged.

"So?" Cangemi seemed amused, which would invariably make Roquelle boil.

"So if someone hurt my assets, they've run counter to my interests. I'm going to need to know who they are. I have a legal team." She turned to Laura. "What was happening here? What were the girls taking?"

"What do you mean *taking?*"

Roquelle snapped open a green microfiber cloth with an embroidered X in the corner, took off her glasses, and wiped them. "You were watching them for drugs and alcohol, or not."

"I'm not a babysitter," Laura said.

The other thing Roquelle was known for was fixing things. When Thomasina had knocked Ruby over on Friday, Roquelle was the one who got the full-page apology in *WWD* on Tuesday, and the interviews with the *Today* show. She also arranged for the German heiress and the designer from Hell's Kitchen to meet at Grotto, where they could be photographed, leaving not a whit of hostility in the public imagination.

Cangemi moved to stand between the women and indicated Laura's seat. "Why don't you sit down?"

"I don't need to sit," Roquelle said. "I have a life to clean up. I have a family to call. Tell me what I'm telling them."

"She doesn't have any family," Laura said, then was immediately cowed by Roquelle's laser gaze.

"I'm glad you know her so well," Roquelle said before turning back to Cangemi. "So."

"So. I'm just a detective. You might want to talk to our media liaison."

"Oh, that's just rich." She spun on her heel and took two steps toward the exit.

Cangemi, who did not like to be outdone in anything, called out, "Excuse me, ma'am?"

Roquelle turned.

"Why don't you sit down so I can ask you a few questions?"

Thus, Laura was dismissed.

September was unseasonably seasonable. Almost a cliché of itself. Snappy breezes that were just mild enough to avoid being called a wind slipped under the leafy drifts that spotted the sidewalks, lifting them like souls carried to heaven.

The thought brought Laura to Thomasina, the big bummer ending at the end of the show. Or was it? Gracie Pomerantz's murder hadn't hurt Jeremy one bit, once he was exonerated, of course. Maybe Thomasina's collapse could be turned into a positive. It would put the name of the brand in front of everyone for a while. And when she got better, the name would be out in front again. And who better to have something horrible happen to them than the awful heiress giraffe, Thomasina Wente?

By the time Laura got to 38th Street, she'd convinced herself the incident was an incredible stroke of luck. The show was done. The clothes looked good. Everyone had behaved, and the room was three-quarters full, not bad for the single worst slot of the week in the smallest tent. It was also not bad for two newbies who were running out of their backing money too fast even to know where it was getting spent. All they had to do was sell to the buyers, and they were set.

Jeremy had been almost too good to be true, and Laura

spent nights looking at the ceiling and wondering why. When the cutting table and cabinets had grown out of the dining room of her house in Bay Ridge, he offered the closed counterfeit floor of his 40th Street factory, with the machines right there. When they needed a showroom space, they started looking for a sales agent to take them on. But he waved off the idea and gave them a corner in his own showroom, constructing an entryway so there would be no confusion from buyers.

All of that created more confusion for Laura. Learning that he had been counterfeiting his own line and using her patterns to do it had shut something off in her. As if he sensed that, he pursued her friendship almost constantly. When she needed something, someone in the industry heard about it and relayed it to him like one of a swarm of carrier pigeons, and he would call with the exact solution. At first, she'd wanted nothing to do with him or anything he had to offer, but Ruby was not one to reject the straightest point between where she was and where she wanted to be. So they had the factory floor at 1970s rent, a tiny, but adequate showroom space at a terrific address, and they had Yoni, Jeremy's production genius, part time, which was the last gift she was accepting. That was it. Really it.

Once Gracie's killer had been put away and Jeremy no longer had a backer with a control problem, he set his heart on complete world domination. Without Gracie to keep the size of the business small so she could hold Jeremy down to her level, he set about exploding it into a lifestyle brand, complete with overseas production and package deals from factories. He found pent-up demand for his clothes, and the glamorous murder that had put the spotlight on him hadn't hurt either. Jeremy carefully orchestrated the company's wildfire growth, slowing it by missing the Winter shows in order to pull the whole operation together. His Spring show coming up on Friday was highly anticipated, possibly overblown, and for the first time in four years, in the second-best time slot, in the afternoon. He'd lost the coveted evening spot to Barry Tilden, a travesty he shrugged off. He had bigger steaks to grill.

There were too many steaks, and she was right next door. She needed money, so she found herself picking up the odd patternmaking job from him to keep the rent checks flowing. Her fee was obscenely high, and he paid without complaint, which made it very hard for her to stay mad at him.

Working for him and prepping for her own show had been crippling, but all she had to do was hold it together until the next season needed to be designed. Two weeks of eight-hour days was going to feel like a month on the beach to her.

She crossed 49th in her reverie, where she felt the weight of the world lifting off her shoulders. She felt a pressure on her leg, then a little burning sensation. She caught sight of something very large and very close out of the corner of her eye. A bicycle messenger turned his front wheel away from her abraded calf, and the moment she registered her surprise and gasped, he apologized and sped away.

"Well, *go to hell!*" she shouted.

Reverie broken. Bike messengers reminded her of Stu, which reminded her that her life was turning into a series of missed opportunities at the tender age of twenty-five. She thought about him just about constantly, and when she wasn't, she was working, which was most of the time.

Which had been the problem.

Exiting the subway, she realized her ringer had been off. She had eight messages: five from Corky, their salesperson, two from Ruby, and one from Yoni, who had gone on emergency medical leave when her secret pregnancy went bad and she was put on bed rest.

Laura returned Yoni's call as she walked. "You rang?"

"I need my projections."

"Yoni, you're just bored. You'll get them after the buy date."

"Let me tell you something, little girl." She sounded terse, which meant she cared, but she was still bored. Laura took the attitude because the hourly rate for a production person was the best she'd ever get. "You talk like you never looked at a calendar before. The wool crepe you insisted on for the Upstate group is spun in China, shipped to a mill in Italy, and finished and dyed in North Carolina. You can hand carry it yourself, and it would still take months, especially if we don't order. If we don't order it early, the mills will not make the opening to do the work. That means even if we order a hundred or a hundred thousand yards, they're going to have other customers' fabrics on the machines, and they have no *time* to put you in. I have to make reservations for *time* in three places, and to do that accurately, I need to know if they're going to spend a week on a thousand yards or a day on a hundred. Do you understand?"

"How can we order fabric if the buyers don't have to put in POs for another month?"

"Projections, Laura. Wake up. I need *projections* by Friday. And by the way, the Chinese won't spin any order less than five hundred yards or they charge you an extra twenty percent. I simply cannot have this conversation anymore." Yoni hung up.

Laura made a mental note to never get pregnant, then remembered Yoni was always like that.

She started to listen to the first of Corky's messages, then stopped. Laura hadn't wanted to hire a sales guy, since André, Jeremy's head of sales, had been a counterfeiter and a killer, and even without all that, he was a real asshole even on a good day. But Corky couldn't have been more different. She and Ruby had known him from Parsons, where he majored in merchandizing and was known to regale the student crowd at Valerie's with tales of his cat. Ruby had kept in contact with him and pulled him up from the gutter of the last financial meltdown to offer him the crappy job at Sartorial. He'd taken it, and despite their ridiculously small showroom and a staff that could fit around a dinner table, he showed up every day as though he were the head of sales at Donna Karan.

When Laura walked into the tiny back hallway that led to their showroom, she saw that Corky had put out a narrow Danish modern table with flowers and candy. A scented candle held onto its flame for dear life. André had usually just put out a box of donuts and a travel box of Starbucks, grudgingly at that.

Corky was on the phone, which was his job, but his voice was loud, and she could hear him cackling down the hall.

"Oh, honey, he was on *fire*. That man. And he had the whole inaccessible thing going on."

She knew he was talking about Jeremy. Corky made no secret of his crush. She could sympathize with the sentiment, but not the lack of secrecy. Between Corky's declarations of the obvious, she heard the bubbling of the steamer. They could only afford to make one sample of each style, so the clothes the giraffes had worn, stepped on, and stretched out were also their showroom samples, and when she entered the showroom, he was steaming out the wool crepe that was giving Yoni such a heart attack.

The rest of the room, which was no bigger than a Manhattan studio apartment, was set up with a big table in the middle, a wire grid to hang garments on one wall, cabinets on another, and two other walls built so quickly into Jeremy's showroom, they were afraid to hang anything on them. Corky had hung prepped samples on the grid. Everything looked wrong. He had a big drapey shirt with the wide pleated pants— red with red, which was impossible to match in production. He'd co-opted the accessories from the show and incorporated them into his presentation, which promised more than the sisters of Sartorial Sandwich could deliver.

Corky spotted Laura and flapped his hands around his face. "It's an *oven* in here." Then, into the phone, "I'll see you later, honey. Text me your lunch order." He hung up and turned back to Laura. "I have Barneys Co-op coming in fifteen minutes, and I swear if I put a piece of raw chicken on the table, it'll be cooked by the time they get here." He pulled off his corduroy jacket and slung it over a chair, fanning himself with his hands. "How's the German bitch?"

"I think she just overdosed." She reordered the red with the brown and put the steeply priced leather jacket on its own rack.

Corky made a *pfft* sound and flung his hand at her. He put the Westchester dress with the black Rockland cape. "She didn't use when she was working. I saw her get out of the cab before the show. She was walking straight in seven-inch heels."

"Maybe she puked one too many times and her body just had enough."

Corky shrugged. "Where's Ruby?" Ruby and he had rekindled their best buddy friendship, as happened with Ruby all the time.

"She'll get here when she's done."

"Is she okay? She was sick this morning. Is she pregnant?"

"She is *not* pregnant."

"Should we cancel our appointments?"

Laura's first assumption was that Corky wanted Ruby around for another gossip session, but then she realized he wanted her sister around to charm the buyers and be the face of the company. Because Ruby could say words like *fabulous* and *gorgeous* and *Oh that is too cute!* without irony, while Laura not only found that type of fakery sickening, she was unable to hide how sick it made her.

"She just had to finish up with the cops."

A voice piped in from behind Laura. It was a squeal or a squeak or a broken car alarm, and her name was Debbie Hayworth. "Laura Carnegie! I can't believe it!"

Laura smiled and swallowed hard. Debbie had gone to Parsons with her and Ruby, and of course, Ruby had stolen Debbie's boyfriend.

"I knew you guys would make it!" Two girls with perfect hair and big black binders followed Debbie. The room was suddenly a thousand degrees hot. Debbie air-kissed Corky. "Oh, my God, and you, too! It's just like old times."

"You look great." Laura felt herself failing at the whole *fabulous* thing. "You're here with Barneys, I guess?"

"The Co-op. I do all the young designer buys, and I'm *so happy* I can support you and Ruby. It's like my dream to help people I went to school with, the ones I liked. But tell me, where did you come up with that name? I mean, the girls had to look it up in the *dictionary*." She slid into a chair, and the assistants followed suit, popping open their binders like law students on the first day of class.

"A friend of mine came up with 'sartorial.' We figured if we paired it with 'sandwich,' it would sound like highbrow and lowbrow."

"Yeah." Debbie looked at the Binder Girl to her left and wrinkled her nose. "That's so relatable. Isn't that what you thought, Tammy?"

"Not really?" Left Binder Girl answered.

Laura smiled. "Well, I guess you came to see the line?"

Corky planned to sell the handfeel, then the merchandizing, and the fit would be remembered from the show. He had done the presentation for Laura once and drawn her into the story of the fabrics and how they were combined. He was good, but only with a buyer who wanted to be told a story.

"Oh, my God, what happened at the end of the show?" Debbie squeaked.

Laura and Corky glanced at each other. They had no strategy for dealing with this. Stupid. They couldn't lie because whatever the truth was, it would be in the papers tomorrow. They couldn't change the subject. Too transparent. They couldn't minimize it because the whole thing had been so dramatic in the moment.

Laura had no idea what her sales guy wanted to do, but she decided the best strategy was to use it to her advantage. "Thomasina Wente was sprawled all over the bathroom floor."

"Oh. My. God. Did she overdose?"

"It is so *hot* in here," Corky said. "I'm *shvitzing*." He tugged at the neck of his shirt.

"We don't know what happened," Laura said, hewing to the truth, but implying that inconveniences were possible. "The worst was being stuck in the bathroom with Rowena, one-word-answer girl."

Corky draped the Westchester dress over the table.

"Check out the handfeel on this."

Debbie manhandled the dress, checking the seams and finishings. "Where's Ruby?"

When Laura had seen Debbie enter, she'd been glad Ruby was out of the office. Six years ago, during the final runway show before graduation, Debbie had made a fatal mistake. She'd left her boyfriend alone with Ruby for a few minutes too long.

The story was more complicated than that, but not by much. Their Parsons final thesis was a runway show they were expected to prepare over the course of the entire year. They each had a committee headed by a major designer, plus some faculty. Ruby had Marc Jacobs, and Laura had Barry Tilden. It seemed as though the committee built late changes into their curriculum to make sure every student could potentially be late. Their mentors had changed everything at the last minute, almost out of spite. In the class of thirty, no one, except for Ruby, had slept the night before the runway show. They had been up basting, trimming, and setting in zippers. Most had gotten by in school by drawing beautifully and sewing like ham-fisted butchers. But fourth year required they stitch every seam personally, and if the sewing machine left little marks in your satin taffeta, well, you'd better figure out a way to fix that because the judges weren't just looking at what they could see on the runway; they were looking at your stitch counts, too.

Laura had approached fourth year with relief because she drew like a monkey, but could sketch with scissors and a sewing machine. She'd already been temping for Jeremy for a year at that point, and as gay as she and everyone thought he was, she had that rush of endorphins every time he was around. That year, she felt like a star, even if she didn't have time to look at a boy, go clubbing, or initiate a drinking habit like everyone else. Had she had time for that stuff, she might have been able to stop what happened with Debbie's boyfriend, Darren.

Ruby's strategy, which was pure genius, was to avoid sewing and patternmaking entirely. First, she presented a normal jacket/pant-suiting thing for her final, drawn as if it belonged in an art gallery, until her committee was in mid-salivation with each draft. Laura wondered how her sister was going to produce the group and was about to tell Ruby that if she expected her sister to jump in at the last minute and save her, she had some hard realities to face. Because Laura had done it for her before, and to such an extent that no one had any idea that Ruby still hadn't sewn a damn thing but her finger her entire college career.

The suiting group had been a ruse. On the last day to present the finals, Ruby declared that she hated it, and presented a group of heavy-gauge sweaters with leggings that a six-year-old could sew from a Butterick pattern. She had enough yarn interest and trimmings to make it fly, and the entire group was approved unanimously by the committee on account of her general genius.

Laura had just been relieved she wouldn't have to do her sister's project as well as her own. The cunning of the final had become apparent as the weeks passed. Ruby rented a used flatbed hand machine and stuck it in the middle of their room. She knitted her heart out, and when fitting time came, her committee made a few suggestions. They didn't know how to correct a sweater fit any more, because sweaters had been made in China and Italy for the past thirty years. There was a black hole in their expertise, and they didn't want to admit it. So she got a pass on mistakes that would never have been overlooked on a jacket.

She ended up outside the Jacob Javits Convention Center on show night, while everyone else was in the back room fixing pockets and buttons. Her sweaters were folded neatly into bags and ready to go, and she could step outside for a smoke. And who was out there too? Debbie's little hipster boyfriend, Darren, fully annoyed with his girlfriend for spending sixteen hours a day hunched over a sewing machine.

The sweaters were a hit. Laura's origami dresses were ridiculous, and the model unfolded one wrong when she did her turn, exposing her bare bottom all over the runway. No one remembered a damn thing about Debbie's pieces, not because of the scene that followed, but because she was never much of a designer. Her boyfriend made the show, but had lipstick all over his white T-shirt. The shade matched Ruby's, so there was no hiding it, even to avoid a drunken, spitting-mad blowout at Club Winnebago, and promises of death, destruction, and decimation at some undefined point in the future.

After graduation, Debbie worked as an assistant designer at Express for fifteen minutes before they shipped her out to Columbus, Ohio, to join the merchandising team, and then everyone lost track of her, which for Ruby was a big mistake. Laura could see from a mile away that Debbie Hayworth wanted satisfaction, and the sooner she got it, the better for everyone.

"She's cleaning up," Laura said. "There were some loose ends back at the tents."

Debbie gave a smile that bared her teeth and wrinkled her nose.

Laura felt as though she were treading water. "Everything will be made in New York. We have some of the best sewers in town on our floor. We're putting a tag in. We think it will be a selling point to the customer."

"Did you make this sample?" Debbie asked.

"That one's mine, yeah."

"That's why it looks perfect. Which it better because it's going to retail for... what now?" She glared at Left Binder Girl, who had the SartSand look book open in front of her.

Right Binder Girl banged on a calculator. "Twelve hundred eighty."

"Did Ruby make any of the samples?"

"No," Laura said, revealing a sore point.

Debbie leaned forward as if telling a secret. "I remember her in third year tailoring."

"Mrs. Dunnegan's class. She was tough."

"Not for *you*, but for the rest of us. And Ruby—"

"Total personality clash. I had the same thing with Eberto

Saffina."

Corky cleared his throat. "Let's not be magpies now, ladies. Did you see this leather bomber? You have to feel this. The fur collar is faux, but you can't even tell."

Debbie ignored him. "Remember the time she made Ruby wear her own pants for the whole class? And she couldn't sit still for five minutes because the crotch was sewn so bad? And she said, at the end…"

Laura chimed in, and they said together, "You don't want your pants to be the thing chafing you on a Saturday night."

They both laughed. Binder Girls chuckled as much as they needed to, and Corky put a smile on his face, but Laura caught him shooting her a look and tapping his watch. Usually, having someone stay late so that they crossed with another buying team was a good idea. It made the line seem popular, and any exchange of stories and gossip in the showroom made it appear to be an industry hub. But the space was so small that one more person would highlight the poverty of the brand.

Debbie, however, seemed in no mood to rush. "Her tailoring final looked good, though," she said, all raised eyebrows and newsy grins. "The jacket? I had no idea she could pull it off."

Laura knew she was being baited, and worse, baited into trash-talking Ruby. If she lied, this woman who understood their past would know it. And if she told the truth using the wrong tone of voice, she would be as good as tossing Ruby under a bus and ruining her sister's reputation. She was not good at that kind of nuance. "I admit I set in the sleeves," Laura said.

Debbie pursed her lips and narrowed her eyes into slits.

"Look, what am I?" Laura asked. "Heartless? You should have seen what she was doing. I mean, she had somehow made a two-inch pleat at the hem. Two inches! Most people forget to put it in, but not Ruby! Ruby triples the depth because she remembered to put it there at all. Then she wants to say it was a design detail, and I'm like, there's no way you can sell that."

Debbie slapped her hand on the table, unable to contain

her amusement, but the comment wasn't meant to be amusing. It was meant to show her sister being diligent and clever.

Laura continued with utmost seriousness, thinking to wipe the smirk off the woman's face. "So seriously, it's let her fail or help her. Come on now. It was just a pleat. How could I have her in crit telling Marc Jacobs she added a two-inch pleat to the bottom of the lining as a design detail? You would have done the same."

"Oh, honey. Everyone knew you did it. And not just the sleeve sets and lining, okay? Including Marc. Trust me."

Laura had to stop before she told Debbie what really happened, which was that she had given Ruby her jacket and remade another from scratch, handing it in two hours late. Laura had taken a beating on her grade, but slept well that night. "Let's talk about the line. Show them the leather bomber, Corks. You're not here just to make the room prettier."

"Let me see that," Debbie said, reaching for the sleeve. "This fur is gorgeous. I can't believe it's fake. You know we can't even sell real fur anymore." She turned to Laura. "You need a hangtag that says something like, 'premium man-made fur,' or something like that, or no one's going to believe it. I love it. Do it. Jess, write that down."

Binder Girl wrote furiously. In Laura's estimation, that was good. Very good. Until her phone beeped.

Ruby texted: *They're bringing me to the precinct. Come get me!*

Laura tilted her screen so no one could see it, but when she looked up, Debbie smiled like a cat over a wounded bird. Laura smiled back like the worst faker in the tri-state area.

It took another half an hour to get rid of Debbie, and another ten minutes to convince Corky to start the next meeting without her because she was off to pick up the magical Ruby, who was suddenly too traumatized to get to 38th Street by herself.

In the hall, she ran into their agent, Pierre Sevion. He seemed to be on his way to Jeremy's, which was weird because Jeremy was the only designer in New York whose profits were safe from Pierre.

"What a show this morning," he said, starting with the positive, which always sounded more French-accented than his more blunt talk. "Out of the park. Yes, you'll be the superstars of Seventh by the end of the week."

"If we get reviewed."

"It's been arranged." He waved to Renee as they approached Jeremy's offices. "She was there. She knows St. James supports you, and I spoke to her."

"Did she see Dymphna Bastille? She looked like she belonged in the Toys R Us catalog. I don't know what I was thinking letting Mermaid send her."

"She said it wasn't a problem."

Laura froze. "What did she say? Tell me exactly. Every word."

"My dear, do you not trust me? When have I let you down?"

She didn't know how to answer. She was at a loss to describe what he had done at all besides spread goodwill and cheer regarding SartSand, which maybe could have been done with a postcard or a letter from Santa or something. Their backing, which was turning out to be completely inadequate, had been secured by Ruby after Pierre told them he had a matching backer lined up, but he/they had to find the initial money. Ruby had hunted down some guy she'd dated briefly in high school who, it was rumored, had made a killing in hedge funds, then "accidentally" ran into him at some swanky party downtown, after which Pierre swooped in and started negotiating contracts and following up with the tenacity of a starving pit bull. He then gleefully took eight percent when he was contracted to take ten, as though it was a favor, as if the money was going to get them five minutes past their first show.

"I saw Ivanah Schmiller. What did she think?"

"That could be a problem for us," he said, using the royal pronoun as if he was any more than a jester in that court.

"If it's about money, there's nothing you can tell me that Yoni hasn't."

"Your backer is not happy with you. Or to state it more plainly, his wife called your clothes boring."

"To whom? The circus?"

"I don't want you to underestimate her pull in this business. She is the wife of a billionaire and quite the designer herself. People listen to her, so no matter who she said it to, it wasn't *nobody*."

Laura crossed her arms, knowing she was about to get hit in the gut. "Okay, tell me what I have to do."

"First, you need your sister here, immediately. You cannot continue to work the showroom."

"What if I like it?"

"You're selling two-thousand-dollar jackets. This is not a game. Get Ruby from wherever she is and take her to Isosceles for a dinner with Bob Schmiller at eight. You can come if you like, but you are not to speak."

There must have been a dark cloud over her face because Sevion leaned forward and put his hand over hers. "This regards a few hundred thousand dollars and the future of your business. It requires personality, not genius. I cannot put it more plainly or kindly."

"Yes, you could."

He glanced into Jeremy's reception area again, holding up a hand for Renee, as if telling her to be patient. His French accent got thicker as the truth got closer. "Hortensia will give me hell. She'll say I treated you unkindly. She has a place in her heart for you that's a mile wide."

Pierre's wife was a notorious silly gossip and gadabout, but Laura had never heard of her speaking a negative word about either sister. She was not so kind with all of her husband's clients.

Maybe she should be thankful Sevion was so frank with her. Of course, Ruby was the face of the business. Laura knew that, and they'd discussed it repeatedly. Why should she be so surprised that Sevion wanted to enforce what was right for them?

"Naturally," Laura said. "Let me go find my sister. After

that, I'm calling Hortensia to tell her you uninvited me to dinner and called me low class. See if you get laid this week."

"See if I don't." He smirked, checking his phone.

Hers blooped at the same time, and since he was being rude, she decided to return the favor. But they both got the same message from two different sources.

Thomasina was dead.

CHAPTER 3.

Ruby was a perfect grouch when Laura met her outside the precinct. She could tell as soon as her sister grumbled a hello.

"You okay?"

"Yeah, I'm fine. I've been in the precinct for hours, and all they gave me to eat was donuts. They treated me like I was a criminal or something." Ruby ran to the next subject like flipping through a magazine of things that bothered her. "And Thomasina, she's dead. Oh, man, I really am going to miss her. She was such a good friend." Ruby stopped walking as if grief took the coordination right out of her.

"I'm sorry, Ruby. I know what she meant to you."

"No, you don't." Ruby put her head down and walked faster, then abruptly stopped. "She has a shoot with us tomorrow."

"Rowena's doing it," Laura said.

"You replaced her?"

"Yeah! Lucky thing because—"

"Who made you? Did you hatch?"

"What? It'd cost a fortune to cancel."

"I'm going home." Ruby stormed toward the subway.

Laura tried to follow, but found herself falling behind. "You're going to Isosceles with Pierre and Bob," she cried. "Pierre needs you to be nice."

"No." Ruby stopped before descending the stairs. "I cannot deal with meaningless talk right now. I can't talk about money and clothes and stuff that doesn't matter. So you go, okay? Can you go for me?" Laura caught up, and Ruby took her lapels, pulling down as if to drag her to the sidewalk. "Please. Go for me. All you have to do is make sure Bob's wife stays out of it, okay? Just whatever he wants her to do, say no and you're good."

Laura had never met Ivanah Schmiller face to face, so she'd never come upon that rule, and she had no idea how to enforce it.

"Please," Ruby implored, "I'll do something so nice for you."

"You have to go. Pierre said."

Ruby stopped talking as they went into the subway. Her face was dark and closed, lips pursed, eyes slightly scrunched. When they got past the turnstiles, Laura headed for the stairwell to the uptown platform, and Ruby went toward the downtown, where a train rumbled into the station.

"Ruby!"

"I'm going home."

"You can't!" Laura shouted over the noise of the train. She followed Ruby and grabbed her sleeve, but her sister yanked herself free without even looking back and got onto the downtown R before the doors snapped shut. Laura watched the train pull out of the station.

Ruby sat in a window seat and put her head in her hands.

Laura returned to the showroom to find Corky in a huff.

"I need someone here," he said. "I'm not an octopus." He held up the Rye and Rockland blouses, rocking them back and forth to illustrate how hard it was to take things off and put them on the racks at the same time.

"I'm sorry. Is anyone else coming?"

"Unlikely." He threw himself into a chair and took out a cigarette.

"You are not lighting that in here," she said.

"Ruby and I had a whole shtick set up. I can't shtick by myself."

"She'll be back tomorrow. She's just having drama time." Laura looked around for something to do, but everything seemed in pretty good order. "Where are the shoes?"

"Back behind." He waved his cigaretted hand. "I had no time."

Back behind were the words used to describe the sliver of storage space behind the display cubbies. It only held one rack and probably violated every safety code in the book. She went back behind and found hangers askew on the bar of the rack, tangled in waterfalls of grabby knots. She hated hangers. If she could reinvent them, she would, but had no better arrangement.

"Did you not show any of these styles?"

"Yeah, because when they came back late from the Ghetto, I had time to steam them, put them out, and pimp them by myself."

"You're being a real snot."

He got up and helped her yank out the rack from back behind. Hangers clacked, bent, dropped, and pulled the clothes out of shape. The shoes were tangled in boxes on the bottom two bars, and one box spilled rented Louboutins all over the floor. She bent to retrieve them.

"I have to get these back before dinner or they start dinging our deposit." She paired them off and put them on the table.

Corky, for all his huffiness, was the picture of helpfulness, and they had the first box sorted in record time. He pulled the shoeboxes from the top of the cabinet and packed while she untangled the hangers.

A phone buzzed.

Laura and Corky sprang into action, rifling through bags and pockets for their personal devices. After checking her phone, she dropped it back in her bag, then saw Corky sliding his own back into his front pocket.

But a phone definitely buzzed. They looked at each other, then around the room as though they were in a haunted house and had just heard a phantom behind the picture frame.

"It's by the rack!" Corky exclaimed.

The buzz stopped a second after she located the source in a box of shoes under the rack. At the bottom of the box was a leather Lacroix tote with uptrending bellows pockets all over it.

"Cute," he said. "One of the girls, probably."

"Should I open it?"

"No, you should leave it and let it draw the owner here by the power of Christian Lacroix."

She rolled her eyes and opened the bag. It was spanking clean. Amazing. Not a dustball, wadded-up tissue, a hair, a crumb, or even a book of old, useless matches. In comparison, her bag looked like a repository of human detritus.

She located a jar of lavender face cream (no label), a worn leather wallet (no brand, oddly), a cellphone (the latest), a notebook, and a bag of makeup. "It's the wallet or the cellphone. Which is less intrusive?"

"Oh, honey, be intrusive. The cellphone."

She opened the wallet. It was old style, with a little folder for pictures and cards, a billfold, and a display for credit cards. She slipped a black American Express card out of the pocket. "Sabine Fosh. Jewish? Did we have any Jewish girls?"

"Only Catholics," he joked, bagging and boxing shoes like a factory worker.

Laura knew he couldn't stand visible disarray in the showroom. She flipped through the wallet: pictures of no one she recognized, all towheads, a wedding photo from the seventies, an old couple in front of a cake, a frequent flier card for an airline she couldn't identify. One guy in his twenties appeared twice.

She poked at the cellphone screen. She recognized Roquelle Rik's number. "Her agent, repeatedly. She called Ruby a lot. Jeez."

"How's she holding up?"

"Bad."

"I'll take her for a manicure after this week. Cheer her up."

"We have seven hundred left in the bank. It's on Sartorial."

Corky looked pleased.

The phone blooped with a message from Bobcat. She had no idea who Bobcat was, and there was only one way to find out. Without consulting Corky, because she was ashamed to be doing it, she listened to the message.

"What are you *doing*?" he exclaimed.

"Being intrusive."

"Baby Bean. I'm back, and I missed you. You're right about everything. I sent something home for you."

He trailed off with a last "I know..." and that was it. Not helpful. She was down in the mire of intrusiveness, so she figured she might as well listen to another message. There was only one more. Obviously, the girl didn't save a year's worth of messages until her box overflowed like Laura did. She tapped and listened.

It was in another language, and the guy talking was stompin' mad.

"Do you know what language this is?" She held it up for Corky. It sounded like *wecken ick eeber eer.*

"Not Spanish," Corky said.

"I think it's German. This has to be Thomasina's."

She tossed the phone back inside and stuffed the bag in an overfull drawer. "I'll call the cops and have them come and get it. Just leave it out here. I have a nightmare dinner at Isosceles in twenty minutes."

"Oh, chic. Can I come?"

"It's with Bob Schmiller and his wife."

"Have a great time," he said, handing her a box of rented shoes.

Isosceles took up half the first floor of the Flatiron Building and, seen from above, was shaped like its name. It was so dark that the staff left little lights by your fork so you could read the menu. Pierre had gotten a seat by the ice fireplace, a pit of broken glass with blazing gas jets underneath that looked like the Arctic Circle on fire. Laura thought it was absurdly on-the-nose and decorator-y, as though designed to be designed, instead of placed where necessary as part of an organic whole. It was cool so that people would say "cool," not because it was necessary. But that was the problem with half the designs she had seen since opening SartSand. Her mind started pulling things apart only seconds after her eyes saw them, and the constant critique in her head got on her nerves and impinged on her enjoyment of details like a stupid pit of flaming tempered glass.

Also, her mood was soured by the whole Ruby/Pierre/Bob/Ivanah debacle that was about to occur and the raised eyebrow Pierre gave her as he stood to say hello.

"Ruby's not coming," she said.

Bob Schmiller, who looked more like a linebacker than an angel backer, stood up when Laura approached. He'd been a heartthrob receiver for USC, then a heartthrob rookie receiver for the New York Giants, then a player with a busted collarbone, then a bootstraps tale of a master's degree in finance and a way of sniffing out the right stock market bets. Laura figured the collarbone was the best thing that ever happened to him.

Ivanah didn't stand. She patted her yellow hair, which stood high on her head with painted enamel clips and combs, and smiled at Laura in such a stiff, perfunctory way it came off as a snarl.

Bob leaned over, the bulk of his upper body the result of too many hours in the gym, maintaining the football player build. He smiled like the charming guy he was and poured her some wine.

Pierre sat and placed his napkin on his lap. "So, did Laura tell you that they've been writing orders all day? Barneys co-op spent how long in your office?"

"About two hours." She didn't mention that most of it was spent stabbing Ruby in the back, and no orders had been written that day. Not one pair of pants. Not one jacket. Not even one of the scarves they cut out of extra fabric ends left on the marker. That wasn't how the business worked. The way it worked was you broke your brain telling someone about the clothes and talking about production lead times, and then you sat around for a month while they sorted their money. Because buyers were given a certain amount of play money to assort their floors, and they wanted to see everything before they gave you a dime. The best Corky was going to be able to do by Monday, after all the shows were done, was to get promises. Those were the projections Yoni was waiting for, and apparently, Sevion thought Bob didn't know that.

He was wrong. Bob smiled at Sevion and turned right back to Laura. "Let's stop with the bullshit." She was initially very relieved to hear that because it was what she wanted to say from the beginning. "You're asking for more money. But I bought this company for my wife, and she's not happy. And if she's not happy, I'm not happy." He put his arm around his wife. Ivanah tried to look coy, but came off looking predatory.

Sevion shifted in his seat, and she wondered if he was thinking, as she was, that it might not be the best day for a business dinner, with or without Ruby. But Laura preferred laser attention and direct questions to obfuscation and social dancing. "How can we make you happy?" she asked, choking on the words.

Pierre made a last ditch effort to wrest control of the conversation from her. "Ms. Sidewinder is excited to review us. She said it's in the cards for the next issue, which is tomorrow."

Bob ignored him. "I'm concerned about my ROI. We charted this out, and since your matching backing fell through,

I'm looking at a loss."

"Can't you take it off your taxes?" Laura had no idea what she was talking about, and Bob knew it.

"I already have tax efficiency built into my business."

Ivanah put down her glass and spoke in her thick Eastern European accent. "This wastes time." She pulled a small leather folder from her bag. "My husband invested in your little company because he thought it would complement my interiors. He did not invest because he believed in you, in particular. This was not for you to do whatever boring thing. You already started, so he let you do what you wanted, but that stops today. Now you will follow my sketches."

The ridiculous charade of Laura's good mood shattered. There was only one road, the road of flashy crap, the road Jeremy had walked with Gracie, where she got to dictate what was what because of her money. Laura didn't know whether to let things take their course, which everyone seemed to do, and let Ivanah have what she wanted at the expense of her vision or hold fast to her vision and lose the company.

Ivanah opened the file and handed it to Laura. The only surprise was the skill with which the sketches were drawn. They were gorgeous depictions of velvets, damasks, and sparkly trims in jeweled pinks, purples, and blacks. She could see before she even picked up a piece of paper that it was a beautiful line, just not for her.

"This is what you want my company to be?" Laura asked.

"My husband's company."

"I'm thinking globally," Bob said. "As a business driver, we may have to restructure to improve our value."

"Why don't you start your own company?" Laura tried to sound encouraging instead of surly, as though she'd just had the most awesome idea, ever. Pierre kicked her under the table.

"It's too late," Bob said. "It is what it is."

Ivanah's body language told Laura just how annoyed she was with her husband. "He told me he was buying a company that did things close to what I need. But he has no sense outside the numbers. He thought you were attached to Jeremy.

This is what I wanted. And here we are."

"Well, no," Laura said, "that's not how it was told to me. And the fabric's ordered already." She lied before she even thought about it, and then built on the lie. Dangerous. "We have an eight-week lead time on some of this stuff. We can't change it now."

They all looked at Pierre Sevion, who had been texting his little heart out. He glanced up with a blithe look on his face. "I don't think there's anything here we can't work out. A touch here and a touch there can bring all of these to the next level. We add a few pieces that represent luxury and indulgence. And next season, we start from scratch with a new, fantastic vision that is a collaboration between extravagance, craftsmanship, and commerciality."

"Commerciality stayed home," Laura said, referring to Ruby, who had the sharpest sense of what would sell.

For the rest of the dinner, Bob stayed upbeat about the "new organization," Ivanah tried not to look like a gloating victor, and Pierre tried to make lemons into peach pie.

Laura felt as though she was giving away the farm.

Laura didn't turn on her agent until they were outside. "You *didn't* just do what I think you just did. You didn't just give Ivanah Schmiller the right to say what goes on the line."

"You seem to think a few million dollars will be easy to come by, because that's what you need."

"Ivanah *Schmiller*? Have you seen her stuff? Have you ever even been in a room she designed? It's like a three-ring circus of crushed velvet and chrome. It's like someone vomited animal skin prints. The place she did for the Flusher penthouse? Did you see? She just took a handful of rhinestones and sprayed them all over the marble floor."

"Calm down."

"No. I will not *calm down*. Sartorial is not about carved teak buttons and chrome belt buckles. It's not silk animal skins. It's not about tinsel fringe. That's what Jeremy's for. It's about beauty on the inside. It's about not being obvious. You're going to kill this line before it even takes its first breath."

Sevion was unflustered as he hailed a cab. "There are two things you need to consider. One, at your prices, you need more beauty on the outside." A cab stopped, and he opened the door. "Two, your sister would have gotten that money without the histrionics."

Laura felt her bottom lip quiver, and as much as she tried to stop it, the snots came, and her eyes developed a mist that enraged her so much, they misted more.

"Don't get upset," Sevion said gently. "I know it feels like this is happening especially to you. But it happens with every designer, every time. I have not once seen an exception. Very, very successful designers go through this struggle every season, not just their first line. Why do you think your friend Jeremy kept sleeping with his backer? Because money was easy to find? No, because he knew what he had in her. Ask him now what he goes through without her. I believe he would do it again in a second."

"I hate this," she said, wiping away her tears.

"I know. Everyone does. Don't worry. You'll do what you have to do. Just make sure your sister is the one in the showroom with Ivanah, and in the meantime, I'll try to find you something else."

He got into the cab, and Laura watched it drive away.

She didn't know who else to call. The more she looked at her short list of contacts, the more his name jumped out.

"Jeremy, I know you're busy."

"I'm home," he said. "Tiffany came in sick."

She had always thought Jeremy was oddly averse to sick people, until she learned he had cystic fibrosis, which meant that a case of the sniffles for a coworker could be nearly fatal for him. She was the only person in possession of his secret, and the only person he trusted to know.

"We never really talked that much about Gracie."

"You want to talk about that *now*? Where are you?"

She found herself walking toward the train station, but feared there would be no way to get the conversation done with before she reached it.

"I know she had control over the line."

"Yeah."

"Because she had the money."

"Right."

She paused. The station was right in front of her, and she wasn't ready to walk down yet. Neither was she ready to ask him tacky questions. "Never mind."

"What?"

"Do you miss her?"

Silence. Then a cough. And another. Which meant he was working too hard. She could hear him breathing, and she wanted to cover her too-personal question with a string of jokes and denials. But she didn't. She waited.

Eventually, as she heard the train roll into the station downstairs, he said, "Sometimes. When I don't know what direction to take. I have no one to ask. She could have managed this expansion brilliantly."

"But she never would have let you expand."

"I don't miss that."

"Ivanah wants creative control."

There was another long pause. A wave of commuters trudged up the stairs, and Laura stood still, getting engulfed by them.

Jeremy finally asked, "Do you trust me?"

"I don't understand."

"It's a simple question." She'd obviously ruffled his feathers. "Do you trust me?"

She watched a woman with a stroller in one hand and a baby in the other struggle to get down the subway stairs. Laura reflexively grabbed the front axle of the stroller and pulled without asking if the woman needed help. It filled the moments between Jeremy's loaded question and her answer, which was, "No."

She expected repercussions, but got only, "You trust me, and you know it. Don't worry about Ivanah. Forget her. Get out there and talk about the line. You have a shoot tomorrow?"

"Thomasina's dead."

"Forget her, too."

"That's not nice." She remembered Ruby's reaction to her quick replacement of the dead girl.

"Welcome to having your own business."

She smiled a little, wanting to tell him that even though she was just down the hall, she missed him and his rough edges terribly.

CHAPTER 4.

Home was no longer an apartment, but a house shared with her mother and sister, which was good. But it was also an hour outside Manhattan, which was not so good. The train ride to Bay Ridge, her new South Brooklyn neighborhood, took an hour, give or take, which was enough time for her to become intimate with every ad, poem, and public service announcement posted in the car. The train she was currently on was dedicated to the new lifestyle brand, Saint JJ, AKA, Jeremy.

The ads overhead, the ads by the doors, and every bit of ad space in between belonged to Jeremy's brand. The color was a washed out orangey-red that looked like the deepest part of a flame, and the logo, the bags, and hats, even Dymphna Bastille's lipstick, all matched. Nothing in the ads was available yet, but they were already highly coveted items. Laura closed her eyes to shut him out, sure that complete world domination was his for the taking.

Her shoulders drooped. The weight she'd been carrying in preparation for the show was lifted. She almost slept. The show had gone off well, despite the death at the end. The papers would run the story tomorrow, and her pasty face against Thomasina's thoroughbred beauty would be all over the news tonight. Then Debbie Hayworth. And Ruby having a four-hour police interview for reasons that were completely opaque. Lastly, she was practically losing creative control of her own line because she didn't have two nickels to rub together, and the last straw was Jeremy basically telling her to get over it.

She ruminated on how she'd started on a high note, and the whole endeavor had taken a dive after Thomasina's death, as if all the months as a muse for Ruby had just been building up to a fine *screw you* at the end, a lovely bookend to how their relationship began. On the train ride home, she vacillated between feeling sorry for Thomasina to despising her. On the walk from the train to her block, she wondered why Jeremy was so hot to nail down her trust, and as she crossed the last street, she was about to start beating herself up over Stu when she saw the news van in front of her house.

Of course, they'd tracked her down. What surprised her were the police cars, one black and white, and one Crown Victoria with big lights. The house was a brownstone, connected to its neighbors on both sides, so there was no access from the back unless she wanted to go around the corner, scale a barbed-wire-topped wall, walk through someone's begonias, and fight off the mixed-breed hound to land in her own backyard. That may or may not have been preferable to the knot of reporters that shone their lights in her eyes halfway down the block, but it was too late to know.

She couldn't see any one face past the glare. There seemed to be a microphone near her, which made her want to shut up more than anything. Questions were thrown at her.

How do you feel about Thomasina Wente's death?
Was she taking any drugs during the show?
Do you know who she was seeing?

She ducked her head. "I really can't answer any questions right now."

They repeated the same ones, making such an effort not to be in her way that they were completely blocking her from getting home. All she cared about was finding out what the police were doing at her house, so she barreled through, which caused them to make stronger efforts to follow, which, again, put them squarely in her way.

She recognized Akiko Kamichura more by voice than face and heard the question loud and clear. "Did you know the police think there was foul play involved?"

She stopped short, truly shocked. "No."

"Were you with Ms. Wente right before the show?"

Her exhaustion and stress boiled to the top of her consciousness. She took a step toward Kamichura, forefinger raised, the picture of aggression. "That's completely over the line, lady. Who the hell do you think you are? Do you have a badge? No? You don't? Oh, that's right. You have a second-rate journalism degree and enough silicone in your body to fill the kitchen utensil aisle at Target. It is *not* your place to ask me about my alibi. Do you understand me?"

Kamichura had taken a step back, but her expression was pure satisfaction. "Any theories on why—"

"I asked if you understood."

"... she might have been killed?"

"Did you understand?"

"She knocked your sister off a runway in the Jeremy St. James Fall show."

The horrible woman was trained to bulldoze her way to the most dramatic on-the-spot interview she could muster. She had no skin in the game. It had already been a win for her, and another emotional outburst wouldn't make the reporter look stupid; it would get her a promotion.

Laura smiled and said, "Excuse me," right into the microphone, then stepped toward her house.

Kamichura moved, but not really enough. The reporters shouted questions and shone their lights, but they could not trespass past the gate. She looked up at the stoop, which led to the middle and top floor where she and her mother lived. The door was closed. The lights were on, but she detected no activity in the windows.

"Hey! You bastards!" The voice came from the top of the adjacent stoop, and she knew right away that it was Jimmy, their landlord. He lived next door and had bought the buildings on each side during the last housing depression. Standing above them with a crowbar and a voice so loud it ripped the time-space continuum, he was the picture of psychosis. "Get the hell away from my gate or your eyes are gonna be lookin' out both sides of your head!"

Kamichura pointed her cameraman, a guy in his fifties who stood at six-five and weighed in at about three hundred pounds, to shoot the nut at the top of the stairs.

When Jimmy came to meet them on the sidewalk, in the light of the camera, they saw he had a weapon more dangerous than the crowbar. He had a phone to his ear. "They're restricting access and blocking a fire hydrant," he said.

Kamichura indicated her van, which had enough satellite dishes for a Presidential dinner on the roof. "It's legally parked!"

Jimmy held his hand over the mouthpiece. "They don't give a rat's ass."

Laura interjected, "Retired cop. PVB comes if you wave a stick at an illegal space." She rolled her eyes as if it annoyed her.

"Why don't you tell the dozen cops in the house?"

"Those goons can't call a tow truck," Jimmy said. "You leave my tenant alone, and I go back inside."

Kamichura took a step back. Laura knew she hadn't seen the last of the reporter, but next time she'd be prepared. "And my sister is ten times more gorgeous than Thomasina Wente, even when she's flying off a runway."

Kamichura and her cameraman exchanged glances, and he lowered his camera. She pointed at Laura. "I'll see you at work tomorrow."

Ruby's downstairs apartment, which she'd begged for, was private with its own kitchen and backyard access. Down a couple of steps, the door was open, and the flashing lights and hubbub of activity drew Laura in.

"Carnegie," Cangemi said. "Welcome."

"It's my house. I'm supposed to be welcoming you."

"Fat chance of that happening," he said. And he was right. The apartment, huge by New York standards, was dwarfed by the sheer number of people wiping surfaces, flipping cushions, and generally poking around where they didn't belong.

"Where's my sister?"

"In the bedroom with your mother. I need to ask you a few questions."

She ignored him. He was more pleasant to be around when he wasn't fighting with his girlfriend, but his recent lack of humor forced her to keep the observation to herself.

The apartment was a railroad, meaning one had to walk through either the bedroom or the bathroom to get to the kitchen, so both bedroom doors were open to allow people in NYPD bunny suits to get through. They had a wonderful view of Ruby crying on the bed where Mom multitasked by rubbing her daughter's back while talking on her cellphone.

"No, I know for a fact she has nothing to worry about, but I won't have her caught short because you need to be hit over the head with a disaster to get your ass moving." The tone of Mom's voice betrayed nothing. The long sentences told her Mom was mad.

She continued, as if the person on the other end didn't get a word in edgewise. "I have never asked you for a goddamn thing. Even when I was raising two kids by myself in a godforsaken ghetto, I never asked you for a dime or a favor, but I made your girls Halloween costumes and taught them how to sew doll's clothes, which was wonderful. I love them. And I need you to get your ass out of wherever you are, get down to Midtown South, and get me some answers with the same pleasure I had helping *your* kids."

Ah. That would be Uncle Graham, the cufflink lawyer.

"I don't want to hear it, I don't want to hear it, I don't want to hear it!" Mom had graduated from long, rambling, calmly voiced sentences, to her prepubescent relationship with her brother. Fantastic.

Laura snatched the phone.

Uncle Graham was already speaking. "... charged with something."

"Uncle Graham? It's Laura."

"Can you calm her down?"

"Probably not."

"If I get involved before Ruby's charged, it's going to look like she's hiding something."

She looked at her sister, who was falling apart in no uncertain terms, and Mom, who was trying not to, and felt as alone as she ever had. "Maybe you can come around after the cops leave and explain what just happened? Or maybe you have a contact in the NYPD you can prod a little? It doesn't have to be a big thing. Just, you know, let them feel like they're not swinging in the wind?"

"I heard you got into some trouble a few months back and didn't call me."

"I had it under control," she lied.

"Don't tell your sister," he said, "but you were always my favorite."

"Thanks, Unca Gee."

Cangemi walked in with a purposeful expression and motioned her out of the room.

"I have to go." Laura tossed the phone onto the bed and followed the detective into the backyard.

Mom had started organizing the soil into borders and beds. A little overhang against the house sheltered a long metal table with boxes of bulbs, pots, and bags of soil and compost. It had all been moved out of Ruby's kitchen after an epic freak-out about personal space and cleanliness versus the ease of using the garden apartment for the gardening. Mom's eviction from her rent-controlled apartment had reawakened her love of flowers, and bulb-planting season would not go by unfulfilled, even if it meant traipsing through Ruby's own little private Idaho.

"You really upset my sister."

"We have a warrant."

She wanted to call him out for being an officious jerk, but it was hard to do that with a name like "Detective."

"You never told me your first name," she said.

"Detective is fine."

"So what do you want?" she asked. "It's been a long day already."

"Did you see Thomasina taking anything? Pills? Shots? A snort?"

"On or off the record?"

"For now, we're off, but I reserve the right to bring you in for an on-the-record talk if I think you have more to say."

Laura mentally reconstructed the morning. She reviewed all the times she'd seen Thomasina in the previous weeks for fittings and blah-blahing with Ruby in the office. She thought of all the times the model's presence had annoyed her and how the gossiping had made Ruby squeal instead of work, times Thomasina could have been out partying, but instead hung around the office for an hour between gigs.

"I think I saw her eat like three times in the past four months. She was a freak about what she put in her body."

"Ever notice what came out?"

"Catty remarks in a German accent."

"Since this is the second murder to take place in a ten-yard radius of you, I'd keep the wisecracks to a minimum." He really was more fun when his girlfriend did his laundry.

"She puked. They all puke. It's like a reflex. Their stomachs are temporary receptacles for lettuce and almonds."

"And you let them?"

"What did you want me to do?"

"You're supposed to report it to MAAB."

"Oh, you know what? The whole model-babysitting thing is getting really old. Who reports high school football players who work out four hours a day to bulk up? Who reports Sumo wrestlers who eat so much they can't wear pants? What about the actor who loses weight to play an Auschwitz victim? Who reports those people? Nobody."

"That's because—"

She'd heard it all before. "Because they're professionals? And somehow these girls aren't? They make five thousand dollars a day, and all they have to do for that money is walk back and forth and stay really, really skinny. That's their job. But we let football players, at any age, mind you, turn into Mack trucks. Why are they allowed to distort their bodies for our pleasure, but the models aren't?"

"Don't tell me. You have a theory."

"Because they're men. We trust that men have control over their bodies, but women don't. Women need nannies. And little girls are supposedly getting unrealistic ideas about body image because, again, they have no control over their own minds. But boys? Do we wonder if they're going to turn their arms into bazookas? Or distort their upper bodies to look like football players? No! Because there's an obesity epidemic *at the same time* we're freaking out about what grown women do to their bodies for a buck. So did she puke? You bet she did. Did she starve herself? Yes indeed. Because that's her job. If you don't like it, you should take a long hard look at yourself the next time you cheer on a linebacker."

Samuelson, Cangemi's partner, poked his head out and, with a nod, told them it was time to go. Cangemi nodded back and turned his attention back to Laura. "I'm not sure if you're an original thinker or very stupid."

"When you figure it out, let me know."

Laura fielded a few late-night texts about the next day's shoot: something about permits, which the safety team had, something else about Chase Charmain's dietary needs, and plenty else about the model change. Rowena's measurements were so close to Thomasina's, no middle of the night fitting was required, and any problems could be adjusted with a little basting and cutting. She went downstairs to update Ruby, but found her on the couch fifteen minutes into a sleeping pill. The cops had taped off her apartment. Her sister would probably be borrowing her clothes for the duration.

Laura went to bed, but she hadn't taken a pill, and she was too buzzed to close her eyes. So she memorized the cracks in the ceiling and wondered what the hell was going on in her own house. The police had been looking for something in Ruby's apartment, and Thomasina had been poisoned. Obviously, they thought Ruby had some of the poison in the apartment. But they didn't know her sister. Ruby wouldn't know poison from a vitamin. Laura was completely confident that they had found nothing in the downstairs apartment, except maybe Thomasina's fingerprints, which was to be expected.

Why would they suspect Ruby in the first place? Someone must have said something. No evidence pointed to her besides the fact that she'd found Thomasina in the bathroom, but since Ruby had been sick, she'd had every reason to be there. It was kind of poetic that Thomasina had collapsed in a bathroom and Ruby found her there. Those two had spent more time together in bathrooms than any other two people Laura knew.

She sat awake as the clock ticked to midnight because she remembered that though she'd been staring Cangemi in the face not two hours ago, she'd never told him about the bag she'd found, and she'd never called the cops to tell them she had it because her mind was elsewhere. Sabine Fosh's credit cards notwithstanding, the bag was definitely Thomasina's. Laura still had access to it, and she wasn't about to let it slip through her fingers without a second look.

Laura called a cab, got dressed, and went to the showroom because she didn't have a choice. Well, she *did* have a choice. She could have called the cops and told them everything, and they'd pick up the bag in the morning. But that would mean she'd never get her eyes on it. She'd never be able to protect her sister if the police got something stupid in their collective heads. Mostly, she'd never *know* what was in the bag, and if she wasn't going to sleep no matter what she did, she was going to satisfy her curiosity.

When she went outside to meet the cab, she saw police tape stretched across her sister's front door. Jimmy was slumped in his doorway, with a crowbar in one hand and a phone dropping out of the other. She could hear his snoring in the silence of the night. She felt a pang of gratitude for him. He cared about the three women who rented the house next door more than any conglomerate could. As she got in the cab, she noticed the big cameraman standing across the street, leaning on an unmarked van. He sipped from a bottle of soda and nodded at her as the cab pulled away.

She'd been in the office at one in the morning before, so the overall desolation and creepiness had no effect on her. The reporters had gone to report something else and might very well be back in a few hours, but it was quiet at the moment.

The elevators exited in front of Jeremy's showroom. The lights were on, so someone was home. Likely, Jeremy was talking to some new factory in China or prepping for his show, which would begin his drive toward total lifestyle brand domination. She resisted the urge to knock on the door to see how he was doing. He was probably engrossed in something, and her visit would not be welcome.

She walked down the hall to her showroom. In the darkness, she almost knocked over Corky's Danish Modern table trying to unlock the door.

The bag was in the drawer where she'd left it. She slapped it onto the table, the buckles clattering against the lacquered wood. Under that noise, she heard another sound, like a clicking, but she couldn't place it. She was aware that she was putting her fingers all over what could be evidence, and Cangemi would give her a hard time. But she'd already put her mitts all over the bag's contents yesterday, so there didn't seem any harm in doing it again.

She started by carefully unloading the objects onto the table, one thing at a time: face cream, cellphone, wallet, three pens, makeup kit to be unzipped and emptied later, three packets of gluten-free Tamari, a little Coach wallet full of receipts.

The makeup bag was filled with little plastic containers of brand new, super-expensive makeup made in Sweden. She pulled out an unmarked amber bottle of pills. She turned the plastic cylinder in her palm and estimated about ten capsules clicking away in there. Putting the bottle to the side, she moved to the wallet. Every card listed Sabine Fosh, which must have been some sort of fake name. Or maybe Thomasina was the fake name. But who would fake-name themselves Thomasina? She couldn't have chosen something less catchy.

The receipts created a problem. She couldn't write down everything about them, and she wasn't so past the point of no return that she'd keep them. She heard a hard hacking cough from the other side of the paper-thin wall. She pressed her ear to it and heard another cough as if it were in her own bedroom, but she heard no other voices. She knocked gently on the wall.

"Jeremy?"

His voice came in from the other side. "I knew it was you back there. Your show is done. Go home. Take a few hours off."

"Can I borrow your copy machine?"

"Come around."

She grabbed the little wallet and the receipts and walked down the hall.

He was already waiting for her at his office door. He unlocked it and stood aside. "You know where it is."

She didn't look at him because she was trying not to think about what she was doing. She was taking receipts from a dead woman's wallet and photocopying them before she handed them over to the police, because... why?

Because she knew in her heart that she was going to try to pull another Pomerantz. She had no time, no space in her life to do it. She had been told not to. It was stupid and egotistical. But her sister was in trouble, and she didn't know why. Though she wanted to trust the system, and maybe she *did* trust the system, she was going to see if she could solve another murder.

She tried not to think about it, and the more she tried not to, the more the truth stamped its feet and demanded attention.

"What are you doing?" Jeremy asked as he pulled a bottle of water from the fridge.

"No. What are *you* doing? You look like hell."

"Thanks." He smiled, and she smiled back, then he coughed again. "Paper needs to be pushed even on a show week. Come on, you used to be full time here. You know the drill." He pulled a pill bottle from his pocket and tapped out a couple.

"Yeah, but I didn't know then what I know now. Are you getting sick?"

"Fighting it. The plane rides to China are brutal. Even in first class, everyone's spitting phlegm. Beijing's a sewer of germs. I met the president of this manufacturing conglomerate and he was hocking in the street." He slid the pills into his mouth and knocked them back with a swig from the water bottle.

"Okay. Gross." She separated the receipts by date, placing them on the glass to fit one day per page. "You can't do this unless you're going to start walking around the office in an iron lung."

She expected an argument, but instead, he said, "Gracie might have been right."

"She wasn't right. She was scared. You just have to do it differently than everyone else. You can't fly all around the world looking at factories, period. You're no good to anyone dead."

He leaned on the fridge with his bottle of water, looking tired and drawn, as though he wanted to say something he was holding back. "When is Ivanah going to start bossing you around?" She sensed that wasn't what he'd really wanted to discuss.

"I'm sure that we're going to have to take money from them in about two weeks, when we run dry. She'll start butting in right after. Figure I'll be in your office in about three weeks to borrow your rhinestone sample books." She gathered the receipts, which Jeremy probably assumed were hers, and stuffed them back into the wallet.

"You know, she has a big PR machine that could help put a lid on the Thomasina Wente thing. Between now and the next two weeks, it would be in her interest to help you with it." He sipped his water and looked for her reaction over the bottle.

On a whim, and because she wasn't ready to walk out of the office yet, she copied the credit cards. "You saying I should draw her in now, assuming she's going to be a creative partner, and ask her to get her public relations people or press agent or whoever to spin the Thomasina thing? Then what if Pierre actually comes up with the alternate backing he keeps promising?"

He shrugged. "The PR firm's on retainer. No loss for her, really."

She had no idea how it all worked, nor did she understand how you kept a firm on retainer, though she knew that was something you did if you were really loaded. What she did understand was that Jeremy was the same manipulative user he'd always been, and she was glad he was on her side.

"How's Ruby holding up?" he asked.

"The cops are grilling her good, and she's supposed to be in the showroom, otherwise—"

"I mean about Thomasina."

"Fine, I guess."

He tossed the empty bottle away. "Well, now that the show's over, you can pay attention to your boyfriend. He can't like your hours."

"Who?"

"The guy in the bike shorts." Jeremy waved his hand, as if to draw the name into his head.

"Stu?"

"Right. The one who interviewed me for some article."

"He's not my boyfriend."

Jeremy sucked his lips in, and the lower part of his face got very tense. She thought maybe he was trying not to smile, but then pushed the thought out of her head.

"Ruby said—"

Laura cut him off. "Ruby subsists on hope and imagination. He and I were over before we started."

"How do you feel about that?" He was smiling again, which freaked her out almost as much as a question with the word *feel* in it. Jeremy didn't ask about feelings, and he didn't talk about them either. Feelings weren't business.

"I feel fine," she said.

"Good. I'm very happy to hear it. Very happy."

He looked as though he wanted to say more, but Laura couldn't think of a practical reason to linger. On her way out, she glanced back at him. He stood in front of Renee's desk, smiling.

When she returned to her showroom, she stuffed the papers back into the wallet. As she was about to put the pill bottle back into the inside pocket, she covered her hand with her sleeve, opened the bottle, and popped a little capsule into her palm. Having gone over the edge into buttinski mode, she saw no reason to hold back and slipped the pill into her pocket. Then she picked up the cellphone and checked for new messages. Nothing. Bobcat had been the last. She guessed everyone knew there was no point in texting a dead woman.

Bobcat.

Stupid. Of course, it was Bob Schmiller. She marveled at the complete douchebaggery of it. She got angry on Ivanah's behalf and wondered if he'd invested in Sartorial to gain access to Thomasina, screwing over Ivanah's desire for her own company. By the time she had the bag repacked, she was mad as hell. She wanted nothing to do with him. Then, she thought, maybe, just maybe, she should get to know him a little better if she wanted to find out who had killed Thomasina Wente.

She put the bag on the table with a note for Corky saying she realized it was Thomasina's. She left Cangemi's card so Corky could call for the police to come and get it. She had nothing else to do, and it was too late to go back to her bed in Bay Ridge, so she went to her shoot.

CHAPTER 5.

The train to Williamsburg was quiet, and she almost missed Bedford Avenue because she was dozing off. When she exited, it was four o'clock, two hours before call, and the bars were just closing. Tuesday night/Wednesday morning revelers strolled, stumbled, and rolled into the street. Gypsy cabs trolled under the lightening sky, radios buzzing, and slowed outside the station, looking for a fare too drunk to walk home.

She found a diner that had been in business since at least the 1970s, so unhip as to be wildly hip. The guy behind the counter looked as if he slept under the grill where the clattery metal cooking doodads were stored when he wasn't counting out greasy bills with Botox-injected fingers. She sat at the counter, trying not to notice the flakes of rainbow translucence floating on the surface of her coffee. A newspaper lay within reach—*The Daily News*, folded with the headline pressed against the counter. She slid it closer and opened it. She had made a point of avoiding the headlines when she passed the newsstand because she knew something she didn't want to see would be on the front page. She was right, but her fear that it would be her face, in all its unmade-up exhaustion, was unfounded. Thomasina's job was to be in print, and she did it even after her death.

SUPERMODEL THOMASINA WENTE DEAD AT 27

Laura realized she hadn't known how old the model was, as that wasn't generally a subject for discussion. The window of opportunity when one should be modeling, between eighteen and twenty-five, was too short. Either a woman was too young and a target for MAAB, or she was too old and a target for indifference. Thus, they lied. All of them. And their agents lied. Because it took two years to build a girl into a full-on giraffe and then the agents wanted enough time to capitalize on it before she had babies or drank herself into an unfittable twenty-seven-and-a-half-inch waist.

If the front page was any indication, she knew more than the reporters did. Sartorial Sandwich, along with her and Ruby's names, appeared at the bottom of page one. Also, Thomasina was featured in her first outfit, a rayon suit that draped on her like cigarette smoke over a coat rack.

The story continued on page eleven, where she was hit full-on with her own face in stunning black and white. First runway show of her life and she couldn't drag a mascara stick over her eyes in the morning? Is that the way things would run her whole life, seeing herself and being stunned at the dishrag eyes and hay-bale hair? And why didn't they print Ruby, who always looked Photoshopped, even when she woke up hung over and cranky? Pretty news in the front, ugly news inside, she guessed. It took her another minute of shaking off her shock at seeing herself to get to the actual story.

"Ms. Wente was the founder of the White Rose Foundation, a rescue mission for young girls in Eastern Europe. She is survived by her brother, Rolf Wente, and sister, Hannah. Both live in Berlin."

The article didn't mention that she was one of the *ostalgie* heiresses, an old guard of East German wealth who had managed to get the mobs of protesters to protect them by saying that the new democracy would help them join the Wentes in the new meritocracy of the rich. Then, they played on the nostalgia of the prewar days and their part in the beauty of the East German countryside to keep protesters at bay. For that, they used the passion and anger of the skinheads, who wanted to return to some past permutation of Germany. Brilliantly played, if ethically questionable.

When Laura saw the picture of Rolf, she knew why his sister had been so ashamed that she'd led Laura to believe she had no family, and why the celebrity-sucking media had only mentioned Thomasina's dead sister. Rolf Wente was a skinhead, and a mean-looking one at that. She hoped he stayed in Germany.

The Lancaster Glass building was a big pig on the waterfront that had captured the imaginations of developers, journalists, and activists. The building was twenty-two stories of fat red bricks and steel casement windows that were mostly broken, not because the neighborhood was "bad," and not because the nearby residents didn't care. On the contrary, the building sat on some of the most valuable real estate in the city. Back in the eighties, when dinosaurs roamed the earth and Williamsburg was the arson center of the city, Lancaster Glass, which had owned the building since 1850-something, abandoned their factory/warehouse and moved their manufacturing operations to China. Nobody cared until the late nineties. Then, suddenly, everyone cared.

Floor-to-ceiling casement windows. Exposed brick. Breathtaking views of the city. Expansive floor space. A description of the building sounded like Realtor ad copy before the first busted window was replaced.

Developers discovered that there was a rub, naturally, because if it was easy, it would have been done already. The property had three lienholders, all of whom wanted to sell or develop immediately, and an heir, Katherine Lancaster, who didn't. Katherine wanted to bring glassmaking back to Brooklyn. She was the only reason the building had not been converted into condos, though the activists who believed New York didn't need one more luxury condo liked to think they had something to do with scuttling deal after deal. The developers, for their part, were patient. They just waited for Katherine to die. In the meantime, she collected nice checks by renting out the space for fashion shoots and movies.

Laura followed South Second to the water. The Lancaster Glass building stood in the middle of an empty waterfront like a big erection at the edge of the earth. Yellow signs with arrows that said, cryptically, LAMPPOST, directed her to the waterside entrance. The elevator operator had a clipboard. She knew him, so he let her in and clicked the doors behind her. Olly was a good guy with a crackerjack memory for faces. He loved operating elevators more than anything in the world, and even put on his uniform for his two-hour moonlighting gig in Williamsburg.

"Hey, Olly," she said. "Who's here?"

"Craft services is on eleven. Safety people. They're the ones with the ropes and nets, right?"

"I guess."

"Your photographer and his assistants got here. He's a little…" Olly rotated his index finger around his ear.

She nodded. "Yeah."

"The model came early, and he smelled her breath. Like a puppy, he did it. Then he whispered in this other girl's ear, and she said, 'Chase thanks you for not puking before the shoot and wants you to know it won't be allowed.' I tell you, I wanted to puke a little on his shoes just to see what he'd do."

"Scream like a tropical bird is what," she said. "The smell makes him crazy."

He slid open the doors and winked at her. "Eleven. Coffee to the left."

Coffee was exactly what she had on her mind. She mixed herself a cup, then went directly to the roof, where the shoot was to take place. At some point, she may even have drunk a little, but the next hour was lost in preparation and details with interns, makeup with Monty, clothing with Maria and Carlos from the sample room, accessories that arrived in trashed wheeled suitcases, and Ruby, who showed up a minute before Rowena came from behind the curtain.

"You all right?" Laura asked.

"They taped off my apartment. I can't even get in."

"Did they tell you anything about why they were there?"

"No." She shook her head as if trying to loosen the gears. "How is Chase doing?"

The photographer, with his signature long mop of curly black hair and pageboy cap, was doing what he always did before a shoot, holding his camera at his chest, standing directly in the way, and staring into space. He spoke to no one, having briefed his all-female team beforehand by whispering instructions in their ears. They set up a net over the edge of the building, and then another, larger one a few stories down, and a dangling shelf for Chase and his silent camera.

"He's not happy about Rowena," Laura said. "Thomasina worked with him a hundred times. She could read his mind. Rowena, he's going to have to speak to. And she was obviously out last night."

He stood there until the sun was in the right place in the sky, and his team, like a well-trained squad of assassins, stopped talking and puttering when he held out his hand. The person in charge of the music started the thumpity-thumps, and Rowena stepped out from behind the curtain in a silk tulle dress that looked like twenty yards of fabric wrapped around her and sewn shut.

"She can't walk," Ruby said.

"That's the point."

"You did that because you didn't like Thomasina. Now how do you feel?"

"I feel like she looks exactly like Thomasina, but with a different face and an accent I can understand most of the time." Laura took the purple capsule out of her pocket. "You ever seen one of these before?"

Ruby barely glanced at it before she said, "It's probably a vitamin."

"Vitamins don't come in lilac."

"How would you know?"

"It looks like someone emptied grape Pixy Stix into a clear capsule. And what's with you getting defensive about a pill that you don't even know where I got it?"

"I just feel bad for Rowena, and it's your fault she can't walk."

Laura suspected there was more to it, but Ruby was sour and puckered, so she let it drop.

The shoot was simple. The model stood over the ledge in the dress she couldn't walk in and tipped over so the view to the city spanned below her. The imagery was going to be gorgeous, hashed out between the four of them: Laura, Ruby, Thomasina, and Chase, who nodded, grunted, or hissed. There would be a net, safety gear, and a dress so tight the tension of the scene would be palpable enough to make the pages sweat. The key to that had been Thomasina's agreement to look as though she were falling twenty-five stories, which Laura didn't realize until Rowena came out of dressing in an ankle-length skirt that she expected to be able to walk in, but couldn't.

Chase motioned with his hands, and Rowena moved all six feet of her fabric-bound legs as far as she could, while looking completely inaccessible to either gender for sex, friendship, or a two-dollar cup of coffee. She turned sideways, and Laura noticed the bones in her arms and thought she might actually be thinner than the last show, as if some internal organs and musculature had been removed so her skin could adhere better to her bones. But what stood out the most was that, for all her lack of preparation, Rowena was dishing it out. If Chase was doing his job, the shoot was going to send girls all over the country tumbling over rooftops.

Laura turned just in time to see Roquelle Rik walking over to her.

"This was slick," Roquelle said, sipping creamy coffee

from a vintage chintz cup. Laura was pretty sure the coffee and the cup had come from Marlene X, the breakfast joint on Third that was filled with models, wannabe models, agents, producers both real and fake, fashion hangers-on, and the occasional hot designer seeking an undiscovered look.

Laura fondled a nondescript paper cup holding her now-cold coffee. She'd been to Marlene X once and had been caught without cash, which was all they took. She had been mortified and never returned.

Roquelle seemed to sense Laura's thoughts, like a cat, and played on them, like a bitch, when she said, "My girl dies, and you two don't miss a beat."

Mortification notwithstanding, Laura's mouth functioned fine as she snapped, "Please, if I'd died on Saturday afternoon, Thomasina wouldn't have missed a Sunday brunch over it."

Roquelle clicked her cup into the saucer, and they watched things progress at the building ledge. "Nobody would, but she wouldn't have been so public about it."

Laura turned to Roquelle to see her expression because the tone was too flat for her to make out the sentiment.

The modeling agent smiled. "She was a class act. And lots of people knew it. Oh, and don't start with the whole Ruby-runway thing. It was a moment of pique. I hear you've had your own."

Laura turned back to the shoot, *her* shoot. Rowena swung her arm up, then down, and made a big circle with her other arm. Laura was sure the woman was headed over the edge. Even with the net, it was scary, and her instinctual mind refused to believe Rowena would be caught. But the model righted herself, swung left, and growled at the camera, which clicked. Even Chase made a shocked sound. Rowena seemed to be getting tired, and he held up a hand. His team dropped everything and scuttled around, picking things up, and one brought Chase a container full of something brown and gritty. Someone handed Rowena a small bowl of almonds.

"Nicely done," Roquelle said. "You make them beautiful, then throw them off buildings. You're playing on public disdain. Everyone else is doing aspiration."

"That wasn't my intention."

"Of course not." Roquelle went over to Rowena. She spoke in a soft voice and stroked the model's hair.

Laura felt a hand on her shoulder and turned to see Monty, Jeremy's special style guy, and now hers by dint of the fact that she apparently had no career outside of her old boss. They air-kissed, but she somehow did the wrong side first, and they wound up pressing cheeks together.

"You were brilliant yesterday," he whispered.

"Maybe you can help me with today?"

"How is Ruby holding up?"

"Great."

"Can I do something with your face?" Monty asked, continuing a line of badgering that had been going on for at least two years. "Please?" His cartoonish pleading wasn't new, but Laura was feeling dish-raggy from the picture in the paper, so she sat in his chair.

The first thing he did was put drops in her eyes. "Your eyes are red as a lobster. Didn't you sleep?"

Laura didn't feel like answering any questions about her insomnia. "How's Rowena behaving?"

"She's forever in the bathroom. Like a diva already."

"Chase is going to freak out if he smells puke on her."

"Rowena? Never. Darling, she just doesn't bother eating in the first place." Monty flicked his brush over Laura's cheeks and said, "Dymphna eats her portions. She just chews gum because there's nothing worse than a pretty girl's breath after a trip to the bathroom. Especially after cheese. They all pretend they're like your sister. Eats like a sow at a trough and loses weight anyway, but no way, honey."

"You know all about these girls."

"Of course. They get to my chair on time from the bathroom or not, so I have to know."

She reached back for the lilac pill, almost getting a mascara stick in her eye.

"You have to hold still," Monty said.

"Wait, have you seen these before?" She held it out.

He glanced at it and went back to work. "Where'd you find that?" His whispered tone was so serious that she slipped the capsule back into her jacket.

"What is it?"

"Diet pill," he said. "It's from Amsterdam or the Netherlands or something."

"Amsterdam is in the Netherlands."

He shrugged. Apparently, geography wasn't his thing. "It's supposed to make you allergic to food. They say, anyway. But it's not like any of these magpies are scientists, if you know what I mean. Where did you get it?"

"I found it on one of the girls." It was the truth, but a truth that might get her a little closer to a little more information.

"Don't tell me," he said, falling right into her evil trap, "Dymphna Bastille."

"Nope."

"Really? I'm surprised."

"Why?"

"She has fat fingers. Ever notice? There's a fat girl inside her waiting to get out, and she's just fighting it tooth and nail."

She was about to ask him what exactly he meant by *fat* and what exactly he saw when he looked at *her* fingers, but Rowena came into view. She wore a matte black body stocking meant to go under the next dress. The dressing order went: undergarments, makeup, hair, overgarments. If the hair was bigger than the opening of the clothes, the hair was finished while the girl stood in her final outfit. Rowena was going to wear an origami number spitefully close to the dress that had almost gotten Laura a failing grade on her Parson's thesis. No small neck on that thing, it was basically a trapezoid with darts and ties.

Rowena held it out. "This works how?"

"It's like math," Laura said as she tucked, folded, and tied. "You wear it according to the first three axioms of Euclidean geometry."

"I missed that class," Rowena mumbled. Monty squirted something in her hair, and she swatted him away. He ignored her and finished the job.

Laura tied the last knot and flipped the back panel up into a hidden hood. "Not like getting an A in the class would have helped, anyway. I was just being pedantic with this group."

"Honey," Monty said, flicking the hood to the side. "I don't know what that means, but you can fuss with the dress when I'm done here, okay?"

Dismissed, Laura found her sister fussing with a paper bag full of bracelets.

"Silver?" Ruby asked.

"Yeah. Gotta be with the heather grey."

"I planned for a lot of them on the left arm, but now I'm thinking…" She held up two.

"That's fine. Hey," Laura said as if some interesting topic had just occurred to her, "I was wondering, do you think Thomasina took some sort of diet pill that was laced or something?"

"I don't know, but here's a great idea. Oh, my God, this is genius! Wait. I have it." Ruby had Laura's full attention to such a degree that she forgot she was supposed to be looking at Rowena. "Uhm, how can I say this so you get the full impact? Okay. This solves the whole thing. What if… you minded your goddamn business for a change?"

"She was your friend. You don't care?"

"I do care. Really I do. But since finding her killer means you try and make her out to be evil, I'd rather let the police do it."

"Taking diet pills is evil? Come on. These girls have to do it or their thighs won't fit in skinny jeans."

"Today it's diet pills, tomorrow, who knows what you're going to find out?" She held up a slight silver charm bracelet that tinkled in the morning sun.

It was perfect, and Laura gave it the thumbs up. "You mean that she was sleeping with Bob Schmiller?"

Ruby froze, and her eyes got imperceptibly wider. She

might have answered in the affirmative, but they were interrupted by a scruffy-looking guy with brown hair mussed to perfection, leather pants worn in exactly the right place, and a sharpness to his green eyes and accented voice that left no room for further gossip.

"Which one of you found Thomasina?"

Laura could tell by Ruby's open mouth that she was about to volunteer information. It could have been his good looks, or maybe the roughness to his voice, but the very things that inspired Ruby to answer immediately inspired Laura to step forward and break her sister's train of thought.

"I'm sorry? Who are you? And why do I care?"

Behind him, one of Chase's assistants, empowered not by her age, but by the orders of Chase himself, stepped in and said, "Mr. Charmain needs you to leave right now."

But Leatherguy wasn't having any of it. He didn't move an inch from Laura. "My sister was missing some items when they found her. If you stole them, I can offer a reward and no questions asked." He offered it like a ticking time bomb.

Laura wasn't insulted by the implication that she had stolen something because, in fact, she had. She was, however, attracted to the open door of opportunity. The guy was an emotional wreck and might say something unwise. He was also Rolf, the guy on the phone screaming, "*Wecken wecken.*" She hadn't recognized him with hair.

"A bag?" she asked.

"A wallet."

"I didn't steal it, but I know where it is."

"How much do you want?"

Chase snapped his fingers so loudly they could hear him from halfway across the rooftop. Rowena stood by the ledge with all of Manhattan spread before her, waiting for accessories as the sun rose and rose, changing the light with every second.

"I want to know who Sabine Fosh is."

Ruby jumped in. "Who the—?"

"It's not important," Rolf said.

"I agree," Laura said, holding up the bracelets as if she

had decided to move on to a conversation about the merits of silver versus platinum.

Rolf stepped around to get in front of Laura. He spoke in a quieter voice, more pleading and less demanding. "Where we're from, we can't go anywhere. We can't leave the estate. Everyone knows us, and there are those who would do away with us very quickly. She needed another name. So did I."

"So she could go to the grocery store, I guess?"

"Sure," he said, as if conceding the point.

She checked her watch as she walked over to Rowena with the bracelets. Over her shoulder, she said, "I had it this morning, but it should be with the police by now."

He paused for a second, as if he wanted more from her, then left.

The shoot had two more hours, and most of that time was spent perfecting Rowena's hair, makeup, and clothing. Chase used real film, not digital, and didn't change it once. Everything shot in those three hours fit on a single roll, which concerned Laura. Photographers tended to press the shutter and keep their finger there, blowing through hundreds of frames to get one shot. Laura asked one of his assistants about it.

The girl, who couldn't have a been a day over the dewiest weeks of nineteen, responded, "He needs five for the spread and takes ten just to give the editors something to choose from. But he always knows the shot, and he always gets it. He's amazing." Her eyes practically welled with tears.

One accessed the roof from a nine-foot-tall shed with a metal door that sat atop the inside stairs. The last bit of the shoot had Rowena sitting on top of that structure with her legs spread as if daring someone to look up her dress, a dark grey rubberized poly draped and rigid at the same time. She ate the camera alive, turning to make sure the red stitching at the hem was visible.

A tinkling noise went off on some glass-covered phone somewhere, and Rowena stepped off the top of the little shed and down the portable steps to the building roof. It was over.

She said goodbye in passing, rushing to Central Park for the shows, taking her platform heels for a canter as she hurled herself to the elevator.

Ruby looked concerned as she watched Chase pack up his camera and leave.

"They say he can get everything in fifteen shots," Laura said.

"Yeah."

"And Rowena looked great."

"Yeah."

"Except for the brown smear on her ankle."

"Yeah."

"Ruby. What's on your mind?"

"Where did you hear that name? Sabine Fosh?"

Laura didn't want to admit she had poked around Thomasina's bag twice, so she hewed close to the truth without admitting that she had turned a corner and driven down Busybody Street at full speed. "I found her bag with the rental shoes and opened the wallet."

"Is that how you found out about Bob?"

"Yes."

Ruby turned and looked her in the eyes. "You always seem like such a cold-hearted bitch, like you don't care about anything but business. But you're not. You say every horrible thing about Thomasina and you go on with your life like she never mattered. But you're going to find out why she died, aren't you? You're going to get justice for her."

Laura rolled her eyes. Ruby held her shoulders at arm's length and said, "Stu!"

"What about him?"

"He knows everyone and everything. We can ask him what he thinks."

"Ruby, we have work to do. Corky's in the showroom by himself."

"Everyone's at the shows. Come on. It's not like anyone has any money to buy anything until next month, anyway."

"An hour ago, you were telling me to mind my own

goddamn business."

But Ruby, the fickle fiend, pulled her out into the street and east to Bedford Avenue, where the hipsters roamed, and the artists and unemployed played.

CHAPTER 6,

Nine in the morning was early for some people, if the bleary eyes and slow gaits down the Avenue were to be believed. A line of bearded boys and persimmon-haired girls staring at their phones curled out the front door of the artisanal coffee joint. After the swill of the craft services table, Laura was tempted to get at the end of the line, but knew she was only avoiding the inevitable. Ruby, sensing her slowed pace while passing the long, trend-forward coffee line, walked faster.

"I don't know what makes you think Stu knows anything," Laura mumbled.

"It's not what he knows. It's what he can find out, and what his brain can figure out."

Under different circumstances, Stu would be her first stop any time something bothered her or didn't seem right. But things had changed between them. Or they hadn't changed in the way that had been expected, and the confusion led to a discomfort she took great pains to avoid experiencing.

After Gracie's killer had been found, everyone knew she and Stu were going to be together. Nadal regularly called them boyfriend and girlfriend before they'd even held hands, and Ruby, having been released from her engagement to Michael the douchebag, passed all her wedding dress sketches to Laura. It was so ingrained that Laura immediately dove into seventy-hour workweeks, and Stu began research on a piece about the Pomerantz murder and her part in solving it. Their time together, which should have been spent in dimly-lit restaurants and locked rooms, was instead spent with Laura hunched over her work, answering pointed questions about the two weeks in February she had spent unraveling a counterfeiting ring and catching a killer. Then Stu went off to write his piece, which had been picked up by the *New Yorker*. They required another five thousand words and three months of research, and the pressure of a byline in the most prestigious magazine in the world—Stu's words—turned him into a hermit. He even quit his bike messenger job, his sound mixing job, and his internship at *Cultcha Bustas* magazine.

Then, while she was pinning the rhombus-shaped crotch of the Parsippany pants and thinking about everything but him, he had called. After the usual niceties, he said, "I have to tell you something."

Still too stupid to be worried, she said, "Good thing you have me on the phone."

"Well," he started, then stopped. It was the first time he had ever seemed uncomfortable saying anything at all, and though she noted it, she did not stop pinning the pants for one second.

"You could be talking instead of doing whatever it is that you're doing now." She said it with good humor, but he had been looking for an opening to the conversation, and she realized weeks later that she'd handed it to him on silver platter.

"We're very efficient, you and I," he said. "We go out to dinner, and I bring my notebook. We meet at your office for lunch so you don't have to stop working."

"Yeah." She wrestled the pants off the form and turned them inside out, stuffing one leg inside the other so she could see the crotch. The shape that looked so bad when worn wasn't immediately apparent on the pattern, but when the pants were twisted that way, she could see the shape had changed during sewing.

"We don't actually act like two people who are dating," he continued.

Her heart felt like a finger had reached out and poked it. Something was wrong, and her answer that they weren't like everyone else wasn't going to cut it. "We agreed to hold off until the article came out and I had my first show."

"I met someone," he blurted.

"What?"

"The last time I kissed you was outside a bar, and you told me to take it back. We've just been assuming we're together ever since, and really, it's not the same as actually doing it."

"Is this about sex?"

"Don't get petty on me. You're too good for that."

"How am I supposed to get? Who is she?"

"I wish I hadn't said this on the phone."

"Are you seriously avoiding the question? Who are you?" She had actually stopped working on the pants and looked out the window. It was night, and most of the office lights were off. She looked at the clock—nine thirty.

"I met her at a protest at City Hall that Nadal dragged me to. She's nice, but it's not about her."

"Right," Laura said, "it's about the non-entity of *us*, right? Which only started bothering you when someone else came along?" He might have said something, but she didn't give him a chance. "What's her name?"

He said something. It wasn't Mary or Jane or Stephanie, but something foreign and exotic sounding.

"Tofu?" she cried. "You're dating someone named after pressed vegetable protein?"

"Laura, please, don't let this be something it's not. We

should always have stayed friends."

"A white square floating in stagnant water? That's who you're with?"

"I'm not letting this get ugly."

"That is unbelievably passive-aggressive, even for you." She had clutched the Parsippany pants so hard she creased them.

As she walked down Bedford with her sister, she thought of the few stilted conversations she'd had with Stu since then, conversations he'd initiated so that their falling-out would be mitigated. She cooked up a few hundred reasons why they should avoid seeing him or talking to him entirely.

"It's too early," she said.

Ruby, who knew the whole story inside and out, knew what she was doing and ignored her completely. Laura would have sworn Ruby walked faster, forcing her to trot to North Fourth Street and turn right before she could think of another excuse or wonder at Ruby's real motivations. They stopped in front of Stu's little brownstone, which looked like every other brownstone on the block and appreciated in value by the minute. She remembered telling him he was overpaying and that he was too classy to rub in how very wrong she was.

Ruby hit the doorbell before Laura could stall, and as the seconds ticked by, she saw herself in the window's reflection. Monty had never finished her face. Her right eye was mascaraed and shadowed, and her left had some sort of base and a little of something else, but didn't look made up at all.

"I look like a Merle Norman ad!" she cried, but it was too late. The front door opened, and there was Stu, fully dressed and showered. Laura suddenly felt tired and worn down.

"Hey, Ruby," he said. His smile when he saw Laura was genuine enough and put her at ease. Whatever happened, he still liked her. That and a full MetroCard would get her a trip uptown.

"Stu," Ruby said, "we need your brain."

"You can have whatever's left of it." He glanced at Laura before he stepped aside and let them in the house.

The dark wood stairway was topped by a skylight that sent shafts of light into the foyer. The effect made Stu look angelic and mysterious, with his pale face cast in shadow and the light glowing in his yellow hair. That was not what Laura needed. She needed him to gain fifty pounds and smell like stale coffee and fresh garlic. Alas, he was still the same Stu she had thrown away. Or more accurately, the Stu she had let fall out of her pocket while she was running for the bus.

"What's on your face?" he asked.

She spun to the mirror. The house was a hundred years old, and the wood trims were exactly as they'd been when it was built. The foyer had a wooden bench with a hat rack and coat hooks attached. A mirror served as the centerpiece, and Laura turned her face from side to side. Monty had gotten her whole face with the powder, thankfully.

"Looks nice," Stu added.

"Which side?" she asked.

"Yes."

Ruby giggled, but Laura didn't think it was funny. His answer made her feel as though he didn't care for either side, but she wasn't about to morph into a crazy broad and press him for more.

"Come on up." He led the way, his old man's slippers chuff-chuffing on the wooden stairs. He wore skinny jeans, a cotton shirt, and a fine-gauge cardigan that was buttoned wrong, hipster-style. The wrongness of the buttoning seemed to improve the fit of the sweater, making it asymmetrical in a controlled way, and interesting. It was hard to not look at him twice because her mind wanted to correct the buttons, then it decided they were okay.

Oh, how she wanted to hate him.

As soon as she got into the apartment, she really did hate him. A fringed leather bag sat on the coffee table, along with banker boxes of files, a laptop, and a sleek little printer. Stu was not a messy guy, as far as she knew, and he didn't carry around fringed bags.

"What happened in here?" she asked.

Ruby punched her arm.

He headed for the kitchen. "I've been doing my piece. Do you want coffee?"

"Does the Pope crap in the woods?"

Ruby glanced down at the papers. "Why hasn't your story come out yet?"

"Ruby!" Laura hissed.

Stu continued as if the question wasn't rude. "It started out as amateur sleuth, your sister, hunts down rich woman's killer. But I'm rooting out a lot of corruption. So it's taking on a life of its own. The whole thing's moving somewhere different. The editors are so cool. They advocate me taking it where it's going to go. As long as it's clean and on time and I loop them in, it's no problem."

"Cool. Hey, I need to use the ladies'," Ruby said. Like a quick answer, a white noise they hadn't noticed stopped, and the room got a little too quiet. It had been the shower, and whoever was in there was finished. Ruby cleared her throat and sat down. The silence was thicker than a down coat.

"You heard about Thomasina Wente dying during our show." Laura despised thick silences.

"It's hard to not hear about it," he replied, his tone implying that there were bigger injustices in the world that might take up more space in the newspaper. "Another rich woman dies, and we're all supposed to drop everything."

"Oh, my God!" Ruby exclaimed. "Are you doing that thing again?"

"You mean standing up for the little guy?"

"No," Laura said. "I think she means complaining about the coverage of rich ladies dying while you write a book-length article for the *New Yorker* about exactly that thing."

She knew that was not what Ruby meant at all. Ruby had just been annoyed and probably hadn't even noticed the duplicity. And though Laura had no intention of raking Stu too far over the coals for it, the rustling sound from the bathroom kept her from dragging out the issue even another five seconds. She didn't want Tofu to hear her breaking Stu's balls over that or anything. For some reason, she wanted the new girlfriend to worry about her, which ran totally counter to her own interests, but she had no control over the perverse impulse.

Stu helped her out by looking at Ruby and saying, "Touché."

"Okay, we all have to get on with our day," Laura said, still worrying about the person about to emerge from the bathroom. "Can I ask you for a favor? Because I know you know everything and everyone."

"Naturally." He sat down next to Ruby on the couch.

"I looked through Thomasina's things by accident."

Stu nearly spit out a mouthful of coffee laughing. Ruby elbowed him. "Sorry," he said. "Go ahead."

"All the stuff in her wallet was made out to Sabine Fosh. Credit cards. EU driver's license."

"Library card?" he asked.

She ignored his joke. "Her brother said this was kind of a persona she put on so she could travel and go to the grocery store and whatever without people knowing who she was. But you know, she was so rich that she probably had her maid go to the store. And she wasn't ashamed one bit of who she was. So, can you find out the deal with this person?"

"Sabine Fosh?"

"No, the brother."

He looked at her as if he was trying to read the book of her intentions. "What else? I'll need all the details. Where and how you came upon this information and exactly what Rolf said."

He already knew Thomasina's brother's name. Very impressive. Yet she didn't want to go too far into how she'd inspected the bag after she knew whose it was, not in front of Ruby at least. She told the story without the one o'clock in the morning visit to the office and the photocopies of the receipts while he poured her a cup of coffee and Ruby a juice. Ruby interjected where she could, telling him what a really awesome friend Thomasina was, how the whole runway thing had just been an unfortunate incident, and how even her beast of a sister had grown to like the German heiress.

As the bathroom door opened, Stu said, "Same deal. I get you whatever you need, if I can. My sources are an open book. But it's my story. I have exclusive first rights to everything you guys do or say regarding what happens with the Thomasina Wente case."

"You're becoming quite mercenary, Stuart." The woman's lilting voice had an accent so slight it only seemed to add music to the perfect speech. Five-nine and not a hair over a size six, she was radiant and clean in jeans and a white shirt. When she smiled warmly and genuinely, Laura felt guilty for hating her so completely.

She held out her hand to Ruby. "I'm Tofu," she said, except that wasn't what she said at all. What she said sounded like an exotic fruit of subtle sweetness. *Tah-fuh.*

Ruby shook Tofu's hand, and Laura realized that Tofu thought Ruby was her, because if someone were to describe her and her sister without pictures, he or she might use the same words. And if one felt threatened by someone, and there were two people in the room, well, one might assume the more attractive of the two was the problem one. One might think the competition was an equal. But no, it was a woman three inches shorter and fifteen pounds heavier. And with half a face made up, as if she were starring in *A Clockwork Orange.* All she needed was to be leaning out of a triangle with a knife. She shook her head a little so her hair covered her eye.

Ruby looked at her pointedly. If she could shoot thoughts out of her eyes and into Laura's brain, her look would have said, "Wear it like you mean it."

Laura brushed the hair away, exposing the overdone eye. "I'm Laura."

Tofu was the picture of social grace as she redirected her attention and shook Laura's hand, firmly and dryly. Like a total bitch. "Nice to finally meet you," she said. *Finally.* As if Laura were Stu's long lost sister or Canadian ex. "Honey," she said to him, showing ownership, "did you get the tent down from the hall closet?"

"It's by the door." Then he turned to Laura. "Tofu's doing an action at the I.I. building today."

International Insurance had been busted for evading taxes and selling fancy financial products that amounted to legalized gambling to investors, hedge fund managers, and the federal government's pension fund. The CEO got a nine-figure bonus, and the pensioners had gone broke. Oldest story in the book. It bored Laura into a coma. Ruby was already picking her nails.

"Our dear should be going, too." Apparently, *our dear* was Stu. Tofu must have had a streak of old lady in her. "But he's too busy using his talents to support big publishing."

"The *New Yorker* is not big publishing." But by the look on his face, Laura could tell he was conflicted, and by the faux-light tone of the conversation, she knew that had been discussed until the issue was raw at the edges.

"Darling..." Tofu touched the side of his face. "A hundred small, struggling papers that support our cause would have your story. Even the *Village Voice*. Not that that's perfect, but at least they put a left polish on the issues."

"Of magazines with any kind of circulation, the *New Yorker* is considered the most progressive magazine in the country, bar none."

She rolled her eyes. "Is there any coffee?"

"Oh, sorry." He pointed at Laura, who clutched the cup that apparently contained Tofu's coffee.

"Do you want more?" Tofu asked.

Laura put down the mug. "I was just going. It was really nice to meet you."

"You, too!"

Ruby said good-bye, but from Tofu's bare-bones reaction, the enthusiasm in her salutations had been based not on warmth, but on the perception of the threat to her territory.

At the bottom of the stairs, Stu opened the door for them. "I'll call you when I have something."

"She'll nag you if you take too long," Ruby interjected.

Laura ignored her. "She's nice, Stu. And pretty."

"Glad you approve."

She heard a touch of annoyance in his voice, as if he either thought she was being disingenuous or she was focused on the wrong thing. So she had to do something to impress him, and the only way to impress that particular hipster was to be honest to the point of pain. "I didn't say I approved."

"I like that you never change," he said.

But she didn't like it. Not at all.

They stood in line for coffee at the hipster place. Her fourth cup of the day. She needed some kind of drug to get her through the next hours, and the medication of choice was caffeine. Ruby tagged along, even though Laura knew she had someplace to be.

"You coming to the showroom?" Ruby asked.

"No, I have to bring Yoni some fabric approvals, or she's going to give birth to a squid."

"Not nice. You shouldn't wish that on her."

"Why? You think I'm so powerful that Thomasina bit it because I wished her dead when she pushed you?"

"You *didn't*!"

"God, you are such a little sentiment fascist. What's your deal?" Laura turned away, making mental notes of what she saw: striped jeans with voluminous geometric tops and old lady glasses, tiny floral prints, muted colors. Teased hair was apparently making a comeback. She dubbed it Geriatric Nouvelle and filed it.

"Bringing you to Stu was a mistake," Ruby said. "I should have dragged you to Jeremy's. That would have cheered you up."

"Anything would have been better, actually."

"He's your friend. You shouldn't cut him out."

"I know," she said, her voice barely audible under the white noise of the coffee place.

"I know it's hard, but—"

She couldn't listen to a platitude, so she interrupted, "You know what *is* hard? That he was it? He was my chance to be with someone who wasn't interested in you, and to have someone you couldn't steal."

"I don't want—"

"Exactly. I liked him, and he was safe, and he was a sure thing, and I blew it. Do you know how hard it is to listen to you talk about real relationships, and I have zero experience? I'm so tired of wondering what it's all like. I can't even read books anymore without getting jealous of the characters who are actually... you know." She lowered her voice too late. The guy behind them had heard, even if he pretended he didn't.

Laura looked at Ruby and could feel a big apology, or compassion that came right from the gut. But she didn't want anything more than to run away from the whole conversation.

Like a blessing from above, they reached the end of the line. She ordered something, but forgot what it was, then babbled about old lady stylings in the hipster set before Ruby could offer a dose of saccharine or sympathy.

CHAPTER 7.

Ruby knowing about Jeremy had not worked in Laura's favor. She dealt with constant winking and nudging, especially after Stu turned out to be such a dud. The innuendos and coy looks drove her up a tree, and more than once, Jeremy had pulled her to the side and asked if Ruby was okay or if she had a case of Tourette's that would damage her usefulness in the showroom. Of course, once he introduced them around and saw how Ruby took control of the situation, how she was inviting, warm, personable, and made immediate friends, he respected her professionally. After that, the favors streamed in, but he never really warmed to her. Laura thought it a pleasing turn of events. Even though she officially wasn't interested in her old boss any more, she still harbored a slight, annoying possessive streak, at least where Ruby was concerned. Her sister had stolen enough boyfriends over the course of her life to convince her that if Jeremy wanted Ruby, her sister would be willing to meet him halfway. And everyone wanted Ruby. She was like a force of nature.

It wasn't even just men. Women craved Ruby's friendship as well. Thomasina had been no different. It was always Ruby's choice to be a friend or a lover or not. Even Bob had purred the first time he met Ruby. Married men were over the line for her, and apparently, she took his vows more seriously than he did. Laura couldn't imagine how Bob thought he had the energy to have an affair with Ruby as well as Thomasina.

What had been in it for Thomasina? Money seemed too easy an answer. She had more than most people would see in a lifetime. He had no prestige, no special knowledge outside of a football field, no access to people she didn't. Laura refused to believe there was some deep attraction there. People like Thomasina didn't go near people like Bob unless there was money or connections to be had. Actually, Laura had pinned her as the kind of woman who would *only* have affairs with guys like Bob because they saw money and connections as the point of having affairs.

It was a long walk out to Tudor City, where her, and Jeremy's, production person was laid up, and she spent that time worrying about whether or not Bob would shell out another dime, with or without Ivanah's interest in the design end, if a certain supermodel wasn't alive to encourage him.

Yoni was not a woman who stood still. She was wildly productive, accurate to a fault, sharp, detail-oriented, and big-picture conscious. She could be running her own company, but seemed too busy to start one.

So Laura imagined the worst when she went up to see her in her Tudor City prewar co-op, and because being around someone who idled at a hundred miles per hour made her forget her problems just so she could keep up. There was no way Yoni was actually sitting still, even if the doctor ordered it, even if the doctor strapped her down. That was why she was freelancing for Laura while on maternity leave. No one could keep a good woman and her fetus down.

A stout woman with skin like a boiled pierogi led Laura to a back room without really looking at her. The apartment went around corners and hallways, where little tables held little doodads that looked perfectly proportioned and painted to be next to the little things beside them.

Yoni lay in the bed with her feet up, her seven-months-pregnant belly barely distended. Her fingers tapped, and her toes wiggled. The TV displayed some relaxing music and ambient abstract shape-changing thing that wasn't actually meant to be watched actively. Books lay everywhere, open a third of the way through, bookmarked, upside down. Yet there was a certain aesthetic order that made even a mess seem somehow right.

"What did you bring me?" Yoni asked when she saw Laura with the cardstock sheets.

"Approvals." Laura moved some books from a chair that was shaped like a brick. The tomes were titled *Taking Down the Enemy* and *Infiltration Techniques for a Better Tomorrow*. No surprise. Yoni's dad had been in Mossad, and there was no proof she wasn't following in his footsteps. Laura plopped in the chair and slouched enough so her legs were straight and her heels touched the hardwood.

"You have projections, I hope." When she saw Laura's face, she slapped the cardstock to the bedspread. "You want your delivery, or no? Tell me now."

"Yoni. You know the calendar better than I do, and you know—"

"We're behind."

"How can we be behind already? We designed the line a year ahead of delivery."

Yoni closed her eyes for a second, obviously trying to remain calm. "How long did you work for Jeremy? Did you think he kept to the calendar for fun? The buyers expect to see product when they expect it, no sooner or later, and the delivery calendar was set by God, so this is your personal hell."

"No," Laura said. "My personal hell is Ivanah Schmiller

having editorial power over the line, a dead model in my bathroom during the show, getting in trouble for replacing her for a shoot the next day, and a sister-slash-partner being borderline non-functional because she was friends with the dead model, who has a brother who is totally hot, by the way, who I don't trust at all, showing up at the shoot. Oh, and the cops totally dusted down my sister's place last night."

Yoni looked up from her cardstock. "Why?"

Laura shrugged. "They wouldn't say."

"They would have lied if they did. Listen to me. You of all people should know better. They came because they think your sister is a murderer."

"No way!"

"Wente dies how? Gunshot? Strangled like the other bitch? No. Poison. Why, then?"

Laura shrugged.

"Get out," Yoni said. "You make the baby annoyed. She wants to come out and slap you."

"Yoni!"

"I'm having a contraction right now. Stress. From you." She pulled a plastic gallon of distilled water from the night table and drank right from the container.

"Do we call the doctor?"

"Why do you kill someone with poison? Why don't you just shoot them?"

"Guns are messy and loud and hard to get."

"Strangle the bitch."

"She's too strong."

"Use a knife." Yoni poured her water instead of gulping from the jug.

"Messy again. And it's hard to kill someone that way. Too easy for them to live and lurch off."

"You can hold your hand like this…" She bent her hand in half so the first knuckles of the fingers stuck out like a wedge. "And hit them hard in the Adam's apple. This breaks the trachea."

"I don't think a normal person could do that in just one

shot. I mean, if they tied her down and got a couple of shots at it, maybe." She imagined herself straddling Thomasina, popping away at her trachea while she said, "*A little to the left. No, my left.*"

"So," Yoni said, "you're saying they needed to poison them because they're strong and you don't want to make a mess. The killer didn't have a gun. So, not a professional. Someone personal. But not an accident. Oh, no. If it were an accident, you wouldn't be seeing that detective at your house. What was his name?"

"Cangemi. I don't know his first name."

"I think he likes you."

"He only likes his own jokes."

Yoni's water sloshed when she put the glass on the night table. "Do you want to feed the poison, inject it? Maybe a pill? This person is maybe on some medications they can mix up?"

"Diet pills, but I'm not sure if they're hers."

Yoni wagged her finger at Laura. "The next time you come to me with questions like this, you should have the details worked out. I don't have time to walk you through what you should know already." She snapped up the pile of swatches stapled to the cardboard, giving the wool crepe a tug. Then she looked at the writing on the cardboard and tugged again.

She waved the cardstock page at Laura. "They used the wrong denier lycra. I cannot stand it." Pulling out a red sharpie like a cowboy reaching for a pistol under her pillow, she scribbled "REJECTED" across the top of the page and signed it. "Tell me something," Yoni said, scribbling more notes on the other cards. "You want to poison someone. Do you force them to eat something they don't usually? Or inject them? How do you get it inside them? Maybe she took drugs already?"

"If I were going to poison someone," Laura said, "I'd put it on the food she was already eating. But I'd need access to her food."

"Correct! Who fed her last?"

"She doesn't eat, Yoni. That's her job. But if she did, it would have to be breakfast. Or dinner the night before." Laura was frustrated with her own answer. "Or a snack, I don't know!"

Yoni held up her hand, and Laura immediately felt calm. She had a window into what kind of parent the production manager was going to be. A stern mother who made her child feel safe and in good hands, as though she knew the location of all the answers and was waiting for the person to meet her there. The exact opposite of Laura's own mother.

"Before that," Laura said, "when I saw her, she looked kind of green, and Monty made a comment about her skin color being off. So she must have come in sick. But she didn't say she was sick all night or suddenly or anything."

"So?"

"So she must have been poisoned already, but I don't know for how long."

"Get me that book right there." Yoni pointed at an art deco table.

Laura placed the fat tome carefully on Yoni's lap because it was about as thick as it was tall.

Yoni flipped through it. "Tell me more about what happened that morning, please. What did she say? How did she act?"

"She was normal. Just a little sick."

Yoni clenched her fist. "More."

"She was cranky, as usual, and Ruby sided with her."

"Cranky about what? My God, you can try a woman's patience."

"She wanted to wear sunglasses on the runway. And Ruby said okay? I mean, really? Not only is it douchey, they weren't rented or signed off. So we could still get killed for infringing copyright."

"How was she breathing?"

"Didn't notice."

"Were her pupils dilated?"

"I missed my second year of med school."

"Was the black part big?"

"The sunglasses... hello, she wouldn't take them off. I

was arguing with her, and she was barely even answering, just making this clicking noise in her throat, which must be East German slang for 'entitled tall rich person can do whatever she wants.' And get this, Monty was trying to work on her, and she wouldn't take off the sunglasses. She's ready to walk down the runway with flaking skin because why? I don't know because he finally just took them off her, and it wasn't like she had a black eye or anything."

"You didn't see her pupils then?"

"There's no eye contact. She's like seven feet tall, so I'm constantly looking up her nose."

Yoni slapped the book closed. "It's too obvious."

"What?"

"You haven't earned answers." Yoni swung her legs over the edge of the bed. "We agree she was murdered because your homicide detective was lurking around, yes?"

"Yes."

"People are murdered for only a few reasons. Love. Revenge. Money. Politics maybe. Poisoning is good for some of these. For politics. Yes."

"Thomasina? The only politics she cared about happened in the fit room."

"Don't exclude it too fast."

"Well, forget revenge or love," Laura said. "Because what's the point of revenge if you're not standing over them, telling them they're dying for something they did? And love, same thing. No one's getting killed for love unless the killer's there to hear the last words. Because they're hoping for apologies or regrets. No. It had to be money."

Yoni hoisted herself and her belly to a standing position. "At least you've turned on your brain. So I'll tell you. The sunglasses were for light sensitivity. The skin was dry. The clicking in the throat was because she couldn't swallow. She was very sick, my dear. You should have been nicer."

Laura pursed her lips. She could have been nicer, just in general. But what was she supposed to do? She had three giraffes puking in the back room, two who looked as if they hadn't gotten their first period yet, a partner as green as a jalapeno, and rumors that Penelope Sidewinder was outside with her eagle eye. So yes, the whole argument over the sunglasses had gotten cruel with words like "entitled bitch" getting thrown around in the heat of the moment. The guilt made her hold her arm out for Yoni as the pregnant woman trudged across the floor. Her offer was rejected, but Yoni made slow progress toward the bathroom.

"It was alkaloids," Yoni said. "All the symptoms. She was already poisoned when she came. You're lucky she didn't drop on the runway. MAAB would have been on you like bombs on a strategic target. You now figure out how they got into her. You can do that?"

"I think I know already."

Yoni raised an eyebrow. They were right outside the bathroom. Laura ran to her bag and fished out the capsule. "Can we find out if this is alkaloid?"

"I thought she didn't take pills?"

"I found it in her bag."

"You didn't give this to the police?"

"I gave the rest to them. But if they're going to start accusing my sister of something and not telling me anything about it, I need to do my own legwork. Don't you think?"

"I am very impressed." Yoni took the pill. "Give me a couple of days."

"You bet." Laura bathed in validation as she let the pierogi take her to the door.

Once in the lobby, Laura realized she hadn't told Yoni about the receipts, missing a huge opportunity to gain esteem with her. She pulled the copies out of her bag and headed back toward the elevator, questioning the maturity of her motivations, the practicality of bothering when she hadn't even looked at them, and the benefit of waiting for a later moment when she actually needed something from Yoni. Right about when she started looking at the pages, she realized loneliness had driven her back to the elevator. She had no one else to talk to. Ruby was too emotionally involved to keep in the loop. Stu was with a processed protein product. Corky was entertaining buyers. Mom was over some kind of emotional edge about Ruby. Jeremy was too close to the business; he'd invariably tell her to back off and sew.

Yoni was a great person to talk to, and she appeared very available where sleuthing was concerned, but she was pregnant and on bed rest. So by the time the elevator dinged, Laura was staring at her copies of receipts and thinking she should just leave. She turned away, but then saw a little scribble on one of the scraps of paper.

The copy machine had done a butcher job, but she could make out a phone number, which had the old school 212 area code. The Kiel's store receipt was dated the day before the show. Before she could talk herself out of it, Laura stood at the curb, dialing the number. And before she could come up with an excuse for calling besides, 'Sorry, I dialed the wrong number,' someone answered.

"Sidewinder here."

It was most certainly not a wrong number.

"Hi, Penel... I mean, Ms. Sidewinder. I... uh... this is Laura Carnegie? From Sartorial Sandwich? I'm sorry to bother you?" She was disgusted with the question-asking lilts on the ends of her sentences. She kicked people like that. They were weak and worthless, and there she was in their company.

"Yes, Ms. Carnegie. I'm heading into a showing. Is there something I can help you with?"

Oh, God. Laura had nothing. "You saw my show yesterday?" Stupid, stupid, stupid girl. It sounded as if she was leading in to a request for a review, which was exactly what Sidewinder expected and the reason for her beleaguered, formal tone. Before Laura could get cut off, she blurted, "I wanted to say, some of the girls in my show, I don't think they were of age. And I don't know what to do about it. I feel so bad, and I don't want to get into trouble, but if I don't speak out, well, that's worse. And my Mom looked sixteen until she was twenty-five so... I don't want to make accusations."

The background noise on Sidewinder's side disappeared,

as if the reviewer had walked into a nearby closet. "Where are you, darling?"

"Tudor City area-ish." God, had she just given away Yoni's location or something? What a crappy spy she'd make.

"Have you ever been to Baxter City? Do you know where it is?"

Those were two totally different questions. No, she had never been to Baxter City because it was members-only and impossibly exclusive, but yes, she knew where it was. But before she could explain that she wasn't a member, she found herself agreeing to meet the reviewer there in half an hour. She called Corky to let him know she wouldn't be in the showroom for a couple of hours and was preparing excuses when he answered the phone in full panic mode.

"Where are you?" he hissed.

"I was dropping approvals to Yoni, then—"

"I'm all alone here."

"Where's Ruby?"

"Not here. I got buyers coming out the wazoo, no time to steam anything. No time to refill the water jugs. I've eaten brunch four times. Bloomingdale's ran an hour late, and where the hell are you guys?"

"Corky, I don't know where Ruby is. I assume you called her. But I can't get there for a few hours, and there's nothing I can do about that right now. I'm sorry, but there are things happening, and it's not like I'm any use in the showroom anyway."

"Is this Thomasina drama?"

"Yes."

"Fine," he said. "Just get Ruby back here."

She promised she'd make it up to him, but had no idea how.

CHAPTER 8.

Laura had heard of Baxter City, but never seen it. It was not visible or accessible from the street. She walked up an alley off Centre Street with a cast iron gate and made eye contact with the guy in the building's window. Unlike every other alley in the city, the cobblestone paving was scrubbed clean and repaired. The dumpsters and their smells were hidden away, and the building windows had not a bar or burglar alarm on them. The guy in the window opened the gate, and she walked through a pair of frosted glass double doors with the letters BH etched in them.

Past the doors, she stepped into a simple lobby about the size of a doctor's waiting room. The room was dark, with candles and a small casement window as the only sources of light. A thin Asian man in black jeans and thick, black Bakelite glasses circa 1923 greeted her from behind a raw wood counter.

"I'm not a member," she said, as if deflecting Bakelite's inevitable derision.

"Very good." He seemed nonplussed by her plebe status. "Who's sponsoring you today?"

Laura blinked. She had no idea what he meant.

"You're a guest of someone?"

His courtesy was disarming. If she had been a guest, it was calculated to make her feel comfortable. If she was an interloper, it was meant to let her know, politely, how one gets in. She felt at ease then, as though she wasn't going to get thrown out on her ear or shamed into leaving before she had her meeting.

"Penelope Sidewinder invited me?" God. With the question voice again. When had she started to feel so small? When had she decided she was permanently the bottom person on a social ladder that could get pulled up any time?

Bakelite checked his clipboard and motioned toward two doors. "She's upstairs already. Elevator to the right. Stairs to the left. Sixth floor. Mandy at the counter will help you out once you're there. There are no photographs, please."

"Thanks."

As she walked the three, maybe four steps to the wall with the different transports to the upper floors, she wondered which method the rich people took, the people who weren't "guests." One would assume a sense of entitlement took them to the elevator. But the truly entitled, those who didn't have to think about their entitlements, would probably take the stairs. And didn't she want to be one of those?

More than what she *wanted* to be, who *was* she? Regardless of money, which method did she *want* to take? She was on the third step, still undecided, almost walking directly into the wall in between, when a couple blew by her so fast they almost knocked her over. She heard a girl giggling and a man mumbling, and saw a leather jacket and bit of pink georgette frill pass her and enter the stairwell. Neither apologized nor even looked back. She decided to take the elevator.

Everything about the place was magical and perfect. The floors were made of an unfinished, distressed wood laid out in a herringbone pattern so irregular and impossible to clean that ten ticks of specialness were added for the simple cost of managing them. The walls were covered with art. Real art. Banksy's scrawled screams, Barofsky's numbers, Ryden's big-eyed mannequins and meats. A Cullen so pornographic she could almost smell it. All were framed and crowded together so close that the wall was almost completely covered. The amount of original art that had to be purchased to achieve the effect was staggering.

At the counter, a Hawkinson soda can/clock sat next to the phone like a knick-knack bought at a thrift store. Mandy looked like a normal person, not a model, not overly made up to out-glamour any of the members.

"I'm meeting Penelope Sidewinder," Laura said, keeping any hint of a question from her voice. The amount of effort required to do that was monumental.

Mandy smiled in a way that made Laura feel like she was in the club, part of their inner circle, welcome and wonderful, and led her down a hall, up half a flight of stairs, and deeper into that new world. Not wanting to miss a moment, Laura turned off her phone.

They entered the biggest living room Laura had ever seen, with islands of tastefully worn couches at discrete distances from one another, rugs that did not cover too much of the raw wood herringbone floor, and floor-to-ceiling windows with a view that could have been created only by accident or pure mathematics. Both New Jersey to the west and Long Island to the east seemed to be visible. The scope of the space and views from the windows gave her a feeling of peace and rightness. She would join the club and have access to that room any time. It was her place as much as Penelope Sidewinder's. She belonged. Even wearing her old jeans, a chain mail belt, and a cropped wool crepe shift she had pieced together from extra Sartorial fabric, even with her cheap shoes and unhighlighted roots, even with one eye's worth of makeup that had rubbed off since the morning, she vowed it was not the last time she'd see that room.

Penelope Sidewinder sat by one of the many windows, sipping something from a porcelain cup. The setting sun glinted off the flyaway strands of hair she hadn't tucked into her bun. At five-ten and built like a breadstick, she had probably modeled in her younger days. She was one of the top half-percent of people who had the face and build for magazine covers, and the other top half-percent of those who could run her career like a business, stay off the sauce and the powder, and survive. What no one expected was that she was also a woman of strong moral fiber and sharp sartorial eye. When modeling started drying up, she took to fashion reviewing, and as she aged into her forties, she spoke her mind frequently and openly. The girls were too young. Their bodies were too thin, and the industry was eating alive all but the top five percent.

And there she was at Baxter City, waving Laura over to a seat.

"I'm so sorry to bother you," Laura said, slipping onto the cool leather. "I didn't know who else to call."

"Oh, I was at the Calvin show. Same thing every season. I can just look at the pictures. Tea? It's rooibos. African red. I take it with cream and sugar, like a chai, but most people take it straight."

Laura accepted the tea and left it plain. "You know, I didn't really think about any of the girls much, since Mermaid made all the right assurances." Laura listened to herself and thought she sounded like an actress in a scene from *Upstairs, Downstairs.* "But Thomasina… with what happened at the end. It's been haunting me all day."

Penelope leaned forward and put her hand on Laura's knee. "Don't worry. If you have the green sheet from Mermaid, you're protected." The green sheet was the boilerplate contract, with assurances from the agency that their girls were of minimum age and weight. It was called a green sheet because the agreement had been first scribbled on a green napkin at Marlene X. "But I do need to know what you saw, especially with Thomasina. The board at MAAB is foaming at the mouth. Someone's going to have their blood drawn."

"I hope it's not us." Laura only breathed the last two words, because in the middle of the sentence, she was pretty sure she shouldn't have said it.

"I doubt it," Penelope said. "But who can say? Things happen. And there's been no time for a full investigation."

Laura felt pensive. What a stupid thing to lose her business over. Nothing was going right. "This is harder than I thought it would be. Starting the line." She realized immediately that she'd spoken too frankly.

"Everyone pays a price. Even people born into it have a piece of themselves missing."

"Thomasina was born rich and wore clothes for a living. I mean, I'm sorry she's dead, I really am, but—"

"Thomasina had dreadfully conservative parents who only cared about their image, and she carried self-loathing in every picture she took. It was what made her face so special. The complexity there, you don't learn that in acting class."

"I never saw it. I'm sorry."

"You did, even if you couldn't pin it down. Every girl has a history in her eyes. The brilliant ones put it right there without saying a word. I took pictures before and after I came to New York, and it's like two different people were in them, because I was different."

Laura looked past the little wireframes and into Penelope's green eyes. She found nothing but warmth and sincerity. She felt accepted and invited, finally somewhere she belonged utterly. "Where were you before?"

Penelope sighed. "When I started out, I was fifteen. From Kentucky."

"You don't have an accent."

"Back then, we had to erase our accents. Obliterate them. Now of course, it would be part of my brand. Are you having a cookie? I can't eat all of them myself."

Laura took one and nibbled.

Penelope watched closely, cutting the warmth of the

moment with a little discomfort. "I was on the volleyball team at East Cherokee High when there were so few girls' volleyball teams. I was a freshman on varsity. Very impressive. I had a spike, which was unheard of on the girls' team." She rooted around in her slip of a bag and came up with a little vial with an eyedropper.

"I tried out for volleyball at Dalton. I was too short."

"Ah, Dalton. That explains the erudition of your line."

Laura's cheeks tingled, and she wished she could ice them down.

Penelope squeezed some liquid into her tea. "Vitamin D concentrate. Would you like some?"

"No, thank you."

Penelope dropped the bottle back in her bag. "My mom made me an extra jelly sandwich on practice days. We were good. Very good. We went to the regional championship in Chicago. My dad drove me up there in my uncle's pickup. He complained about closing the store and the cost of the gas the whole way." Penelope sipped her tea, as if for effect, smiling a little.

"Did you win?" Laura asked.

"I don't remember. It didn't really matter. There was a scout there named Dianne Gorbent. Not a volleyball scout or a college scout. Oh, no. A scout for tall girls. And where better to find thin, tall white girls than a volleyball tournament? No one ever underestimated Dianne and lived to tell about it. She approached my father after the game, telling him about all the money a girl like me could make in New York. Of course, we were relatively... well, I want to say, we lived in the back of my father's drugstore. And imagine, my mother wouldn't have to make any extra jelly sandwiches. My father said he would miss me on the ride home. Who would listen about the evils of OPEC if I wasn't there? He wasn't the crying kind. But you could tell he was proud I was making something off my looks. Before I left, and got on a plane, of all things, he said he expected the next time I came home, I'd be with a man of my own. His words were, 'Someone richer than your old man.'

This being the scope of what a woman could achieve in Kentucky in the 1970s.

"I got to New York with a duffel bag full of gym shorts and sports bras, and Dianne took me shopping." She sighed. "Those days. It was like a dream. Like a movie. I lived in a guest apartment off Central Park. She fed me like I have never been fed before. Three hot meals a day. If I could, for one minute, recapture the feeling of constant gratitude and happiness I felt for that first week. Over the simplest things, too. I didn't have any chores. I didn't have to take care of my brothers or sweep the store. She took me to Donna Carnegie's party on Fifth Avenue, with some of the most sophisticated people I have ever seen. Are you sure you're not related? I see a little resemblance."

"I never looked into it."

"You should. Anyway. I hadn't even gone on a call, and I knew I had found my purpose, at fifteen years old. Those were the best weeks of my life. Dianne let me call home, which was very expensive at the time, and I told my parents not to worry, everything was great. My sister said everyone at school was simply green with envy."

In the twenty minutes Laura had been there, the sun had crested its apex and started down toward the horizon line, lengthening shadows and warming the world with yellowish light. She wondered if Ruby had ever made it to the showroom, if Rowena had looked haggard for her other jobs, and if Chase had sent his selects. She didn't really want to hear the rest of Penelope's story. There was nowhere to go but downhill.

"Ms. Sidewinder, I—"

"I went on my first shoot on a Monday, absolutely high from the weekend. I came out, as it were, and Dianne said she was already getting bookings. She couldn't make that shoot, and she said it was simply to have some photos to show. His name was Franco. He was relatively well known, she said, and she didn't have to go with me. I never knew if she knew what he would do. But that doesn't matter now."

"I think I get it." Laura didn't want to hear another word.

"It was in this studio downtown, before downtown was what it is today. I can't tell you how many rats I stepped over. But I thought, 'Ah, this is the high and the low. I'll see everything and do everything,' and it added to my happiness. Well. He couldn't have been more average. Short and scruffy. I did my makeup and went into the lights. And he adjusts the camera, takes a few shots, and tells me I look great. And I believe him. And then, looking through the camera lens, he says, 'Have you ever sucked a man's lollipop before?'"

Laura almost choked on her cookie.

"Exactly," Penelope said. "When I reacted, he snapped a picture, and then he said, 'You realize, before you leave here today, you're going to suck my lollipop.' And he's click-clicking pictures, and I think I must have misheard him, but he says, 'You like sucking lollipops,' and I say, 'No, thank you.' But he ignores me. And he's saying the filthiest things I won't even repeat. And right before I start crying, he takes the last picture and says, 'What am I telling Dianne when you leave?'" She sipped her tea and placed the cup on the table. "Laura, I knew I was going to have to do it."

"No."

"What was I supposed to do? How was I supposed to go home to Kentucky? With what in my bag? Shame? Failure? And what would I do? Play volleyball for varsity, marry some man from my class, and have children? No. I wasn't from there anymore. I'd changed in that week. Not enough to have a friend to turn to and certainly not enough to refuse him. All I had to do was get through it."

"I'm so sorry."

"When I got back to the apartment, I was going to tell Dianne, at least to ask her if this was normal. But as soon as I got in, she sat me down and said she didn't realize how little I'd eaten at home. The rich food of the past week had gone straight to my gut, and I was going to have to cut down. After she told me that, I couldn't tell her what I'd done. What if it was the wrong thing? What use was I then? I would be a whore, and a fat one at that. On the bus back to the Midwest with nothing to show for it. I started making sure I ate well at dinner parties and puked thoroughly afterward."

Laura felt a little sick, and it must have shown because Penelope, who had already been warm and inviting, softened even further. "Plenty of women have gone through worse, and plenty of models, I daresay. I came from the Midwest; some of them come from countries I wouldn't even want to talk about. No citizenship and no one to protect them. No birth certificate with their legal age. Their passports are fake. It's terrible. We can't even track half of them down. Which is why it's so important for designers to be on board."

Laura had walked into the meeting ready to talk about Dymphna's pre-adolescent cheeks and pubescent attitude. She was going to say she had a funny feeling about that girl, but after hearing Penelope's story, she decided to say something else entirely. "Rowena Churchill. I was at a shoot with her this morning, and... God, I'm realizing there's no way I can prove this. She couldn't walk in the heels. She seemed so young. She was looking at Chase like he was a celebrity."

Penelope leaned forward like a reporter getting the big scoop. "She's from northern California, I believe. Sequoia country. Did she say anything, maybe about school?"

"She said she never took geometry."

Penelope's eyes looked far away, as if she were gazing inside herself. "Tenth grade. In my era, that was tenth grade."

"How old is that?"

Penelope just said, "Roquelle can be careless."

Laura was about to answer in the affirmative when she heard a gasp behind her. Then a swallowed giggle and she had to turn. Rolf stood there with a girl in an equestrian-printed pink georgette scarf. When he recognized her, he raised his eyebrows. Laura recognized the clothing. He wore a brown leather jacket. They were the two who had almost knocked her over on the way to the stairs.

"Laura Carnegie." Rolf nodded at her. His breath was so unnaturally minty fresh, even from a more-than-adequate distance, that Laura flinched a little.

The pink georgette girl with the meatball-sized brown eyes turned to Penelope. "I am such a fan of yours." Her Euro-accent was so thick, she was hard to understand.

"Frau Sidewinder," Rolf said, using the German formal, which Penelope seemed to appreciate and understand. Apparently, they knew each other, like typical rich people, traveling in circles. "This young lady eats, sleeps, and breathes modeling. Her name is—"

"How nice," Penelope said. She looked at the girl, but again did the thing where she was actually looking deeply inside herself. It was disconcerting. "I haven't modeled since you were about four years old."

Laura changed the subject to something she considered safe. "Did you get your sister's bag from the cops?"

"They won't release it."

"You just have to wait."

"These American cops—"

She had no idea what he was going to say, but was sure she didn't want to hear it, so she interrupted with, "I'm sure in Germany they're pussycats."

Penelope snapped out of her middle-distance reverie and patted the seat next to her. "Sit here, young lady, and let's talk about modeling."

"Maybe next time," Rolf said. "We were just leaving."

But the girl with the meatball eyes squirmed out of his arms and sat next to Penelope with childlike delight.

Rolf took the seat next to Laura. "Your sister is all over the news. They think she did Thomasina in. I want to tell you, I don't think it's true."

She didn't want to give him one word he could use against either of them. She suddenly felt she was in the wrong place, at the wrong time, with people who wanted to hurt her.

"I have to go," Laura said. "It was nice talking to you." She shook Penelope's hand and nodded to Rolf and Meatball Eyes.

As she was leaving, Penelope called out, "To be continued."

Roquelle is careless.

Laura sat in the very nice bathroom, looking at what may or may not have been an actual Manet hanging over the sink, and recalled the conversation.

Why the interest in Roquelle? What had she done, or at least gotten caught for? Did Roquelle have a reputation Laura wasn't aware of? Out of curiosity, she went back to the room with the big windows and the bays of couches. Penelope was gone, but Rolf and Meatball Eyes were hunched close in front of her unfinished rooibos tea. She took a long stroll around the lobby, looking at the art, and the orchids and paper whites on the tables, letting three elevators pass before she finally bit the bullet and left the club.

CHAPTER 9.

Laura had heard a gruesome story and little else, and the train ride back uptown was the perfect time for a little self-immolation. She got so embroiled in the Kentucky volleyball player's metamorphosis into a savvy New York blowjob provider that she hadn't gotten an ounce of information about Thomasina. She did, however, make a contact out of Penelope Sidewinder, which was no small thing, so if she ever had anything more specific to ask during an intentional phone call, maybe she could ask it. By the time she got to the 38th Street office, she was feeling pretty good about herself.

She slowed by the newsstand and was about to glance over the headlines when she saw a face she recognized.

"Fancy meeting you here," Kamichura's cameraman said. He wore a huge tweed jacket with ballpoint pen stains at the bottoms of the pockets and a straw hat. He held out his hand.

"Name's Roscoe. Roscoe Knutt. You might remember me from Channel Four. When you were a kid."

"Vaguely." Actually, her mother's news-watching habits meant Laura knew the names of every broadcaster to grace a screen in the past twenty years, but she was in no mood to encourage him.

"Might recollect me from your front sidewalk last night."

"That, I remember." She took half a step toward the revolving door.

Roscoe took it with her. "I wanted to get a jump on my partner. You know, she's young and ambitious and on a camera like white on rice. As it were. Pushed me right outta my job. Can I ask you something?"

As frustrated as she was, she was a sucker for regular people who got the shaft from someone more attractive. "One question, and I may not answer it."

"The coroner's report says Wente was poisoned that morning between seven and nine."

"What? They *gave* you the coroner's report?"

"No one *gave* me nothing my whole life." He shrugged. "We have a channel, lady, please. We're not new at this, but listen, I got half the office saying she was at your sister's that morning, and me, myself, I'm saying she wasn't. So, can you prove me right? Please?"

"What else did it say?"

"I didn't read it," he said. "I just got a guy who tells me stuff, which is more than I can say for the girl getting all the credit for my job."

"Well, I can't help you. The morning of the show, I was at work at six thirty, basting the Hudson dress to fit Thomasina. She lost a pound and a half, which on a percentage basis, meant I had to take in seams."

"One more question. You see anything wrong with anyone's eyes that morning? Maybe a scratch on 'em?"

"What?"

"They found eyeball membrane under a nail. It'd really help if you thought about it."

"I will."

"One more question."

She moved quickly enough to sidestep him and get into the building.

She exited the elevator, expecting a day's recap from Corky. What she saw once she turned the corner was Pierre texting as if his fingers itched. He was leaning on the doorjamb, as if he couldn't commit to being either in or out of the room. He looked up at her pointedly, and Laura realized she'd never turned her phone back on after she left Baxter City. Too late. But she *had been* in a meeting with Penelope Sidewinder. He couldn't get on her case for not working.

She couldn't have dreaded the meeting more. Her short encounters with Ivanah had yielded little in the way of good will or comfortable rapport. The scene at Isosceles had done absolutely nothing to improve things. The woman was pouty, coquettish, rich, and well-respected in interior design for reasons Laura feared she would never unravel.

Ivanah had a toy poodle tucked under her left arm, and with her right hand, she held up an unlined Spring jacket with real shell buttons. "This here? The buttons can be rhinestones. Or gold at least. Why do we charge so much for something that looks like I can get it at Target?"

"Hi," Laura said, hoping to inspire politeness, if not a tiny bit of backpedalling.

"Darling," Ivanah said, "where is the other one?" She looked truly puzzled.

Laura held out her hand. "Ruby's not here, apparently."

Ivanah shook hands with her left, as her right still cradled the dog. "You're the one who makes the clothes? The one with the seams? You do a good job, but designing is more than tailoring."

Laura didn't know whether to argue or to let her talk. Did she want to disagree so soon? Or should she let the woman say her piece and give her yeses and noes where applicable?

Pierre must have seen the lack of decision in her face. "Can I get you coffee, Ivanah? I can call for it."

"I'll go!" Corky practically jumped out of his seat; not good salesperson etiquette, but if he didn't want to be there, she figured he'd better go.

Ivanah mentioned a mocha-frappa-something as she picked a Kate Spade men's gym bag off the chair and threw it on the table. It made a big rattling noise as if full of pebbles in cans. "This is how we keep the showroom?"

Corky slung the bag over his shoulder.

Ivanah splayed the jacket with the faux fur on the table. "This is fake. I can tell."

"Barneys Co-op loved it," Corky said. "And every buyer we had in yesterday wanted to know what Barneys liked."

"They'd like it much better if it was real." Ivanah looked under the collar and then dropped it like a used tissue. "Did the Co-op write you an order?"

"Well, no," Laura said.

"That's right. Their money hasn't been allocated. So talk is talk, and it's free to talk."

"We have nothing else to go on right now."

Ivanah turned to Corky who, for all his general good cheer, seemed suddenly out of his depth. "Weren't you getting coffee?"

He slipped out as if a vacuum attached to the door had been turned on.

"Sit down," Ivanah said, as though it was her office.

Laura sat.

Ivanah put her dog down and put both palms on the table. "Do you need money or not?"

"Sure."

"Last night, I was very hard on you, I admit. But I think you have a shot at greatness, my dear. A big shot. And I want to make it happen."

"Honestly, Ms. Schmiller—"

"Ivanah's fine."

"Ivanah. With what you said last night being true, and Thomasina dying at our show, well, I mean the news people are accosting me everywhere I turn, and the cops are scrutinizing everything. I think we're finished here anyway."

Pierre took in a heavy breath. "Of course, you mean…"

Laura shot him a look that shut him up immediately.

Ivanah's gaze did not leave Laura. "You're worried about the police and the newspapers?"

"I'm not worried," Laura said. "'Worried' means I'm wasting my time concerning myself with things I can't predict. In fact, the police dusted down my sister's apartment, and mine is probably next. So I can predict pretty well that something smelly is hitting the fan, which means we're not going to have time to give this the attention it needs. And I know Akiko Kamichura's doing a story throwing accusations at us. I just don't have the resources or the time to fight this and still run a business. So, can you tell Bob I'm sorry we wasted his money? I feel terrible about that."

Ivanah waved her hand as if at a pesky gnat in the room. "My husband doesn't know how to waste money. His losses make profits. It's a sickness." She seemed both truly annoyed and truly proud.

Laura held her breath, then held out her hand. "I'm so sorry, anyway. It's been nice working with you, but we're closed for business."

As if blown in by a surprisingly strong wind, Jeremy walked in with a fur swatch in his hand. He looked surprised to see Ivanah there. "Ivanah! Incredible. I was just thinking about you."

During the fake hugs and air kisses, Laura realized what Pierre had been texting and to whom. When she looked up at him, he winked.

"Can you believe the quality these girls got into their line?" Jeremy asked. "This fabric…" He pulled down the magenta wool crepe. "Hundred fifty a yard and dyed in North Carolina because the flower that makes this color only grows in this one Appalachian valley. Feel it."

"The color is lovely, but—"

Jeremy cut her off. "I can't believe it." He pulled the leather bomber out of the pile. He chuckled in a way that sounded real, but Laura knew was put on. Jeremy didn't laugh that way. "I was just bringing you this swatch." He held the fake fur in his hand against the fake fur on the collar. "Well, looks like I can't use this now. Look at this, Ivanah. Feels real, doesn't it? But we use it and we don't have to alienate our younger customers. They don't want to kill animals."

"Oh, please," Ivanah squeaked. "This is a leather jacket."

"They think the rest of the cow is eaten."

Ivanah and Jeremy laughed at their customers' stupidity, and Laura could see what he'd done. He'd spoken her language. He'd walked into the room, looking for a way to agree with her, and he immediately found it. Whatever that thing was that he had that could assess a person in half a second and use it to get what he wanted, she needed. He did it with the workers in his design room by playing on their fears, and he did it in the showroom by playing on the buyers need to feel like they were "in," and he did it with Ivanah to show her the things about the line that would appeal to her and downplay the things she didn't like.

"Jeremy," Laura said, "this is fun, but we're dissecting a corpse. We're closing up."

"I'm sorry?" His back was to Ivanah when he turned to look at Laura, and she became acutely aware of the fact that he knew exactly what was going on. "Oh, right. You're going out. I'll see you tomorrow. Come by for coffee in the morning."

"No," Laura said, "we're going out of business. We're done here. Between the money running out and Thomasina, it's too much to handle."

"She's dead. What can she do to you now?" Jeremy asked.

"Akiko Kamichura and her team or whoever are totally on us. They're running a story on our relationship with her that I think is going to imply we had something to do with it, and the cops are all over Ruby."

"How is this more than a PR problem?" He looked from Laura to Ivanah and back. "Hire Tintell & Ives, and they'll turn it into an asset."

"What?" Ivanah exclaimed. "They'll botch it. No, darling.

We have to use Greyson. They're mine, and they're fabulous. Yes, of course, you're right. This is no more than a PR problem. We'll have it sorted out in no time."

Laura folded her arms. "I can't afford to hire Greyson Management to spin this."

"Don't insult me," Ivanah said. "I have them on retainer. I'm paying them to do nothing. It's decided. We stay open, and Greyson is on this tomorrow morning."

Laura felt pretty sure that had been decided without her, and she was okay with that. Pierre and Ivanah exited in delightful moods, leaving her and Jeremy alone in the disaster of a showroom.

She picked up the wool crepe dress and gave herself a proper mental beating. "God, I feel like such a whore." She drifted off, thinking about Penelope's story. Not a fair comparison. "She's going to put glitter on everything, and I have to let her now."

"She's more useful close." He hung up the leather jacket, leaning over her to do it. The movement was completely unnecessary, since there was plenty of room on his side.

She looked into his face and saw that he was sharing a deep secret with her, the secret of how to use people to get what you wanted. She felt a little queasy, and she didn't know if it was because the idea was repugnant or exhilarating.

"Her ideas aren't bad," he continued, "but they need to be reined in. Use them. Your trick is to take your own ideas and make her think they're hers. If she's invested creatively, she'll use her clout to get people in the door. And she has clout, Laura. Don't underestimate how important that is. There are no prizes for purity."

"Can I have just one season be right?"

"You're having it. And you can't make your fabric minimums." Only Jeremy could make the phrase "fabric minimums" warm and inviting and an opening to a kiss. He leaned in and did what she had wanted him to do since the day she met him. He did it smoothly, like a cat, or a snake striking, or a man who had not a cell of insecurity in his whole body.

He kissed her. Or she kissed him. Or there was some silent communication from one to the other, some change in the intensity of their pheromones, or a look or glance coded to mean *now*, and they understood that *now* was *now*. Now was *it*. Now was the end of the line for her, the time when wondering and pining and candle holding slid off her, and something new started. Something undefined. Now was the pause between the wanting and the having, where the wanting was all she knew, and the having was suddenly possible, but unanticipated, unimagined, frightening in its unpredictability. It was a closet door that opened by itself in the middle of the night or a dark alley that was a shortcut. It was a wrapped package given by a practical joker. That moment, that *now*, that moment when she saw the door creak open, or considered the alley, or received the package, came before the surprise, which would be pleasant, or unpleasant, or unimagined, but different.

Their kiss went on forever and ever, when all she wanted to do was sit alone in a dark room and remember it, ask what it meant, bring it to heel. Her mind went blank, and she existed solely inside her own mouth, where he was, with the warmth, taste, and feeling that he surrounded her inside and out, and when she thought she couldn't take the pleasure of it anymore, she gave him a little push and opened her eyes.

"Do I need to apologize?" he asked, all French roast eyes and black widow lashes.

"God, no. I just… I thought of something."

He kissed her neck and she thought she would die right there when he whispered, "Tell me," into her ear.

"You're using a wool crepe for Spring. Can I tack onto your fabric orders and drop ship here? I can make my yardage if they'll ship greige."

"Yes. What else?"

"I… ah… nothing."

"Anything. Name it."

"I can't think."

She surrendered fully to his lips, letting him pull her close.

"Oh, Jesus Christ!" It was Corky with a tray of frothy

coffees. "About time."

They separated, and Laura felt prickly heat rise to her cheeks.

Jeremy slipped Ivanah's mocha-frappa-something out of the cardboard cupholder and handed Laura hers, saying, "I'll be at the cutting table."

Once he was gone, she asked, "What do you mean 'about time'?"

"You've been mooning over him since senior projects."

"Well…"

"Well?" he asked.

"You thought he was gay. Even you said he had some gorgeous inaccessible thing going." She was speaking in sentences and hearing herself say things, but her mind was dulled by the taste of him and the desire to crawl into a corner and relive the moment over and over. But Corky was looking at her as if trying to figure out what she was talking about, and it was disconcerting. "After the show, you were on the phone, talking to I don't know who, and—"

"Oh, honey, I wasn't talking about St. James. I was on about Thomasina's brother, Rolf. He was at the bandshell that morning, and he is searing hot. No, no, the hunk next door is all yours."

She rolled her eyes. Rolf was good looking, but somehow unattractive to her. Her phone rang, saving her from having to answer. Corky began straightening the showroom, making little kissy noises just to irritate her. She punched him in the arm before answering.

"Hi, Uncle Graham," she said.

"How are you, favorite niece?"

"I'm fine," she said, leaving out the part where she had just kissed the love of her life, even though she had thought he wasn't anymore. "Why are you calling me at dinnertime?"

"Your sister was taken in this morning, and the police want to talk to you."

Laura abruptly left Corky with a messy showroom and mocking kissy faces.

CHAPTER 10.

He kissed me.
She kept thinking about it and feeling the pressure of him on her lips. She walked to Midtown South, but nothing about the blocks between stuck in her mind. She had trouble paying attention, smacking into a parking meter and stopped dead by a cab door opening. But she just kept walking and staring into the distance, wondering if the feeling of his lips on hers would ever go away.

She wanted to go home and tell Ruby and then warn her away from Jeremy forever and ever, but Ruby was at the precinct, and Laura had to have her wits about her if she was going to get her sister out of custody. She had to shake off Jeremy. It was nothing. It was going to lead to ickiness and discomfort tomorrow. She had to just move on immediately.

She almost got hit by a bike messenger when she tried to

cross Broadway against the light. She wondered if that was why things hadn't happened with Stu. Had she known, deep down, that Jeremy would come around? Had she needed another few months to see if coming out as a heterosexual changed anything for him? Or her? To see if the stolen glances and gifts of coffee had been more than appreciation for hard work and loyalty?

She walked into the lobby of the precinct as if the whole operation was an interruption of some other, far more entertaining series of events. She scanned the room for Uncle Graham, who was usually easy to spot with his white hair and snappy suits. He stood beside a pillar in the center of the room. The column had a wide, wooden shelf built around it, and he had made it into his own personal space by opening his briefcase on it and spreading papers. His suit was custom-made and his wire-framed glasses were made of some lightweight metal used in spaceships. He waved her over when he saw her, putting down the phone as if it had a cradle and the lobby was his office away from the office.

When Laura greeted him, he held her at arm's length, saying, "I'm not happy with you."

"Why?"

"You've been asking questions."

"I just talked to... wait, who do you think I was asking questions?"

"Next time," he said, wagging his finger, "you call me."

"There won't be a next time." Though standing in the lobby of Midtown South again, she wasn't so sure. "Where's Mom?"

"I sent her home. I wanted to talk to you before you went in."

"Is that allowed?"

"You're my client. They can't stop me." She couldn't help but feel annoyed that he'd made the presumption, yet she felt warm and fuzzy at the same time. "They also can't stop me from telling you why they have Ruby. I just need to elicit a verbal agreement from you first."

"Okay?"

"I do not want you getting involved the way you did this past winter."

"Uncle Graham, I can't—"

"You have to."

"You know what my sister means to me?"

He nodded as if he did, but if he truly understood it, he wouldn't have asked in the first place.

She tried to explain. "When we were kids, and Mom was working late, and we got home ourselves from Dalton, we were our own world. The rich white kids wouldn't talk to us, and the other scholarship cases didn't know we had anything in common with them. It was just *us*. If something happens to her, it would be like cutting my heart out."

"That's very dramatic. Also irrelevant."

"Why do they have her?"

"I need you to promise. For her sake, not yours."

Laura crossed her arms. "I cannot tell a lie. I'll do whatever I want. And if you don't tell me, I'll get whatever information I can from wherever else I can. The reason I almost got killed last time is because I was missing a piece of information about the location of a certain sample. Because Detective Don't-Know-His-First-Name Cangemi was protecting me. If I'd had that piece of information, I might have avoided the whole mess."

"A compelling argument. And unprovable." But he smiled.

She shrugged.

He said, "You could have been a lawyer."

"It's a lot of reading."

They paused, as the subject had worn itself thinner than the knees on a pair of pre-distressed jeans. She wasn't good at silences. "I can't believe they think Ruby killed Thomasina. What could they have found in the house? I mean, Ruby squeaked by in chem; I hardly think she'd mix up a poison and put it in a capsule."

Uncle Graham waved his hand. "No. I think they're aware of that. Poison on her countertop or not."

"What?"

"Who would be in her apartment, Laura? Who could have done something, mixed something up maybe, in her kitchen?"

"Uncle Graham, seriously? Thomasina and me. That's all. I think Stu came for an interview a month ago about the Pomerantz case, but otherwise? Nada." It was crazy. Ruby? Something was wrong.

"And they're telling me Ms. Wente was at Ruby's house for dinner the night before? They have her saliva on a spoon."

"No way. Ruby washed her dishes like she was going to perform surgery. This is a complete set-up. What are they holding her for, some… what do you call it kind of evidence? Begins with a C."

"She can be held for circumstantial evidence, my dear, just not convicted on it. I've been with her in all of her questioning, and personally, I don't think they have enough to arrest her. Yet."

"Did they tell you about the coroner's report? That Thomasina was poisoned that morning and not the night before?"

Uncle Graham nodded. "They're aware. It's not relevant."

Cangemi came out and had the nerve to smile at her. Laura didn't get to ask why night and morning were the same thing.

CHAPTER 11.

"We are not going to talk about your sister at all. Whatever you need to know, you can get through her lawyer. I'm going to ask you things, and you're going to think they implicate her. So I want you to know, I'll see it if you're lying to protect her." Cangemi put two fingers to his eyes, then used them to point to her.

"She's not a murderer."

He slipped a booklet from a manila envelope and slid it toward her. A naked female waist, as seen from behind just above the butt cleavage, made her think immediately of pornography. But the rest sparkled in soft pink, floral and lace, strawberries and cream. The script at the top, rendered in deep mauve with a lens flare in the corner, said *The Pandora Agency*.

"Okay?" she asked.

"Have you ever seen this before?"

She took the opportunity to flip through the booklet. It was about thirty pages long, in an expensive matte finish. There were about twelve girls, each with a two-page spread. The photography was totally professional, as was the presentation of the girls, despite the lascivious cover. She flipped to the back page, where the real information would be. She caught an address in Belgium, a couple of funny European phone numbers, and a New York address—277 Park Avenue, 17th floor, the building with the atrium. Below that were three names. She only caught the head of the agency, who was none other than Sabine Fosh.

"Oh, look," Laura said. "No pictures of Ruby, and Thomasina's fake name right here. What do you want? A cookie?"

"You're a pit bull, you know that?"

She couldn't help but be flattered. "My sister spends half an hour picking a nail color." She pushed the modeling catalog toward him. "Ruby isn't Sabine Fosh. That was Thomasina. You know that from the wallet. I mean, this is like… wait. You think they were in on this whole thing together, and they had a business dispute, and Ruby killed Thomasina over it? Really? Have you *met* my sister?"

"What I think isn't important."

"Yeah, and did you talk to Bob Schmiller before throwing my sister under the bus?"

Cangemi cringed and shifted in his seat, as if jolted by a shot of discomfort.

"You okay?" Laura asked.

"Just this huge pain in my ass since you walked in the room."

Everyone's a goddamn comedian. Laura tapped the top of the booklet. "I've never seen this before."

He pushed it back toward her. "What about the girls? Seen any of them before?"

She took the book back reluctantly. She wanted to see the girls, but she didn't want to look too eager. Cangemi seemed to know her and her curiosity streak all too well. The girls were a uniformly feminine type, with yards of sheened, slightly curled hair. The agency was apparently not for supermodels or runway stars. Big eyes. Perfect skin. There were no exceptional looks. No girls with a big honking wedge of a nose planted on an otherwise perfect face. No characters. Nothing striking or shocking.

Except their ages.

Laura held up a picture. "Do you think she got her period yet?"

"Third period math?"

She huffed. They were babies. Totally not MAAB-ready. Photoshop could take years off a middle-aged woman, and slutty makeup could add a couple to a girl, but the babies in the brochure were dewy and sweet. Possibly they were of age, but no man with a heart or moral compass would take one to dinner. And no man with a fear of the law would take one to bed.

"I know her," Laura said, pressing the page open on a girl with brown eyes the size of meatballs. "I met her at Baxter City. She was with Rolf Wente."

Cangemi took the booklet to get a better look. "Baxter City, huh? You're washing windows on the side?"

"They have this really nice red African tea. You should try it next time you go."

He smiled. It was the best reaction she'd ever gotten from him after a wisecrack.

"So, were she and Rolf business or personal?" he asked.

"Depends on what business you're in."

"Catch her real name?"

"No, unless it's really Susannah, which I doubt. She was just giving Penelope Sidewinder the fan treatment."

He nodded as if he knew the reviewer by name, and maybe he did, working Midtown South. He had to pick up something from the garment center.

"Did you ever tell me your real name?" she asked. "The first? The one your mom uses to call you?"

"I told you."

"Your mother calls you Detective?"

"Only when I bring her in for questioning."

"So," Laura said, knowing she sounded like a guy making a pickup line to someone completely out of his league, "you think Thomasina and my sister were repping underage girls and putting them on a runway? Then my sister got pissed and killed Thomasina because she's just like that."

"It's a cutthroat business."

"I thought she was poisoned."

"You're just a pistol. Who signed the contracts for your girls?"

"To be honest, I picked girls for their body type. Once I laid that down, Ruby was in charge of the models. She said she was getting everyone from Roquelle's agency, and all the contracts I signed were from Mermaid. I didn't count the contracts, and I only read one. So I'm not saying one or two didn't slip through from somewhere else, but I think if we were getting girls from Pandora, Ruby would've mentioned it, especially if she was a partner or whatever you think she is."

He leaned back in his chair and laced his fingers together. She saw from his expression that he was trying to weave together strands of knowledge, and what pissed her off was that it was knowledge she didn't have.

"I could help you if you'd tell me everything," she said, swinging for the fences.

"You think?"

"Yeah. I could tell you something."

"Odds are pretty good I know it already."

"You sure Bob Schmiller didn't do it?"

Cangemi had absolutely no reaction. His face was either dead from the boring nature of the information or the hard work he put into looking like he didn't have a reaction.

Laura pressed on. "He called her, yeah, and I know he was away, but if he just put one bad pill in her bottle, he could afford to wait until she took it. Even better if he was away while it happened and he called her like she was alive. He could be patient, right?"

Cangemi held up his hand. "You can have all the fun you want making guesses. We don't do that."

Laura was undeterred by his perch at the higher moral ground. "Bob had to get rid of Thomasina. Ivanah was starting to get involved in his garment business, and they were bound to meet. There's more gossip than a soap opera. The secret would die, and what would happen? A divorce? It would cost him a fortune. That woman isn't stupid; she'd rake him for everything he has. And the fact that you're looking at me like that means I hit on something, doesn't it? I mean, just because I haven't heard you brought him in for questioning doesn't mean you haven't. And whatever he said, you believed him, because he has the money to cover his tracks. And there's Ruby, who has, maybe, a pot to piss in."

"I know you don't get that these accusations are serious. You think you're just talking. And you got this whole problem with not having a filter."

"Just tell me you spoke to Bob Schmiller. He could have planted poison on Thomasina and left on some business trip and waited it out. The question is, when did he plan that trip? Before or after she threatened to tell his wife about them?"

"Isn't he your backer?"

"So?"

"Maybe you should stop talking about him like that." He slid the Pandora book back into the envelope and stood. "You should go before you say something really stupid."

He unceremoniously walked her to the lobby and left her with Uncle Graham like a father giving away the bride. Then he walked away as though he had more important things to do.

"They're releasing her in an hour, maybe two," Uncle Graham said, tapping on his BlackBerry. "You can wait if you want."

"Have they questioned Bob Schmiller?"

He looked at her suspiciously. "Why do you ask?"

"Because he was having an affair with her, one. And two, he could have done it."

He put his phone in his pocket. "Is this what you did

earlier this year? Grasp at straws?"

"As a matter of fact, yes."

"Thomasina was not having an affair with Bob Schmiller, I promise you."

"You're hiding something from me."

"When Ruby comes out, you can ask her about it. But for now, leave it alone."

"I can't."

"Yes, you can, and you will. I'll wait here for Ruby and make sure she gets home. Why don't you get some rest?"

"I'm not tired."

He put his hands on her shoulders. "Do you trust me?"

"Yes."

"Then let me get you a cab."

She let him because he was her uncle, but she didn't go home.

CHAPTER 12.

She held onto a sliver of spite and used it to get her uptown, that and the cab, which had a Jeremy St. James ad on top. Saint JJ. Coming in Spring. As much as her heart tried to hold onto the rage that pushed her to the Schmillers' house, her body kept remembering Jeremy.

Central Park West had never had a renaissance like other neighborhoods. There had been no metamorphosis from dangerous to dumpy to hip to satisfactory to desirable to inaccessible. It had always been a fortress for money, even if the walls around it were in the imaginations of the citizens of the rest of the city. There had always been a doorman, an awning with brass stands, and a no-parking zone right in front because the residents could not be inconvenienced by a parked car outside their building.

Naturally, the Schmillers lived in the shiniest building with the gargoyles and stone balustrades on the top two floors overlooking Central Park and 73rd Street. She wondered about Bob's part in choosing the condo. He didn't seem like a polished, shiny guy. He seemed like an ex-football player with the talent for turning lemon-drop companies into lemonade-flavored cash. If she'd been his real estate agent, she would have pegged him as more of an Upper East Side kind of guy.

Laura had a million reasons to be there, yet she still needed to come up with an excuse to show up after sunset. And she needed flowers. She took a detour to a Korean market and bought the loudest, gaudiest bunch she could lay hands on.

"Hi," she said to the doorman, whose nameplate advertised his name as Harvold. "My name is Laura Carnegie. I'm here for the Schmillers."

"Are they expecting you, Ms. Carnegie?"

"Nope."

"Lovely flowers." He picked up the handle of a circa-1970s wall phone. He said her name and Ivanah's without judgment, hung up, and pointed her to the elevator. "Press the button marked 'P.'"

She did, and the brass doors slid shut with a rickety creak. They probably paid extra for that little sound of authenticity, like the wood paneling inside, and the wool carpet, and the tungsten light. The elevator coasted, then halted, opening onto a small hallway with one door. Their apartment took up the entire floor. Nice. She knocked.

A short man in a grey wool suit with a blue tie and wireframe glasses answered. He held a leather folder in his hand and stopped short when he saw her. "Are you the lady Harvold called up about?"

"Yes. I'm Laura Carnegie?" Damn that little question mark lilt.

"One of the Sartorial sisters, I presume?"

"Wow, that is such a better name than what we came up with."

"Not a stretch, actually. She's up in the garden. Would you like to follow me?"

He led her through the biggest apartment she'd ever seen. Quite possibly, it was bigger than Gracie Pomerantz's house, or the same, but more horizontal, and either tasteless or suffering from an overabundance of taste. The crushed velvet couch was as deep a pink as ripe strawberries and the pattern was perfectly not too big or small, with a matching loveseat, and both had black trim that Laura realized was leather. Everything had chrome or Plexiglass, and every room they passed had some sort of animal skin.

"I'm sorry," Laura said. "I didn't get your name?"

He turned around with his hand out. "So sorry. I'm Buck Stern."

She tried not to laugh. Buck Stern was a good name for a deep-voiced radio broadcaster or a soap opera star. Not this pipsqueak.

"How did you know about me and my sister?" she asked.

Buck slowed down, and they took the rest of the journey through the house at talking-pace.

"I do Miss Ivanah's books. I have for twenty years. Your company is on her ledger."

"Really? I thought Bob—"

"Oh, yes, of course. But it's her company on paper."

"No, actually…" She stopped walking. "It's my company."

Buck just smiled and held out his arm to escort her up a windowless staircase. "These were built as the maid's stairs."

"What are they now?"

"Much the same." They went up the stairs, which were alabaster because these maids were apparently too good to walk on wood.

"So you manage her design business?" Laura asked.

"No, no. Ivanah's designing concerns aren't under my purview. I'm more of a manager, if you will. I move what needs moving and make sure the gears are turning smoothly. It's a full-time job."

"You said twenty years? She hasn't been married to Mister Schmiller more than ten years, I think." They exited onto an expansive roof deck with a wall of pink orchids to the right, a greenhouse to the left, and modern, dark wood benches everywhere. It was the most gorgeous corner of New York City she had ever seen.

Ivanah stood at the edge of the roof, letting her dog sniff a purple orchid. She was done up and perfect, and Laura saw something in Buck's eyes that was a little more than respect for a long-time employer.

"Ivanah started as a model and invested very wisely. She never makes a wrong move."

"Never?"

"Never. She has magic in her."

Such a statement didn't fit with the name or image of the man in front of her, but she took it at face value. When the ex-model-turned-investor saw them and put down the dog, Laura felt a little warmer inside, thinking about how the woman, who never misjudged the success of another enough to make a bad investment, had invested in *her*. Maybe Ivanah wasn't such a hideous bitch. Maybe she had a few redeeming qualities. Maybe she'd seen something worthwhile in Sartorial, even financially redeeming, that Laura could extract and use and highlight. By the time she reached them, she had forgotten that she thought Ivanah was a hack, and that her goal was to collect information to exonerate her sister. All she felt was the white heat of her now-worthwhile, somehow magical validation.

She handed the flowers over as soon as Ivanah was in arm's reach.

"These are lovely," Ivanah said. "Thank you. Come sit." She motioned to a table overlooking the Park. It was assembled from twisted metal wires, meant to look like a bird's nest. The chairs had cast iron stems across the back, and tiny birds perched on them. The seat, for being a mass of twisted iron, was comfortable.

"I came to tell you we're starting on Fall in the next couple of weeks, and if you want to look at the boards, we can set up an appointment."

"Oh, how nice." Ivanah looked over the expanse of the

Park. "I can look at your boards. Then what? I hate those things. They're a waste of time. Sticking last season's magazine pages on a piece of cardboard with some fabrics you might use? Silly."

She had a point, as Ruby's description of the inner working of big companies sounded much the same. Every season, design teams created boards, some floor-to-ceiling with cutouts, sketches, trims, and fabrics arranged in an aesthetically-pleasing manner so CEOs, company presidents, creative directors, and investors would say "oooh" and "aaah" and string together clumps of relatively intelligent questions that didn't matter a goddamn. The boards were for mood and tone only. What was someone supposed to say? "I don't want to 'fun in the sun' this year?" "Too much brown?" No. Because none of it mattered. It didn't matter what was on the fun in the sun board; it was going to turn out the way it turned out. The colors weren't set in stone. Nothing on the boards was intended for production. It was just to make the bosses feel like they had their mitts in the design process, so nothing was getting past them and there were "no surprises." But they learned about boards in school, and Ruby had produced scores of them at Tollridge & Cherry, a catalog-driven company with executives strolling the cubicles, pretending they knew what to tell people to wear. Laura had only ever worked at Jeremy's, and what was he going to do, make them for himself? He only worked with actual bodies and fabrics. Every day, Laura realized the luxury she had worked under when she was at the house of St. James.

"I also wanted to thank you," Laura said, "for coming today. We could use your help. I really want to make this work."

"I am so glad to hear you say that," Ivanah said. "You need it. I hope you don't take this the wrong way, but you are on the brink of having no company."

"Yeah, the Thomasina thing was bad luck."

"And your sister? Is she still at the police station?"

Laura was past worrying about how her backer knew. She

was sure it was all over the gossip channels. "Yeah."

"I have Greyson on it already. They're talking to that newswoman. You must have really thrown her a good bone sometime in the past, no?"

"I got mad when she was outside my house."

"She smells a story. We're using this to our advantage. We're letting her paint it like Ruby killed Thomasina. It's brilliant. Your name will be on everyone's lips."

"What? No! You can't do that."

Ivanah looked at her as if she had just gotten upset that it was going to rain tomorrow. "How else would you do it? Boring denials? No, no. If she didn't do it, there's no problem. It's a PR firm. The P is for public. This is who they influence."

Laura couldn't shake the feeling that the plan was a bad idea for Ruby. Her sister was being used like a dishtowel, and even if for her own good, it was too risky. What if Rolf got wind of it and flew off the handle? What if his skinhead side got the better of him and he decided on a little vigilante justice? How long would that strategy keep Kamichura and Roscoe Knutt on their doorstep with their little pissing match over the story?

"I was at the precinct today," Laura said. "They wouldn't even let me see her. I'd want to run this by her first."

"It wouldn't matter what she says, darling. You can do it yourself any way you want. When you ask me to do it, I can do it any way I think is best. And this is best. The best in the business are doing it this way. So that's what it will be."

"How can letting the public blame her for a murder, even for a second, be to her benefit?"

Ivanah must have seen Laura's hurt and confusion because she reached out and grabbed her hands, which shocked Laura so much she didn't move them. "Sometimes, blame is the best thing to take."

"Not if you didn't do anything."

"In Czechoslovakia, we were so poor, my mother made us dinner with this little piece of meat." She let go of Laura long enough to hold her fingers two inches apart. "She cut it into pieces and made it in a sauce so all of us could taste it. Also, it was so my two brothers wouldn't eat everything and leave me with nothing. But my oldest brother worked all day in a lamp factory, and he had no lunch, so one day, he ate all the meat while my mother was out. I saw him there, standing over the counter, with this tiny piece of meat on a stick, burning it on the stove and shoving it all in his mouth. The juice dripped off his chin, and I thought, 'Oh, he had better lick that, or it's going to go to waste.' He saw me watching, too. And how do you think I felt? He was a big man, even at thirteen, and when mother saw the meat was gone, I told her I ate it because she would beat my brother, but she wouldn't touch me. Oh, my God, it was like a bomb hit the house when my father found out. Throwing this and that, and my other brother hiding in the corner. I got the beating of my life. I thought I'd never breathe out of my left nostril again. See? Look." She pressed her right nostril and took a breath. Her left nostril squeaked slightly.

Laura nodded.

"My mother picked me up and left. Just like that. She carried me to the church, and after one good night's sleep and bandaging me up, she picked me up in her arms, and we started walking. We walked forever, days and nights. We slept on the side of the road and ate whatever we found growing. One day, she stopped in a small town, and she started our new life. Shall we compare that to this? I took the blame for something I didn't do and look." She flung out her arms to encompass the brutally expansive piece of real estate. "You can't take the hard things too seriously, really. It all works out in the end."

Laura had lots to say about that, so much in fact that the words got jumbled up in her throat, and nothing came out. That may have been considered complicity in thinking that because Ivanah's bad times had been temporary, they were thus potentially temporary for everyone. Or that it was okay to perpetuate a lie because telling one years ago had happened to work out for her. Or that the lie a person told out of his or her own choice and the lie a person told about someone else was, in fact, related in any way whatsoever.

Mostly because the story was told in good faith, she was really sorry about what happened, she was in the woman's house, and she still wanted to ask about Bob's last business trip, Laura paused. She couldn't find a way to call Ivanah a bunch of names fast enough.

Bob strolled into the garden. "Carnegie," he said, sounding truly happy to see her, "the truth teller. What brings you up here? You ruining our surprise party?"

Ivanah folded her arms and looked up at him crossly. "You..." she said with mock rage, then she turned back to Laura. "He forgot my birthday is coming this Sunday and planned exactly nothing. He will pay." Laura could see from her face that he wouldn't pay any more than he could afford. Despite the fact that she knew Bob had been sleeping with a supermodel, the couple really seemed to love each other.

"I wanted to talk to you about your trip," Laura said. "We've been thinking, we're so limited in the quantities we can produce on 40th Street that we're having a problem making the production line worthwhile. The way to slice this thing might be to move production overseas so we can make more. I heard you just got back from Shanghai." She came up with the city very fast, and almost said "Milan" instead, so it came out more like *Mi'Shanghai.*

Instead of diving in and correcting her assumption that he had gone to China, he said, "If you're producing more, it'll cost more to do the run."

She had to remember he was in hedge funds, rows of numbers, not manufacturing. "The biggest cost of producing anything is the set-up. So the more you make, the more the cost is spread out. The thousandth pair of pants costs less to make than the fifth."

"But your desirability takes a beating."

She swallowed. He was right, and it was what she'd argued from the beginning, when Ruby wanted to call in every Chinese, Turkish, and Pakistani factory she'd ever done a favor for at T&C. "I'm just looking into it. Did you make any good contacts?"

He sat down and put his arm around his wife, who draped her hand over his knee. "I was in Northern Europe. You can't afford to produce a glove out there."

"Bobby was taking care of some business with a foundation I help from my home country. They help girls leave very ugly situations," Ivanah said.

"Oh." Laura didn't know which question to ask first. She caught a mention of Thomasina's White Rose foundation before it left her lips. She didn't want to be too forward. "In Czechoslovakia?"

"That place is dead," Ivanah said. "He was in my real home."

Laura nodded. "Right, you were saying—"

Bob jumped in with half a laugh. "Was Ivanah regaling you with her mother's walk to East Germany? Good times, baby. Good times."

Ivanah slapped his knee.

Laura thought that in her twenty-five years in one of the most international cities in the world, she had never met more than two people who had lived in East Germany.

She almost fell asleep on the train.

It would have been nice, actually, because home was going to be unpleasant at best, and dramatic at worst. Unless they were both out and the house was empty. Maybe Ruby was still at Midtown South and Mom was in the waiting room, twisting tissues into knots. Then it would be quiet, and Laura could stare at the ceiling, worrying, without either one of them turning a sleepless night into a drama-fest.

There were too many strands floating around the web, and none tied together. A German foundation that both Thomasina and Ivanah had their fingers in. Pandora modeling. Rolf, the brother of the dead woman, showing up with a meatball-eyed girl from the catalog. And Ruby, of course, with poison all over her sink, which could not have been less like her. If Ruby were going to kill someone, she'd charm a guy into doing it. She'd never do the chemistry herself, and Cangemi must have known that because there was no arrest pending, from what she could see, just a seemingly indefinite holding pattern.

CHAPTER 13.

Laura avoided the news van parked across the street. The police tape was still across the garden apartment door. She walked up to Mom's apartment and there they were, sitting at the dining room table, looking sad and dim, with two sets of puffed eyes and a general attitude of the put-upon.

Ruby ran into her arms, and Mom went back into the kitchen for another teacup.

Neither Laura nor Ruby cared much for tea, outside the odd red African variety served at a thirty-grand-per-year social club, but they warmed their hands on the cups and let Mom give them as much sugar as she thought they wanted.

"They swabbed me," Ruby said. "Do you know how humiliating that was? They wore gloves and scraped the insides of my cheeks, and Uncle Graham let them." She worked herself up into crying.

Laura put up her hand. "If you're going to make this into a CBS drama event, I'm going to bed."

Shockingly, she got no resistance from Mom or Ruby, and she realized it was because they were utterly rudderless without her. She was in charge. Talk about putting the blind guy behind the wheel.

"Rubes, I just need to ask you," Laura said, needing to get some preliminaries out of the way, "were you running a modeling agency of underage girls with Thomasina?"

"Where would I find time to do that? I was working on Sartorial, like, all the time."

As far as Laura was concerned, one could easily work Ruby's hours and run an agency or two on the side: a few phone calls, some air kisses at a party, have a lawyer draw up a contract or two. "What about Thomasina?"

Ruby shook her head. "Nope."

"What about the White Rose thing? For the orphans in Eastern Europe? It was in Thomasina's obit, and I just found out the Schmillers were involved."

Mom fussed with the teaspoons and sugar. "I don't want you upsetting your sister, dear. She's had a bad day."

Laura was never one to be deterred by Mom. "Did she do it alone, or was there someone else in with her? Or was it you?"

Ruby answered tersely, like someone who had no choice but to comply for her own good. "I don't know, I don't know, and no."

"Didn't you give to that foundation or something?"

Ruby sniffed and nodded, noisily sipping less than a drop of hot tea. "We both did."

She'd almost forgotten—a dinner and a speech, before Ruby and Thomasina had kissed and made up, back when Laura carried a forty-pound grudge in the door and laid it on the table like a sack of lard. The model, having suffered the barbs of the public and nearly losing Roquelle as an agent after knocking Ruby over, had taken them to dinner and laid out her case. Thomasina wasn't evil. She had a lot on her mind, specifically the situation in Eastern Europe for beautiful young women. The horrible suffering. The rapes. The killings. The aftermath of wars, and the worst, of course, being the economic distress that the western world ignored because the victims were white and beautiful. The suffering of young girls in the third-worldish parts of Hungary and Slovakia was brutal, even compared to what was happening in Africa and the Arab world, apparently. Laura, who had walked in sour and was determined to stay that way, pushed her food around on her plate. Ruby, bless her, love her, misted over like a fast-moving low cloud, and as coldhearted as her reputation had her, Laura could not stand her sister's tears. Laura had gotten roped into writing a check.

"There was a brochure, wasn't there?"

"I have it." Ruby waved her hand toward the floor. "It's in a box in my apartment."

"Well, that takes care of that," Mom said, picking up all three teacups in one hand. "The police taped it off. Uncle Graham can help you get down there. We'll call him tomorrow."

When Laura looked at Ruby, she knew Uncle Graham could sleep in late for all they cared.

Mom protested every inch of the way. In the name of a good night's sleep. In the name of protecting themselves. In the name of their security deposit. In the name of the law.

There was only one way down to Ruby's apartment that wouldn't break police tape, and that was through the broom closet. The house had been built as a vertical living space with a kitchen in the basement, living space in the middle floor at the top of the stoop, and a top floor with bedrooms. It was meant for one family with a dumbwaiter to move food around. When the bottom floor had been converted into a separate apartment sometime during the Great Depression, the stairs had been closed off. The space under the steps to the top floor was converted by adding a floor, a door, and some wall. In Ruby's downstairs apartment, she had two closets, the original one that had been under the stairs coming from the top floor, and one over the stairs. When she opened the door to the closet, there were steps she used as shelves. Had Jimmy taken them out, Ruby would have had one long closet. But he didn't, and that was to their benefit.

Laura stormed into the broom closet and removed dozens of cleaning products, nondescript shoeboxes, a set of vintage Samsonite luggage no one would ever travel with, and rolls of shelving paper. Once the floor was clear, she looked at the edges of it. The 1950s abstract linoleum curled up at the corners where the glue had lost its stick power, and she was sure the dirt she brushed away had settled on a clean floor fifty years ago. She grabbed the most promising corner and yanked it as far back as she could. Then she did the next corner, and the next. The last corner was tough, and she used a pair of pliers to pry the linoleum from its place. That was so successful, she used the tool on the other three corners, making a ripping, cracking, grunting racket that made her glad the walls between the buildings were stone. By the time she'd hit all four corners and the cutouts at the doorframe, there was nothing but a two-foot piece of linoleum stuck to the center of the closet and a curling mass of aged flooring making it nearly impossible to get in there.

Mom stood behind her, arms folded. "Don't do this."

"I'll help," Ruby said, arms out.

"No, I got it."

But Ruby would not be deterred, and Mom, seeing that her daughters were about to do exactly what she told them not to do, emitted a resigned sigh.

Laura scanned the mess in the hallway and found the cordless drill. She checked the charge, which was 65 percent dead, or 35 percent charged if you were a glass half-full type. The tool *whirred* like a seven-pound cricket when she pulled the trigger. She passed the drill to Mom.

Mom crouched as the drill groaned when she jammed the bit into the screw holes that had been there for sixty years, give or take. Naturally, pulling up all the screws revealed nails, which needed to be pried up with a screwdriver, or the back of a hammer, or a butter knife. Some required all three, and Laura bumped backs with her mother in the closet removing them. The last one was in so tight, Mom chiseled the plywood around it until she could use pliers on the entire thing.

They were sweaty, and exhausted, and in too deep to give up. Mom used a crowbar to pry up the wood, which she couldn't do while standing inside the closet, so she did it from the hall, which had become a wild junkyard of crap from the broom closet and pieces of linoleum they'd scrapped.

The plywood came up, then slapped back down with a *huff* of stale air. Mom pried it up again so they could get their hands under it, then shoulders. Mom yanked it toward the door, which got her nowhere because it was bigger than the frame at that angle. So Laura, who was shorter, got in and twisted, and turned, and called on more strength than she actually had to turn the wood around and gently ease it toward the door. It wasn't coming out, but she'd made enough room so she could look at what was under there.

Ruby's broom closet was as neat as everything else in the house. The cleaning products, which were used on a regular basis, lay like sleeping children in cute plaid boxes. If Laura went into the corners, she was sure she wouldn't see sixty years' worth of someone else's dust.

Mom had flashlights ready. "I'm going to bed," she said. "I don't want any part of this." She walked upstairs as if she could make that statement true retroactively.

Ruby was ready to go. Laura stepped down, kicking boxes of cleaning things out of the way before she opened the closet door. They didn't dare turn on any lights or point the flashlights out the windows, where the snoops in the news van could see. Her sister grabbed her hand and pulled her into the bedroom.

Ruby yanked a polka-dotted box from under the bed and, kneeling in front of it, threw off the lid. She pulled out a pile of paper and handed half the stack to Laura. "It's in here," she said, flipping through her half. "Somewhere. Ah! Here." They huddled in the corner and held their flashlights close to the paper. The brochure was an eight-page full-color foldout for the White Rose Foundation, an organization dedicated to moving girls sold into prostitution in Eastern Europe out of harm's way.

"Flip to the back," Laura whispered. There, they saw Thomasina's picture over a plea for donations, with a signature that was boldly capped and broadly finished, and mention of an unpictured co-chair, Randolf Fosh. "Rolf?"

Ruby shrugged and flipped over the brochure. On the cover, a pretty young thing, smiling and gloriously backlit, unselfconscious about her simple hair and tattered clothes, looked at them with big, meatball eyes.

Laura recognized her immediately. "This is Thomasina's foundation, which Ivanah and Bob are involved in. I saw Rolf with this girl the other day, and she was also in the Pandora modeling catalog. She's the link. She can tell us what all these things have to do with each other."

"Okay. Like what?"

"Someone is pissed at someone else for something to do with this, and if they were pissed enough to kill Thomasina, your problems are over." She was making it up as she went. Her mind was a pure blank. She was tired, frustrated, and restless, and her thinking was a web of nonsense.

Ruby, for having had one of the worst days of her life, was on the ball. She snapped up the brochure and stuffed it in the box. "Let's bring it all upstairs. We need to look at everything."

Laura nodded, but knew she wasn't going to make it. If she didn't sleep, she was going to collapse in her own spit and sweat. Mom, who was waiting for them in the hallway, walked her up to bed while Ruby gathered makeup, shoes, and other necessities from her closed-off apartment. The sheets were cool and dry, and Mom pulled the covers over her as if she were seven years old.

"Mom?"

"Go to sleep."

"I kissed Jeremy today."

"The one you used to work for?"

"Him."

"That you still work for?"

"Just sometimes."

Mom paused as though she wanted to say something. Laura knew what her mother would say. Jeremy was a user and manipulator. He'd never be with her unless he wanted something from her. But she was quite willing to give it. She'd pined after him for six years and finally had the opportunity to be with him. If he wanted to use her, she was his. And manipulation was barely required.

Mom closed the door softly without saying a word. Laura didn't tell her about the wool crepe order tack on because she was tired. But Mom would be proud to know Laura had found as much use for Jeremy as he could find for her. Maybe more. She fell asleep to the sounds of the cordless drill whirring as the floor to the broom closet was replaced as if nothing had ever happened.

CHAPTER 14.

Laura wasn't one to act on dreams. She didn't cuddle crystals or entertain talk about past lives. No tarot cards, palm readings, or talk of Jesus. She worshipped at a sewing machine and prayed to the pattern. Even the idea of "style" or "fashion" was hard to get her head around because it was ethereal and subjective. She preferred an out-of-style jacket that fit beautifully to an up-to-the-minute garment from H&M, a chain that would put intricate beading and embroidery on an armhole shaped like a highway off-ramp.

But insofar as dreams were catalogs of the previous day's events, a meatball made an appearance. No, it was the idea of a meatball, because she and Stu had been searching Central Park for it, but finding only globs of horse poop that looked like meatballs.

She went downstairs to find Ruby sleeping on the couch and her polka dot document box on the dining room table.

Last night's observations had happened quickly and in low light. The documents could have said anything. The girl on the back of the brochure could have been anyone.

Right?

No. It was Meatball Eyes, definitely the best looking of the bunch. A picture was emerging. Thomasina chaired an organization to help young women, bringing them into the country and getting them jobs as models. How Roquelle Rik allowed it with her territorial leanings was the source of Laura's bafflement. She snapped up her phone and dialed the number on the back of the White Rose brochure.

She heard a couple of harsh beeps and a notice that the number had been disconnected.

Behind her, Ruby stirred and sat up, groaning.

"Good morning," Laura said.

Ruby threw herself in a dining room chair and put her head down. "I don't want to go into the showroom today."

"You have to, sorry. And you have to play it like you're annoyed by the whole thing. You can manage. Ivanah's PR people are out there screwing you anyway."

Ruby hugged her pillow and groaned as if hung over. "We saw the eleven o'clock news. I was on at eleven fifteen, falling off a runway. They didn't even mention my shoes weren't buckled. They blamed it all on Thomasina."

"And you for the murder."

Ruby got up and stood beside her, looking over her shoulder as she shuffled through the papers. "Are you going to work on this while I'm in the showroom?"

"Yeah."

Ruby hugged Laura from behind. "Thank you."

"For you, anything. If it was just about Thomasina dying, I'd be working on Summer and letting the police do their job."

Ruby, maybe half as gorgeous as usual on account of exhaustion and worry, poked through the papers, which Laura organized across the table. Modeling contracts for runway. Modeling contracts for fit. Modeling contracts for print. Invoices for each.

"You saw her the night before?" Laura asked. Ruby nodded. "Dinner?"

"Yeah."

"What did you make?"

"We ordered DiBennedetto's." That made sense. Ruby didn't cook if it could be avoided.

"Did anything happen? Did she say anything? Get a phone call? Did she talk about anyone bothering or annoying her?"

"She got a call. She was talking in German. Kept saying 'nicked,' which I think is German for something. She was pissed."

"What time did she leave?"

Ruby didn't answer, so Laura plowed on. "Because whoever she saw afterwards could have poisoned her. Or there could have been some kind of fight or business meeting or something. Did she say where she was going, even?"

Again, Ruby said nothing.

"I can't reconstruct Thomasina's movements without you."

"She was poisoned from the pills in her bag, right? So doesn't that mean someone put the pill in there before, like weeks maybe? So what's the difference what she did the night before?"

"What are you hiding?"

"Nothing, I'm just saying—"

"What time did she leave?"

"I don't know. Do you think I look at a clock all the time?"

"Did she leave at all?"

"What's that supposed to mean?"

"Did she stay the night?"

Ruby looked stricken for a second, and as she and Laura looked at each other, an understanding passed between them. The sudden attached-at-the-hip friendship. The knee-jerk defensiveness. The giggling in the office late at night. The truncated work hours. Jeremy asking how she was holding up.

He'd seen it a mile away.

"Goddamn it, why didn't you tell me?"

In answer, Ruby stormed into the bathroom and slammed the door behind her.

Fantastic. Ruby and Thomasina were doing it. No wonder the police swabbed her.

Laura knocked on the door, then banged. "Rubes, come on! Did you tell the cops?"

"Of course I did, and it makes it look like I did it even more."

"Did she see anyone else between you and the show? Did she say she was going anywhere? Ruby? Come on. Please."

There was a sniffle and a shuffle that sounded like a body moving against the other side of the door. "I made breakfast, and I sat and ate by myself. I don't know if she was mad at me or what, and now I can't even ask her or apologize."

"You don't know where she went?" The question seemed inappropriate, but Laura didn't know what else to say.

"She bitched that she had no cash in her wallet, and I offered, but she wouldn't take it. She had a total breakdown over it, and I couldn't even do anything."

Laura felt as if she'd missed a whole era of her sister's life because she had no idea there had been a relationship. So she had a hard time relating to Ruby's pain. Of course, she first had to come to terms with the fact that Ruby had been with a woman, then that she'd apparently fallen in love with said woman. Then, worse, that her sister hadn't told her. The murder seemed paltry in comparison.

Ruby didn't come out of the bathroom, and Laura felt there was no point in trying to squeeze more out of her without a couple of glasses of wine and a nice dinner. She tucked a folder of choice documents under her arm and walked to the train. Yoni called as Laura was coming out of the Italian deli with her coffee.

"What do you have?" Laura asked, dispensing with a greeting.

Yoni, who was perfectly comfortable without niceties, replied, "Your pill. It's made of alkaloids. Not enough to kill you. Maybe if you took twenty or thirty. It is used to induce vomiting."

"Perfect for bulimic models." She tried to keep her voice down, but a bus went by, and she had to yell.

"Yes, and amateur-made, too, which I could have told you just by looking at it. The clear part anyone can get at a health food store. They stuff it with herbs. But this powder? Not amateur."

"So you're saying the powder comes from some place, and then someone put it into the capsules?" Laura pressed her finger to her opposite ear to close out the ambient sounds.

"Yes."

"And the powder, any guess where it's from?"

"We could guess, but—"

"Czechoslovakia?"

"Oh. You've been busy. Yes. It's made from a daffodil bulb grown mostly in Eastern Europe."

"Anything else?"

"My ankles hurt. I want to shoot them off. I will bleed water, my God."

"Thanks, Yoni."

"Get me fabric orders."

"The wool crepe is taken care of. I'm tacking onto Jeremy's."

Yoni took in a sharp breath through her teeth. "Our Jeremy?"

"Yes, of course. Who else?"

"I don't know what you did, little girl, but Jeremy, our Jeremy, never tacks on his fabric orders. He thinks it can hold him up, and he doesn't like entanglements. He must like you more than I thought."

"Maybe he trusts me, is all."

Yoni, who enjoyed goodbyes as much as hellos, hung up unceremoniously.

Jeremy liking her more than Yoni thought was good news,

she guessed, but it made her feel as though he'd agreed to do it for the wrong reasons, because he liked her, which gave her a weird sense of power and made her uncomfortable. Very uncomfortable. She wanted to call him and tell him he didn't have to tack the order, and she'd asked him at a really bad time.

She heard the train pull in underground as she was dialing, and she had to run down the stairs or miss it. Luckily, she couldn't get a signal underground.

The person Laura really wanted to find was Meatball Eyes. The model could tell where she was from, who represented her, how she got to New York, and whether or not she'd been saved by a goddess in shining armor named Thomasina or Sabine, or whatever. The girl could also tell all about Rolf, and his involvement with the foundation.

But Laura had no access to the girl outside of Rolf, who never left a phone number or slip of information anywhere. And she wasn't about to stand outside Baxter City, waiting for him to show.

Roquelle Rik was the only connection Laura could make at the moment. A modeling agency, be it U.S.-based or otherwise, did not open its doors without Roquelle knowing about it, and the prettiest girl in any such agency would be immediately poached like an egg at Sunday brunch.

The offices of The Mermaid Agency stressed sexuality and sexual power, without yield or surrender. The women plastered over the walls, floor to ceiling, were aggressive, confident, and as inaccessible as the mythical creatures after which they were named.

Thomasina's face gazed at Laura from behind the reception desk, with grainy black and white eyes literally as big as stop signs. Piercing. Perfect. She looked angry and hungry, like a tiger that hadn't eaten in weeks. Fresh flowers, lilies, orchids, in wickedly expensive arrangements, dropped petals on the floor beneath her chin. Soon, their dead star's picture would be gone, replaced with another angry thoroughbred who had to have the busted capillaries under her nose

Photoshopped out of existence.

Laura was intimidated for a second, as always when she walked into the office. Then she reminded herself that those eyes were dead, and she was there to avenge the death on behalf of her sister, who had been having sex with the owner of the stop sign eyes.

The receptionist smiled with lovely, natural teeth that were the product of good genes and better habits. Her eyes lit up the room with an approachability that must have been planned to counter the aggression in Thomasina's snarl. "Ms. Carnegie, how are you?" She had obviously been hired for a cracker-jack memory in addition to the sunny disposition.

"I'm good. Is Roquelle available?"

Sunny's brows knitted, and her gaze went to her computer screen. "Do you have an appointment?"

"I need to ask her about the Pandora Agency."

"I'm sorry. It seems she's in a meeting."

"I'll wait." Laura sat on the leather bench with a seat higher than any other bench she'd sat on. She could only guess it was because of the height of the women coming through there. She texted Roquelle:

—*I'm in recep. Need 2cu re a White Rose girl*

Then she waited. Thomasina stared at her, and Laura imagined the snarl turning into as much of a smile as one could get from a giraffe within ten feet of a camera. The smile said, *Your sister fell in love with me, and she didn't even tell you. She was scared of you. She did whatever I told her. She dropped all that work in your lap because she was with me. And I was with someone else, too. Because I could.*

The taunts were circular, running from subject to subject, and cause to effect, and cause to cause in no productive order. In fifteen minutes, Laura went from hating the heiress, to feeling sorry for her, to being mystified, to curious, to disgust, to rage, to sympathy, to intimidation, to intimacy, and all the way back again.

And where it landed was: *You should have seen it, but you were too busy working.*

She hadn't been too busy to miss a new pair of shoes, however, especially not a pair of Jimmy Choos on Ruby's very own living-off-her-savings feet. They weren't a pair of vintage Choos, either, but that season's, spanking new from not even the back of Otto Tootsi Plohound on Fifth where the size elevens went to die.

Laura had stopped being surprised or excited when Ruby walked in with some new, wildly expensive accessory, so she just looked at her and said, "Nice Choos."

Jeremy followed from the hallway with a fabric swatch for a stretch panel and glanced at the expensively shod feet. "You got the red," he said, tossing Laura the fabric. She caught it in midair.

Ruby tilted her leg so Laura could see the shoe from the side. It was a stiletto, naturally, with straps shaped like an art deco window panel and a heel curving at an angle made possible by some technology that had been unavailable two years before. "The black was too serious," she said.

He stepped behind her and looked from behind. He and Ruby had developed an odd relationship, like siblings who tolerated each other because Mom was watching.

"There were five pairs of those in the entire city," he said, "in your size, I mean." That was a lovely taunt. Ruby wore size eight and a half, big even for her height at five-seven, which Jeremy knew from the gold shoe-buckle incident six months prior. "Did you hear?" He slipped the pattern Laura was working on across her desk. "Dymphna Bastille had them special ordered, and Thomasina Wente went to Plohound and managed to get them instead. There was a scene at Grotto."

Laura spread out the foot-square of fabric. He stretched the fabric, and she measured it, punching the number into a calculator.

"Oh, a scene at Grotto," Laura said dryly. "Imagine." She handed Jeremy a ruler.

He measured across the widest point of the bust. "I don't know how either one of them got the spoon out of their nose long enough to fight about shoes. Add another quarter here,

149

and I think we're okay."

Ruby chimed in, "Don't say stuff like that."

"She not bothering with the spoon anymore?" he asked.

"It's not right, Jeremy. You shouldn't spread rumors." Ruby's sense of social right and wrong wouldn't let it drop as a joke.

Laura glanced at Jeremy, hoping he wouldn't make another cutting remark because she couldn't stop her sister from being who she was. Laura needed his help, and she needed things to be pleasant between the two of them. He took a second to regard Ruby, looking at her a little sideways, pursing his lips slightly as if he had to keep words from tumbling out.

Laura couldn't stand the silence. "Oh, Ruby, come on! You know Thomasina gossips with the worst of them and spends forever in the bathroom like all the other girls. And Jeremy, you know better than to say anything to Ruby about her friends. I mean, my God, just try and say anything bad about me, even if it's true, and she'll take your eye out with one of those heels. Now, get out of here. I have work to do."

Maybe that last bit took it too far. He didn't like being told what to do even if she was half-joking. Or maybe she'd given him the moment he needed to think of a way to make his point and, quite possibly, he was making that point for her benefit, because she was blind, dumb, and tired.

"Thomasina's an eight and a half, isn't she?" Without waiting for an answer, he winked at Laura before heading back to his own factory floor, which she knew he managed to keep going by taking handfuls of drugs while no one was looking and maintaining a five- to ten-mile a day running habit to strengthen his lungs.

He had been trying to tell her something. Either Ruby was borrowing Thomasina's shoes, or the model had snapped them from under Dymphna because Ruby couldn't afford full-price limited-run Jimmy Choos. Nor did her sister have the connections to get them. Anyone could see that. Anyone could see that the relationship between the designer and the supermodel had gone rogue, except Laura. She had just put her head back into the pattern and thanked the stars above and the gods of geometry that the tension had left the room.

"Laura Carnegie!" Roquelle interrupted her reverie, standing over her, a bit too close, with a smile a little too stretched. "You left before the cleanup yesterday. I was looking for you." To Sunny, she said, "Push my nine up half an hour and shift the rest. Shift my eleven thirty to tomorrow lunch and move that to the usual breakfast at Marlene X." Without waiting for a response, she led Laura past reception, into the guts of the agency with its matching cubbies and equally well-coordinated assistants.

At the end of the line was an office. Unnecessarily huge, like an Escalade where an Accord would suffice, it had the look of a room that wasn't used fully. The wood floors weren't worn anywhere. The leather on the couches was pristine, and the desk looked as if nothing on it had been moved in months, except a duster flicking across it.

Roquelle sat on a couch and indicated for Laura to sit in the one opposite. The air had a sharp, distinct peppermint smell. On the table between the sofas, a tray was filled with hot coffee and tea, juice, rolls, and an ashtray shaped like a crescent moon. A turquoise globe was suspended above the ashtray by a brass rod the circumference of a pencil.

Roquelle pushed a button at the top of the globe. "Smoke?" The globe snapped open with a mechanical click, and a variety of cigarettes protruded like sunrays drawn by a meticulous child.

"No, thanks." She was disconcerted by the cigarettes, a fact her host seemed to relish.

"I love showing off this thing. Nineteen twenties. Of course, it's illegal to smoke in here, but most of the new girls are from countries without uptight rules. It makes them comfortable when they see their brand in there."

"It doesn't smell like smoke in here at all."

"We keep after it. So. What was it you wanted?"

Laura, incapable of lying outright, had to find a way there

by strategic use of the truth. She took out the White Rose brochure. "I found this in my sister's things. This girl here, on the cover, I met her at Baxter City with Rolf Wente, but I didn't get her name. I want to use her, and I was thinking, if you could track her down or if you represented her or if you wanted to represent her, well, she's exactly the right thing."

Roquelle studied the photo. "A little pretty for your brand, don't you think?"

That actually was not an insult to the girl or the Sartorial brand.

"Maybe, but we're trying sweet-as-edgy instead of edgy-as-edgy."

"Interesting, and is she represented?"

"Have you heard of the Pandora Agency? I think this might have been a Thomasina thing, and since she's not around anymore?"

Roquelle smirked. "That's not a modeling agency, dear."

Laura paused, cleared her throat, and ticked off everything she could have meant.

The agent cut off her thoughts with, "Why don't you just use Rowena? She was fabulous for you, and she's an untapped commodity. Poor girl hangs with the other hopefuls at Marlene X every morning like a lost puppy. The other morning, she was hovering around Penelope Sidewinder, eating a crème brûlée, and then she sat there, like she was saying, 'Look, I'm not puking.'" She laughed, then sighed.

"What kind of agency is it?"

"The kind with girls, dear. Pretty ones. Really, you can't be this naïve." She would not be sidetracked.

"So, you never saw her here? No headshot?"

"No, sorry. You can still run her through us if you find her. Better to have someone agented for all the usual reasons." That was the common line. Using agented models protected designers from lawsuits and entanglements. It also protected them from worker's comp payments, insurance, 1099s, and other gnarly tax forms. Fifteen percent of salaries were lopped right off the top for the privilege. Over the course of a generation, designers, models, and magazines had bought the logic hook, line, and sinker without questioning what the occasional lawsuit would cost versus the additional salaries negotiated by the agents. There seemed to be entire economies built around middlemen and gatekeepers, but every time Laura tried to think of a way around it, the actual job of designing got in the way.

Roquelle stood up as if to let Laura know it was time to leave.

Just as she was thinking that had been the biggest waste of time of the week, she spotted a wet bar in the corner. On it were two upside-down chintz teacups with saucers leaning in tribute, and a pile of compacts and lipsticks. Roquelle was quite the klepto.

CHAPTER 15.

Laura exited the elevator in the 38th Street building, passed Jeremy's showroom, waved to Renee, and turned a couple of corners to get to her own showroom.

She heard voices: Corky talking about dye methods he knew nothing about, a woman's mumble with a deep southern accent—must be Nordstrom's, their buyer was from Kentucky—and finally, Ruby's laugh as she reacted to whatever the Southern Belle had said.

Suddenly, Laura was sure she would die a thousand deaths if she went in there right then. She wasn't needed, only obligated. The elevator dinged as she rounded the bend in the hall, and a herd of giraffes poured out, all legs and necks and nice smells. She figured they must be there for a Jeremy fitting. His show was the next day. She caught sight of Rowena and Heather Dahl, and turned right around to head toward the bathroom.

Inside a stall, she sat on the cold seat and put her head in her hands. What the hell was she doing chasing down an Eastern European model who didn't have an agent when she could be in the office resuscitating her business? Her failing business. She got up, determined to drop the whole thing and go help Corky, but then the door of the stall next to her slapped open, and she heard the unmistakable sounds of a woman hurling.

Laura checked under the stall. Nice shoes. Lacroix bag on the floor. A few seconds later, there was a cough, a delicate spit or two, and the rattle of the toilet paper rolling out. She decided to help by leaving before the puker did, but no luck, the stalls opened at the same time, and she was faced with Dymphna Bastille looking fresh-breathed, even if she didn't smell it.

"Hi!" Dymphna cried as if she wasn't a first class bitch. "How are you?" The fact that Dymphna actually took a second to ask such a question meant someone must have been watching.

Laura looked around but saw no one, just the underside of Dymphna's chin as it masticated a wad of gum. "I'm good. You?"

The model shrugged. "I have a fitting with Jeremy in ten. They fit me when I was on a juice fast so, duh, the zipper's pulling." They stood at the sinks, washing hands, talking through the mirror.

"You know," Laura said, "I was wondering, I'm trying to lose a little weight. Ruby told me about these capsules she got from Thomasina that helped."

"Oh yeah?" Dymphna stopped making eye contact.

"They were a purply color?" Dymphna waited, so Laura made something up. "I know you don't need any of that stuff. You're one of those, 'eat anything you want and lose weight anyway' types. But me? Not as much. Anyway, I thought you might know from some of the other girls who are less, you know, natural about it."

Dymphna looked under the stalls to make sure they were alone. "Yeah, well, they get them from Roquelle, but if you say I told you, I'll deny it."

Laura waved her hand. "Don't worry. I'll tell her Thomasina told me. What's Roquelle going to do? Kill her?"

They laughed, but Laura felt dirty.

As she was about to leave, Dymphna said, "Hey, can you tell Ruby I'm sorry about Thomasina? I mean, she was a bitch, but whatever. Takes all kinds."

Dymphna was the child of a hippie commune on East Hampton, so her street language mixed with openness to human diversity wasn't surprising. What was shocking was that she seemed to know Ruby and the world's most expensive supermodel were... how should she even talk to herself about it in her mind? Intimate? Sleeping together? Doing it? It all seemed weird.

Dymphna interrupted her train of thought. "What's this?" She tapped the brochure Laura had left on the vanity.

"You know this girl?" Laura asked.

Dymphna took a closer look at the photo, jaw working like an oil derrick. "Never seen her." She looked more closely. "No, wait." She stopped chewing her gum for a second.

"What?"

Dymphna shook it off. "I saw her at a housewarming. Senator Machinelle just had her penthouse redone. God, it was all mirrors and marble. And the decorator was this blonde carrying a poodle. Oh Em Gee, I'm so not voting for her next time." She handed the booklet back and started away. "I have to go."

"Wait! Who was she with? This girl?"

Dymphna called back, "She was the decorator's assistant."

CHAPTER 16.

"What's going on with your face?" Ruby asked.

Laura realized she was standing in the hallway outside the bathroom, staring at the floor. "I'm thinking."

"Does it hurt?"

"Thomasina wanted to bring girls here, right? Find them jobs?"

"Pretty much."

"Did she say she'd actually done it yet?"

Ruby shrugged. "We didn't talk about that sort of thing a lot."

Laura walked toward the elevator, pulling Ruby with her. "Are you ever going to tell me about you and Thomasina? Or are you just going to be embarrassed forever?"

"I'm not embarrassed."

"Then, what is it?"

"You didn't like her, not from the start, because she was rich, and rich people make you uncomfortable."

"She was also a bitch." She was sorry the second she said it, and Ruby didn't waste that second making a point.

"You'd never say that about my lover if it was a man. Especially my dead lover."

The Nordstrom's buyer came out of the showroom just in time to hear. She had thick black glasses and red lipstick, and she smiled as if she and her two Binder Girls hadn't heard an argument over a dead lover. As they crowded into the elevator, Laura had not one word to offer that could ease the tension or change the subject. Ruby mentioned something about her next appointment, and Nordstrom's said something about lunch, and they were all out in the autumn air sixty seconds later.

"I'm sorry," Laura said. "I suck."

"Yes, you do. I still have to pee." They went to Veronica's and ordered sloppy pasta dishes.

Once Ruby got back from the bathroom, Laura asked, "Thomasina knew Bob?"

"Ivanah, mostly. She helped us get the backing if you remember."

"No, she didn't."

Ruby shrugged. "Having her around didn't hurt. It gave a good impression. Overall. That's important even if you don't believe it." They ate in silence for a minute before she broke in, "You want to ask me things, but you're afraid. Specific things, not that stupid, 'What was going on?' which puts all the responsibility on me to figure out what you mean. I don't know what you're afraid of, but it's, like, coming off you in waves. It's freaking me out."

"It's a little heavy, Rubes."

"Yeah."

"Did you love her?"

Apparently, Ruby expected a more mechanical question because she looked taken aback. That, however, was exactly what Laura wanted to know, not only because it could help modify the tone of subsequent questions, but because it would clue her in to how much she'd missed while her head was buried in her work.

"I did," Ruby said, blowing cold air into the balloon of guilt Laura carried.

"I'm sorry she died."

Ruby twirled some pasta, then pushed her plate away. "She was so nice to me. And she valued me and bought me things. She treated me better than any man I've ever been with, and she respected that I wasn't ready to come out with it, and she was a total lesbian. Total. Modeling was the only thing she had that was her own, which is why she had the freak-out on the runway, but I can't tell you how bad she felt. She had all this money and showed me her bank account and said, 'What am I going to do with all this money if I don't give it away?' She was paying the rent and would have paid yours too, but you'd never have taken it. You keep talking about fair. But how was it fair that she had so much, and we're always hurting?"

"That's my point—"

"No, it's mine. Because when you talk about fair, it's about how you have less, and how you're going to take less because of some idea that you refusing help balances the books. But it doesn't. Taking Thomasina's money balanced the books. Throwing it back at her does nothing. It continues a cycle of unfairness."

"I cannot believe you're sitting here talking about a cycle of unfairness when you got what you got because you got these pounds of unfair gifts, like being tall and beautiful and still approachable and so freaking sweet people love you right away."

"And your gifts? How is it any more fair that you were given all this talent that you get to use to make money? And she had beauty she used for the same thing? Some people get neither. So, what should I do? Not love someone, then, to keep everything equal? God, when did you get so about appearances? She was good to me, but like a grown up. She didn't act like some stupid puppy, like a guy. It wasn't, I don't know, gamey? Like she just knew how I felt even before I did. And it wasn't creepy or anything. She was all in. Once she had me and she knew it, she didn't pull a punch."

"Don't get graphic, Ruby."

"Oh, shut up. I'm not getting graphic. I'm just saying. She was... I don't want you to get mad, but you will. Well, she kept buying me things, and one day, when we were going to talk to Jimmy about the rent?"

"Like every day in April?"

"She said, 'Let me take care of it.'"

"You *didn't*." She felt the world was about to fall apart. She paid the rent from her patternmaking side thing, Mom paid from her retirement, and Ruby paid from her magical savings, which she suspected she was about to find out were pretty magical in that they didn't exist.

"Well, of course I said no," Ruby continued, "but then she showed me a bank account, *one* bank account, and you can't believe how much was in there. She said, 'All the money does is make more money.' And what was she supposed to do with it? She could have bought the house from Jimmy, and it wouldn't have made a dent. So why wouldn't I just let her pay so we could have a good time together instead of me worrying and her feeling guilty?"

"You let her?"

"I would have let her pay the whole thing, but you would have known then."

"And did Mom know?"

"Yeah."

The compassion Laura had felt minutes before was gone. Her feelings could only be described as an overall emotional shutdown followed by a boiling rage that burned white hot from the inside out. So intense was the sensation that the backs of her thighs tingled, adrenal glands firing as if she were the slowest camper in a bear attack. It was fight or flight. Fight or flight. Fight or flight. The path out the door looked good, but Ruby was right there and ready for a verbal beating.

"You know what they call that?" Laura asked, pulling a longer, sharper scalpel than she intended. "When you have sex with someone and take money?"

"Don't you even!"

"Well? You never thought about that? It never occurred to you while you were 'falling in love' or whatever, that this rich bitch could spare a little for you in exchange for—"

"Shut up!"

"You never showed any interest in women until you go broke, and then it's Thomasina Wente?"

Ruby stood up and wielded her finger like a weapon, jabbing and thrusting, speaking through tight lips with a voice that cut at the edges and bulged at the centers, her volume just below the threshold for making a scene. "You tell me you didn't want to have Jeremy because he's gorgeous and rich. There's no present in that package, and you know it."

Laura slouched. Her sister didn't know she'd kissed Jeremy, making the words even more hurtful.

Ruby, seeing her opening, continued, "You judge women by how much money they make and how hard they work. And you think Thomasina was privileged and didn't work hard, but what you don't know is that she judged herself as harshly as you did. She felt completely inadequate. Why do you think half these girls are the way they are? It's because they know what they're doing is too easy, and inside, they're not fulfilled, and they're scared all the time they're not good enough, and they don't know how to get better. You'd throw up and starve yourself too, just to feel like there was a job to do and you were doing it. You especially. You'd turn modeling into a seventy-hour-a-week gig."

"I feel terrible now. Are you done?"

"No."

"Can you at least tell me about White Rose? Or Pandora? Or whatever, instead of telling me how hard it is to be a model? Because really, I'm convinced. If society would just give them the opportunity to clean toilets for a living, they'd take it in a second."

"God, you make me so mad!" Ruby looked as though her adrenal glands were the ones firing on all cylinders.

Though Laura didn't feel bad for egging her on, she did detect the need to dig the conversation out of a hole while she was on top. "What was going on with Thomasina and Bob Schmiller? I thought they were sleeping together, but then..."

Ruby laughed so loud it was an interruption.

"What?"

"Even if Thomasina had ever slept with a man in her life, which she never did, Bob wouldn't be that man. Oh, my God, what on earth made you think that?"

Laura told her about the phone message and the trip to Germany. Then she told her about Meatball Eyes and her job as Ivanah's assistant.

Ruby sat down, seemingly cowed. "You've been trying to help me this whole time."

"Well, yeah. What did you think? I was going to let Uncle Graham and Detective Cangemi do all the work? I mean, talk about paper pushing."

"I should have told you everything right away. I was trying to protect Thomasina, but God, that was so stupid." She rubbed her eyes.

"Was the White Rose Foundation legit? Or was it a tax haven or something?"

"Tax haven? Do you even know what that is?"

"Rubes, if you don't stop dodging and start talking right now, I won't forgive you. Ever."

So Ruby told the story and twirled her spaghetti, shoveling it in with bread while lunchtime came and went, and the room cleared out like a bathroom with an overflowing toilet.

While Laura had been working the past six months, doing patterns for Jeremy and putting together her own line, Ruby had also been busy.

Indeed, she had been doing what she was partnered to do: generate good will, attend parties as the smiling face of the company, and hobnob. She had also been falling in love, which Laura forgave her for because, unlike her, people didn't usually plan their personal lives around a convenient time for their business.

Her lover, closeted lesbian supermodel Thomasina Wente, who had knocked her off a runway six months earlier for motivations that got more and more complex the more Laura learned about her, had been trying to set up a post-modeling life. The woman's mid-thirties were creeping up on her like a centipede that looked small and slow until it got close and one realized it had a hundred legs to run with, and she didn't want to be known as an heiress gifted with money and looks who lived and died by both of those. She wanted to make a mark, which Laura saw as an ego trip worthy of someone with the heiress's gifts, at the same time as she felt the sting of bitterness that Thomasina's money and beauty allowed her to do more of what Laura thought she should be doing herself.

Coming from what used to be a poor country smack in the middle of one of the richest continents in the world, and having lived off the backs of the poorer class, Thomasina wanted to do something that fell within her power. Had she been a farmer, she would have taught them to farm. If she had been a plumber, she would have gotten the slums fresh water. But she was a model, and thus, she wanted to help beautiful, poor girls become beautiful, rich girls.

"They're not just poor," Ruby said. "They get pulled into prostitution when they're twelve. I mean, internet porn sites are all Eastern European girls, and the former East Germany is the worst."

"You are talking about a bunch of crap you don't know anything about."

"And you do? Why don't you look into it before you shoot it down? Because who was Thommy pissing off? I mean, she told me she had girls she pulled out of the worst situations. There was a fourteen-year-old who had been bought by three brothers—"

"What did she do with them?" She interrupted to avoid gory details, which she didn't need keeping her up at night.

"She brought them to safe houses like convents, and she was trying to set it up so they'd be placed in jobs here. But there were people who didn't want her doing it because they make a lot of money grabbing girls off farms and on their way to school."

"You told the cops all this?"

"Of course."

Laura was comforted for a second. Maybe two. Then she realized the cops weren't going to do anything based on the ranting of an accused designer, and Uncle Graham's fondest desire would be to get Ruby off and move along to the next billable hour. Maybe that should be Laura's fondest desire. Maybe she should just go back to the drafting table, do her work, and let Thomasina's attempts to unravel all her bad press die with her.

"Are you going back to the showroom? Corky's totally overwhelmed."

"Yeah. It helps to be busy."

"Is there anything else you want to tell me?"

"Not that I can think of. But I promise that if you ask another question and I can answer it, I will. And right away. And without leaving anything out."

"Okay, go away. I'm tired."

They hugged, and Ruby trotted toward Broadway. Laura headed for the 40th Street office, thinking maybe she'd work on Fall or prep Spring production. She passed the jobbers with their windows of slinky, out of style fabrics, and the sandwich places inserted between them. She walked the line of shadows in the sidewalk, avoiding cracks like a kid, getting in the way of everyone in a hurry to get where they were going. Laura wasn't in a hurry, she had something on her mind, and it was the erasure of an assumption she'd been making.

If Ruby was to be believed, and she was because she wasn't so blind or stupid as to dismiss Thomasina's affair with Bob if she thought there was the slightest possibility it had happened, then the message meant something totally different than she'd thought.

"Baby Bean. I'm back and I missed you. You're right about everything. I sent something home for you."

If she skipped the obvious romantic implications of "Baby Bean," the *I missed you* really didn't have to be anything more than a missed meeting. It could refer to a missed meeting at Marlene X or something the day before, not necessarily a romantic yearning.

You're right about everything. He was returning from the former East Germany, where both his wife and Thomasina were from. Was there some different idea of the reality out there that had caused a disagreement between Ivanah and Thomasina? And Bob had gone to check the details? For him to take off to Europe, it must have been something for which he had either a financial or emotional investment.

I sent something home for you. Maybe not a gift. Maybe a person. Maybe he'd sent someone back to be Ivanah's assistant.

Meatball Eyes must have been the latest girl to get a job on the White Rose repatriation program. Bob and Ivanah must have been investors. Bob went to check stuff out in Europe while Ivanah trained Meatball to be a bad interior designer. How many were there, and what were they doing? She guessed if she were a more important person, she could go to the State Department and ask a few questions, but she was a small fish, and she'd likely wind up answering many more questions than she asked.

She called Ivanah with a white lie prepared. Buck Stern picked up.

"Hi, Mister Stern?"

"Buck, please."

"Okay. I hear Ivanah's birthday is this weekend. We wanted to surprise her."

"I believe Mister Schmiller has something prepared in the way of a dinner."

"Yeah, okay, but I was talking to Senator Machinelle and she wanted to amass her clients for a bigger thing. I was wondering if there was someone I could talk to about contacting them? Getting them all in the same room, well, it would be a party, that's for sure."

He gave a little laugh. "Let me give you her assistant's

number."

It was that stinkin' easy. When she called the number from a bench in Central Park, watching the garmentos go by, a young girl with an accent answered, "The Ivanah Schmiller office."

"Hi, um, this is Laura Carnegie. I was looking for Ivanah's assistant?"

Pause, then, "Oh, we met."

"At Baxter City?"

"Yes."

Laura performed an involuntary and embarrassing fist pump. "I was wondering if I could talk to you about a surprise party for Ivanah?"

Meatball Eyes gasped with delight. "I love this! We can meet, but I'm going to be in East New York all day looking at a space. This is for the artist, Franco Finelli. The sculptor, he is gorgeous, have you met him? And rich, too. He makes big, big coffee cups with coffee in them. Ten feet high."

Good God, Meatball Eyes was a chatterbox. She was going to be a fantastic fount of information.

"I've never been to East New York. Why don't I meet you out there?"

"Oh, it is absolutely awful! I can't wait! I've been here two weeks, and already everything is so exciting!"

CHAPTER 17.

Laura often forgot there were areas of the city in the last reaches of the train system, like fingers straining to stretch south and east. She would call it the subway system, but the farther out she got, the more she took her ride above ground. The Outliers. The Edges. The blank, white places on the map that may as well have been Baffin Bay. They were suburbs that weren't really suburban by any other standard in America. But in New York, it was as close to sprawl as had ever been built. The only way to get to the address Meatball Eyes listed was to take the L train to East 105th Street, which she had never heard of, and walk a mile or take a bus. It was going to be a long ride to get to a juicy conversation that would be loaded with details. The prize was certainly worth the cost of admission, but she didn't want to go out there alone. The reason everyone forgot the double-fare zones is because poor people lived in them.

"Hi, Stu," Laura said into the phone as she made her way to the blue trains. "What are you doing for the next couple of hours? I have a potential story on philanthropic immigration."

"You just made that up," he said.

"No, you did."

They met at the 14th Street platform. He was leaning on a pole, and when her train pulled in, his hair blew all around. He hadn't cut it in months, and while she blamed Tofu for everything about how he'd changed, she forgot about the girlfriend just then and appreciated the man's hair. It made him look like a little boy, even with the scruff on his jawline. Having kissed Jeremy, she felt as attractive as she ever had, which gave her the distance she needed to see him, and every other man, as if they were hers to be had, long-necked girlfriend or no.

Then Laura noticed that particular girlfriend standing on the other side of the pillar. Once she thought of taking the trip out to meet Meatball Eyes, she'd been looking forward to the adventure, and to some answers about Thomasina's life and death. She also admitted that she'd been looking forward to a couple of hours with Stu, whom she didn't realize she missed until she saw his blond hair flying around in the train's wind. The trip to East New York was looking less and less like fun as the seconds ticked by.

"Hey," Stu said. "You remember Tofu?"

Tah-fuh. Of course. Laura tried not to sneer because the girlfriend looked so cheerful and happy. "Of course. Good to see you again."

"I can't wait to see you two in action. Stu's been talking about what you guys did with the Gracie Pomerantz murder, and I thought it was so exciting!"

"I didn't do anything," Stu said. "It was all Laura."

Tofu smiled, in what seemed an indication of encouragement, but her eyes were cold, hard stones.

"I looked up the address," Stu said as they traversed the tunnels to the L train. "It looks like an old strip mall. Cutting edge, that guy."

Laura grumbled. She didn't care anymore. Stu and Tofu were holding hands. She was more annoyed at herself for caring than either of them. She'd given him up, so she had no business wanting to blow a two-foot hole right through his skinny little girlfriend.

"I read about East New York," Tofu said. "It's so far, and I can't believe it's even in the city, I mean, a borough. That's really where the poorest of the poor live. It's like that's where the ninety-nine percent happens, isn't it?"

Oh, great. Not only was she a brick of calcified bean protein, she was a chatty Patty.

Tofu switched sides to be next to Laura. "I was telling my dad all about Stu and how he went with you to Staten Island to meet a mobster. Pops looked at him differently after that."

Code: My family likes him.

She continued like a playing card clothes-pinned to bike spokes. "It was hard before, you know, because of the activism. We don't have that in Greenwich. Dad takes it personally."

Code: I'm rich.

"He had someone all lined up for me. Not someone who cared about social justice, believe me, but I think, since Stu got the *New Yorker* job, he's making some headway with Pops. Right, honey?"

Code: I have plenty of other men. They're rich, too. But I chose Stu, and I have so much to offer him that you don't.

Stu looked eager to change the subject. "I filled Tofu in on all the deets, and she feels like this might be somewhere where she can do some good."

"Yeah, okay, except that someone was already murdered, so it's not a jaunt for Miss Polly Pocket." Oh, damn. Too harsh. Too direct. "So," she said to Tofu, "you left her at home, right?"

Tofu smiled, which was unfortunate, because Laura was pretty sure she was down a couple of points after a called foul. Tofu was going to be hard to beat.

When they got on the train, there was only one available seat.

Stu stood beside it in such a way as to make sure everyone knew it was his, but he wasn't sitting in it. Then he motioned for Laura to sit. She knew better than to argue feminist politics with him. He'd been raised to be a gentleman with every ridiculous affectation that went with it. Stopping him would be like asking rain to come down, but be a little less wet, if you please. So she thanked him and motioned for Tofu to take it. Tofu wouldn't. So they all stood, and a guy in a plaid biker jacket sat there.

"So," Tofu said with a fat smile and an arched brow, "who are we meeting?"

Laura wanted to kick her. "What I learned from last time is that if you want to find out why someone was killed, you have to find out what they were doing in their life."

"If you read more," Stu said, "you probably would've already known that." That might have been an insult if it didn't simply prove they were close enough to tease each other.

"Experience is better than reading."

"Touché."

Big points. In a better mood, Laura turned back to Tofu. "This girl we're meeting might be the only one who can, or will, tell me how a foundation for abused girls in Eastern Europe and a second rate modeling agency relate to each other. Because Thomasina was involved in both."

"Okay, I got it."

"This is going to be awesome," Laura said, "even if I end up having to throw a party for Ivanah."

When they got to Broadway Junction, most of the passengers cleared out, so standing looked stupid. They sat together, with Stu and Tofu holding hands in the front-facing seats perpendicular to the window and Laura opposite them. The train trundled to an outside track, and the afternoon sun blasted in through the window.

"I never understood the window seats when I was little," Laura said, "because I'd only ever seen trains in tunnels. So when I was like twenty, I went to a boat excursion out of Sheepshead Bay, and on the train there, I could see the houses and backyards and streets out the window of the D train. It was better than television."

Code: I was born hipper than you.

Stu didn't give Tofu a chance to retaliate, even if he saw what was going on between the women. "This is the second time I'm escorting you to an outer borough on a murder investigation."

"You're supposed to demand full access and exclusive rights to the story."

"I demand it."

"You have it."

Code: You have nothing to offer, bitch.

Tofu rolled her eyes. "It's all about work for you guys."

Code: Game. Set. Match, to the soaking brick of calcified vegetable protein.

Bad neighborhoods in New York could be identified by a few key factors. Laura didn't know if those factors translated anywhere else in the world, but to her, they were starkly clear. Strip malls. Wide streets. Tall, matching apartment buildings spread far apart. There were other markers for the denser neighborhoods in the Bronx, but in Brooklyn and Queens, those were the rules.

East New York, which was in the southeastern-most part of Brooklyn, had all of the above and a landfill to the south. There was really nothing else that could have been done to make it worse except maybe a jail nearby or a training yard for roosters and pit bulls. Every street had a strip mall, and every strip mall had a check-cashing place, and every check-cashing place seemed pretty busy. Starrett City towers peeked over the low horizon like the few last teeth of a rotted-out jaw. The planned community for working class tenants had turned into a low-rent housing project in spite of itself.

Like any war zone in the city, artists had found it by simply looking at a map and drawing lines of acceptability from Manhattan outward. The first affordable place they hit where generous space could be had became a target for the bravest.

Since there were no warehouses or light industrial zoning,

East New York had escaped the wedge of gentrification. Moving there would require more imagination than most people had, but it only took one person to have an idea and thousands to follow, and strip malls were the last big idea. They had space, big windows up front, and small backyards where one could spray paint a sculpture or smoke a cigarette. The parking lot in front could be used as a loading dock for huge objects, or well, just to park the cars and pickups that had become more hip and acceptable since Manhattan had become inaccessible. That so many had been vacant after a few domino financial crises that hit the poor first and left the poor last made them cheap. Many were owned by foreign investors who would fix up the bathroom and floors but never check to make sure the tenants weren't living illegally in the back room.

The store that owned the address Laura had been given used to be a photocopy-slash-fax joint. The one next to it rented little brass mailboxes, which if you looked through the fogged window, still resided there. Walls had been broken down between the stores, making a huge space.

Stu yanked on the front door, and it opened with the violent creak of metal on concrete. Laura entered first, while Stu and Tofu followed. The room probably hadn't looked as big when filled with copy machines. From her quick count of the clean spots on the industrial carpet, there had been twelve in all. She felt a slap of sadness as she thought of a once-thriving business unable to keep up with technology, or the neighborhood, or the rent, or whatever it was that had killed it, then shooed the feeling away with the idea that the owners might have expanded and moved to a better location.

"Hello? Susannah?" she called out, walking deeper into the abandoned store.

"Maybe she went to lunch," Tofu said.

"Laura," Stu said, "this doesn't seem right."

The smell of a thick Turkish cigarette came from an open back door. The yard out back was wide, and she could see a little crabgrass patch where a few dandelions had found a home. Laura figured Meatball Eyes must be getting a smoke, so she picked up the pace. "Susannah?"

No answer. Probably on the phone.

When Laura got outside, she thought a store mannequin had been thrown on the ground. But mannequins didn't smoke thick Turkish cigarettes or drop lit ones nearby, and they didn't bleed from holes in the chest.

In the second before she fell apart, she saw that the one eye that hadn't been beaten closed was brown and as big as a meatball.

Falling apart was too kind a term for what happened. Complete emotional collapse would have been a better term, except that the description didn't encompass the physical. Stu practically caught her with one hand on her way to the glass-dusted ground, missing the opportunity to help Tofu, who screamed like Laura had the first time she'd tripped over a murder scene.

Three dead people in six months. All women. Who did that happen to? Didn't most people live their whole lives without seeing a murder? The details of all three marched across Laura's mind's field of vision, and she was attacked by grief emanating outward from her sternum. It was too much. Too much death. Too much hurt. Too many people on the floor with physical harm done to them. She knew she was crying, maybe for the women, none of whom she'd liked or known very well, maybe for herself and her foul luck. Maybe she was just crying because she could. Stu was somewhere far away, asking her to get hold of herself, though without an ounce of impatience, and she wanted to answer, but her grief had turned into colors that appeared before her eyes. A salty taste that couldn't have been anything but tears dropped into her mouth.

Bright, angled light came from the horizon, which must have been from the setting sun in the front parking lot. There was a little cool breeze because even crappy neighborhoods got the benefit of good weather. She then saw flashing lights. She was getting cold, but didn't have much else on her mind, even as the water she found she was drinking made its way down her throat, into the wrong pipe, making her cough.

When she came back to herself, the sun was gone, and the sky was graded shades of teal and cyan. She sat on the back bumper of a police car with a bottle of water in her hand. Stu was talking to a guy in a jacket that had bulges all around the waistline. A cop. Not Cangemi. Weird. He seemed like the only cop in the world until Stu stood there, talking with another as if they were compatriots or college roommates.

The cop, a super young guy of no less than six-four, wearing a bulletproof vest under his jacket, looked like a gargantuan monster, but when he came closer and she saw the proportion of his head to his shoulders, she knew he was just a normal size under all that gear. She figured she could make a fortune custom tailoring suits for plainclothes cops.

"I'm Detective Yarisi, with the sixty-ninth. Are you okay?"

Her eyes hurt, and her mouth was fighting a coating of phlegm and spit, but she nodded anyway.

"Your friend tells me you're Laura Carnegie? You got the sister all over the news?"

She shot a look at Stu. They hadn't looked at a TV or a phone in hours. "We pissed off a reporter." She pointed at the ambulance with the closed back doors. "Her name was Susannah," she said, then had to fight back a crying jag. She held out the catalog for the White Rose foundation. "And you have to figure it out. Because I can't do two at the same time, okay?" The overwhelmed feeling made her want to fall down, and she was relieved to find Stu right there to hold her up. "I can't keep finding people and then trying to find out what happened because it's making me *upset*. Do you understand me?"

"Sure."

"You have to do this yourself, okay? You have to call Ivanah and explain to her and you have to find out how Susannah got here and you have to do all that stuff because if I try to find another killer, I'm going to find more bodies. And what I'm saying is, if I'm not being clear, just in case, that I am going home and not making any stops, and I'm not asking any questions, and I'm not even going to crack a single joke with you because I am cursed to find dead people, and I'm afraid the next person I find is going to be someone I care about, and then I'm really going to have to ask questions. Are you understanding? Because I see you nodding, but I don't know what that means."

"It means I understand. The paramedics are here. They can give you something to help you calm down."

"No! I don't want anything." She turned to Stu. "Where's Tofu?" She said the name with her thick New York accent that had no time for mediation and made his girlfriend sound like bland, greyish food.

"She went home."

"I want to go home, too."

Alas, she had found another body, which meant another round of questions. She already knew what they were going to ask before they did, so she answered clearly, thoughtfully, and in great detail, careful to explain any contradictions. She and Stu were in a gypsy cab an hour later.

Their driver, by his own admission, was from a village in southern Sudan, and Laura steeled herself for another horrifying childhood story, which could put her right over the edge. But he talked to himself, and then into his headset in a constant musical patois. He didn't expect answers or validation. He was just doing his own thing, man, and if she was okay with it, he was too.

"I don't have a lead," Laura said. "I know that sounds heartless."

"Why don't you ask her boss?" Stu asked.

She glanced out the window. She recognized nothing in the blackness, but could smell the salt of the ocean, which reminded her of Jeremy.

"Because I think she might have done it."

"You think she beat and stabbed her assistant?"

"No, poisoned Thomasina. I don't know what happened to Meatb—Susannah. I almost hope it was just the neighborhood. But Thomasina, that was premeditated and done so the killer wouldn't be near her when she died. And also to mimic a popular diet pill the girls are taking. So it was a practical matter. Not some crime of passion."

"Passion can be very cold."

She huffed, then hoped he wouldn't ask her what she was huffing about because she didn't want to tell him the statement made her think of their short-lived relationship. "Whatever killed her was given in the morning. She saw my sister in the morning is all we know, and I think she saw Rochelle Rik at Marlene X. Rochelle was involved; she had Susannah's scarf right there in her office, even if she denies it. So yeah, there could have been some conflict. Like Thomasina was signing the girls into an exclusive thing with Pandora instead of putting them with Mermaid, which would have made Rochelle bare her teeth. But kill her? No way. She wouldn't harm a hair on that woman's head. Thomasina was a cash cow, so to speak. The Mermaid Agency was built on her skinny back, and yeah, they'll survive without her, but she brought in serious bank." Laura turned fully toward Stu. "But Ivanah? Now think about this. She's a real business shark. Her business manager talks about her like she craps Krugerrands. So listen to my theory."

"This is going to be awesome."

"Thomasina approaches Ivanah about getting involved in White Rose because she knows the drill over there in the former East Germany, and she's a closet tycoon, which is important because either Thomasina just felt comfortable around her own kind or needed money."

Stu gave her a quizzical look.

She held up her hand. "Yeah, I know Thomasina has a buttload of money, but go with me here, because for some reason rich people never use their own money to do anything. They always have to tap someone richer or just someone *else*. I don't know why."

"I think it's a tax thing."

"Whatever." She rubbed her eye and noticed how much it hurt. It was incredible how quickly she'd put the pile of bodies out of her mind. "So anyway, Ivanah's like, all right, I'll help the people. Young girls? Sure, I was one once, and she gets involved, and her husband flies out there to check out the deal and make sure it's clean. But it isn't."

"Like how?"

"Use your imagination. They're selling babies. Or they're just shipping out random women. Or the government isn't getting their kickbacks. Or the girls have swine flu. Or they're addicts. I have no idea. Let's just say Bob calls Ivanah and says, 'This thing is a no-go. It stinks to high heaven, and we need to bail immediately.'"

"You better wrap this up before we get to Williamsburg."

She had him, body and soul, leaning forward at full attention. "They can't bail."

"They can't bail?"

"Nope."

"Why the hell not?"

"Thomasina's dead."

"You're twisting this into a knot, Carnegie. Murder is rarely this complicated."

"Ivanah and Bob are involved with White Rose and possibly Pandora, and they're not saying a word, Stu. Don't you think something's wrong with that?"

They pulled up to his row house on North Seventh. He flipped her two twenties. She didn't take them, and he didn't open the door. Tofu was upstairs, and Laura was in the cab. She had a few hours left in her, and in a moment of honesty with herself, she wanted to be with him.

She looked at the twenties and slid the glass back on the cab. "How much to 48th and Park?"

Manolo shrugged. "Another twenty-five."

"What are you doing?" Stu asked. "You said you wanted to go right home before someone else died."

"Go home to your girlfriend. I'm wide awake and chasing geese."

"What's the name of the goose on Park Avenue?"

"What about your girlfriend?"

"What about the goose?"

"The White Rose Foundation."

He looked down, sharpening the crease in his twenties. "You're a world of trouble, you know that?"

"I have to work tonight, so either you're coming or not, but I have to go."

Stu rapped on the glass. "Go ahead. Wherever the lady says."

"Okay!" Manolo took off for the Williamsburg Bridge.

CHAPTER 18,

Two Seventy-Seven Park Avenue had a three-story atrium in the front with actual trees and recordings of non-actual birds singing. Her mother told her the atrium once had real birds, but the poop situation had forced management to turn to the recorded loops. Laura never knew whether someone had lied to Mom or if she'd just made it up to get her and Ruby to take lunch with her there, as it was right between the Scaasi offices and the actual garment district, but Laura doubted a live bird had ever been brought into a New York office building.

The atrium was a refuge for workers in the neighborhood the way Bryant Park was for the garmentos in her neighborhood. The chirping blasted even louder at eight at night, apparently, because the squeak of their sneakers was drowned out by the aural, if not corporeal, presence of multiple bird species. She and Stu didn't speak, such was the cacophony of the atrium. They browsed the directory and found neither Pandora nor White Rose. The elevator ding sounded like an incongruous technological leap, and a lady in a business suit exited, whispering into her phone as if she too wanted to respect the majesty of the absent birds.

Laura hit the button for the seventeenth floor, and the doors whooshed closed behind them. Birds, out.

"We're going to go up there and find a locked door," Stu said.

"Then I can go finish Jeremy's pattern, and you can go home to your girlfriend."

"I have a deadline, so infer what you will."

The hallways were much like those in any other building in the city, with rows of doors and placards marking the company or entity. Since the building had been erected in the '70s, there were fewer vestigial pipes and conduits, and the layers of paint didn't encroach on the width of the halls, but there was the sense that the building was at the turning point of its life, the style falling between "updated" and "vintage."

Laura didn't have a suite number for the Pandora offices. The brochure had only contained a floor number, giving readers the impression that the company took up the entire thing, window to window. But there were just endless rows of doors.

"I think we have to go back down," she said. "Process of elimination. We'll see what numbers are missing from the directory."

"Waste of time. Some companies take up two suites." But even as he dismissed her idea, she saw his attention drawn elsewhere, like a bloodhound catching a scent.

Then she caught it, too, a tingling vibration in the walls.

Music.

Throbbing stuff that hummed in time. The beat wasn't loud or close enough to rattle the sconces, but it was palpable enough to follow, which they did, without speaking, like Green Berets in enemy territory. The sound got ever louder, or deceptively smaller, hitting a fever pitch behind a lonely door in a cul de sac of a hallway. Neither number nor name hung on the door, just a doormat on the floor in front of it, with a border of decorative white roses woven into the hemp. It could have been a closet, but apparently wasn't because it was surely the source of the thumpy-thump music and voices. Many voices. Too many for a closet.

"It's Thursday," she whispered. "Haven't these people heard of weekends?"

"Weekends are for amateurs."

"Could this possibly be the only entrance?"

Stu reached for the doorknob and picked off a dust bunny. "Apparently not."

Laura had no real sense of direction without the island of Manhattan to follow. Seventh and Broadway went South. Sixth and Eighth went North. The rest followed. Once inside a building without traffic to guide her, she could be anywhere.

Luckily, Stu didn't have the same problem. Like a force of nature, he took off with the same bloodhound instinct, around corners and through stairwells, until she feared they were hopelessly lost. But then the music got thumpier again. The voices came through loud and clear as she walked up a secret flight of stairs Stu said might get them past a locked door in a newer wall on the seventeenth floor.

The stairwell was little used. She'd seen filthier in her life, but it was narrow, beige, and utilitarian, the kind of place where one might just hurry up the concrete stairs to get to the next place, so quickly, in fact, that a person might just barrel into three half-naked people doing... Laura covered her eyes, but burned into her memory were a middle-aged male butt, a woman's bare back pushed against a fire extinguisher, and another woman on her knees, her face buried somewhere Laura didn't want to think about, at all, ever again.

Stu gripped her arm, which was held rigidly straight in order to keep her eyes from seeing anything else she wouldn't be able to unsee. She just let him drag her wherever he wanted. She heard grunting and smelled smells, as if her presence was of no consequence to the grunters or smell-makers. The stairwell door clacked, and the voices got louder. The music was still coming from someplace else; however, a layer of voices became clearer. They stopped. It was dark behind her hands, but she wasn't ready to move them.

She felt Stu move to stand in front of her and take her wrists. "You're committed now," he said. But when he moved her hands, she kept her eyes closed. "It's just a club. Come on, we've seen some crazy stuff. Remember the night Heyday was all pornos all over the walls? Just pretend you paid thirty at the door."

"Can I pretend we were on the list?"

"If that helps you function, then fine. Just let's go. If this is the Pandora office, I'm going to have another story to pitch to the *New Yorker*."

Nothing soothed discomfort like doing a favor for someone else. Someone she cared about. Someone she'd still like to date, except he had a girlfriend too pristine to discover a sex club in an office building. And Jeremy, of course, whose kiss should have erased any feelings for Stu.

"Am I getting back to work tonight?" she asked.

"Not likely."

She opened her eyes. It was dark. No, that was Stu's face filling her vision, looking at her as if to let her know everything was going to be okay if she would just chill. So she nodded, letting him know that she was totally chilled, the very vision of chill, that if he looked up "chill" in the dictionary, depending on the dictionary, he'd probably find the definition of a transitive verb for cold, but anyway... she was calm.

"I'm not taking my clothes off," she said.

"I agree." He took her hand, and she checked out the scene.

Like any New Yorker, she looked at the windows first, since they defined place, affluence, and orientation. The view was of the office building across Park Avenue, on one wall only. So they were in the middle of the building because she didn't see any passage to a corner office, and the proximity to the offices across the street, where someone was probably working late, increased the excitement of what was going on in the windows. Against the walls, pushed akimbo as if in a hurry, stood folded cubicles and oldish computers. Half the grey fabric chairs were pushed under the desks. The other half were being used.

She has once seen a Tom Cruise movie where he entered a sex club he'd been trying to get into for most of the movie. It was supposed to be the hottest, sexiest scene ever. People were doing it on pool tables and in threes and fours, wearing big masks, but no one looked as if they were having any fun. So the scene wasn't sexy. It was boring. She thought that the lack of sexiness was intentional. She didn't know if the same could be said for the Park Avenue office.

Stu scanned the room and pointed to an unappealing door with a red EXIT sign. That was the front, with the rosy doormat, the door no one used.

"So it's got a door through a back hallway and another up utility stairs?" she asked.

"Yeah, but people work here."

"Apparently." She was making a joke about the work going on right then, which she took great effort not to see. "We're sticking out." They were the only two fully clothed people.

No, there were two more dressed people across the room, a man in a leather jacket and another man in a suit. A woman in a gold string bikini hung on Leather Jacket as he and Suit shook hands. When Leather turned his face to the light, Laura recognized him.

"Rolf?" Because of the music, she said it louder than she meant.

Rolf looked up and directly at her. She was on his turf, safeguarded by the skinniest guy in the five boroughs, surrounded by people who had something to protect, and she was terrified. Stu squeezed her hand, which told her one, to be calm, and two, that he wasn't feeling too cozy himself. She couldn't see Rolf's face too well, as the windows were behind him, so she was surprised when he shot toward the rosy doormat exit.

She was even more surprised when she went after him.

She couldn't help it. She hadn't just seen a woman's face buried in some guy's ass so she could walk away and say something like, "Wow, Rolf was there. How interesting." No, she was going to catch the asshole and rip information out of his throat, the fifty pounds he had on her notwithstanding.

She'd seen people in movies run down halls and flights of stairs, and it always seemed quite easy. When Rolf took a turn, she took it. When he barreled down a long hall, she ran at top speed, noting the minty gum scent he left behind. But there was the matter of her slippery vintage Via Spigas to consider, and in the three seconds she took to wipe out on the shiny floor, right herself, and kick off the shoes, she almost lost him. He cut a hairpin turn to the elevator bay and seemed gone. When she caught up, the stairwell door was clicking shut, and the elevator buttons were lit. She headed for the door at full speed, her bare feet giving enough traction for her to launch herself toward the stairwell door. She noted the elevator ding in the back of her mind.

Her velocity worked against her when Rolf, obviously having planned the little trick, opened the stairwell door all the way and dodged her thrust. It was too late for her to stop, and the full weight of her body slammed against the bottom corner of the fire extinguisher box. The glass shattered and, when she rebounded, stuck in her arm as it was smashed against the cinderblock wall. Glass shards rained as she *oofed*, the air exiting her lungs.

She didn't go fully unconscious. The fire alarm could be heard in The Bronx. The stair door clicked shut. The elevator motor churned through the wall she had her back against. The room turned sideways.

No. That was her, falling.

He was getting away. From what, she didn't know. But she wanted to know, and he would disappear like a phantom, with his billions of dollars and his dead sister, and whatever was going on with White Rose, Pandora, and the threesome in the back stairwell would go with him.

Stuff was broken. Bones, perhaps. Skull, maybe. But it was too soon after she lost a fight with a stack of cinderblocks to feel it, and she functioned enough to get herself to the next elevator and crawl into it.

Lying on the floor, staring at the lit-up metal mesh at the top of the elevator, she wished she'd taken a look at some of the girls she'd seen in the White Rose offices. The girl with her back against the fire extinguisher, the one with her face where no face should be, the gold bikini chick, they were all blank to her. If she'd seen just one, she could at least look for them in the catalog she'd found under Ruby's bed eons ago.

The connection between White Rose and Pandora didn't seem so farfetched anymore. They found girls in scrubby, impoverished parts of Eastern Europe, brought them to Germany, which was part of the European Union, and somehow brought them to the U.S. to be prostitutes. Maybe they promised them modeling jobs, and the girls jumped at the chance.

But Thomasina wouldn't have gone for it. How could she? And more importantly, why would she? She had enough money to do whatever she wanted; she didn't need to operate a prostitution ring to put food on the table. So, Rolf. He tried to sneak his sister's foundation away from her. Maybe he seduced the girls and maybe that was what Bob had seen on his trip. When Thomasina found out and tried to stop Rolf, he killed her.

But where was Rolf going now?

The elevator stopped with a ding, and with a whoosh, the doors opened to the cacophony of the fire alarm. The birds chirped, buzzed, whistled, and grunted.

No. There were no grunting birds, at least not in the atrium's audio loop.

She dragged herself out of the elevator. Her legs seemed okay, but her right arm had lost its ability to hold her weight, so she got her feet under her. The grunting was close, right under the elevator button. Two men were wrestling and one was Stu, who had blood all over his forehead. She didn't think about who the other guy was, so strong was her impulse to protect her friend.

As she was lining up her shot, maybe a hundredth of a second, Stu, getting a micro-moment of upper hand, got on top. She saw her opportunity and raised her right foot. Rolf's face flashed red when the fire truck pulled up outside, and Laura brought her foot down onto his trachea.

One thing for sure. Laura wasn't a covert Mossad operative. Rolf was stopped for only half a second, but that time gave Stu enough of a leg up to wrestle him face down— the fifty pounds of weight difference between them notwithstanding.

Laura stepped on Rolf's head so he couldn't move. He cursed in German, and she moved her foot a little so his mouth was squished. No more guttural garbage from him. The cops and firemen arrived like a brigade, turning keys and talking into their black boxes. The siren wailed, and the birds chirped, and Stu put his arm around her to keep her from falling down again. She leaned into him and would have laughed if the whole thing wasn't so ridiculous.

CHAPTER 19.

"A broken humerus," Cangemi said with a smirk. "You sure it wasn't cracked at birth?" He had a captive audience, in the so-very-public-corridor of the ER, with some battle-ax of a nurse placing Laura's right arm on a stack of pillows.

"You'll note my inability to even get your stupid joke." She was tired, work was piling up, and the bastard was after her sister. "Where's Stu?"

"On four getting an MRI. I couldn't believe how many questions that guy can ask when he's concussed."

"He's a journalist."

"What's your excuse?"

She didn't answer right away, deciding instead to wonder how she was going to make patterns, or use a pen even, with her arm in a cast. When she did speak, she bypassed blabbermouth and instead took a page from Stu's book. "What did I just see?"

Nurse Battle-ax had no interest in either lively banter or manners and jumped in without a how-do-you-do, asking, "You comfortable?"

"Yes." Laura's tone fell somewhere between blunt as a falling coconut and sharp as a scalpel.

"I'll be in with a technician to plaster this up. Can you sign with your left?" She held out a clipboard and put a ballpoint in Laura's left hand. She signed without reading anything, something she had to stop swearing she never did.

Unfazed, Cangemi continued his questioning. "What do you think you saw?"

Nurse Battle-ax flipped pages, and Laura signed where she pointed.

"Okay, my mom did that when I asked her if there was a Santa Claus. She said, 'Do *you* think there's a Santa Claus?' and I said, 'Yes, I believe in Santa Claus,' and I did until I was like, ten, which is too old, in case you don't know. So when someone asks a question like that, basically, that means they're hiding some kind of lie they've been telling for years."

He pointed at her broken funny bone. "You really broke that thing, huh?"

"That's it. No more answers until I get a first name."

He held both hands up in surrender, but she put on an expression meant to tell him no treaties would be brokered. She probably looked constipated, but she did her very best to appear serious and mean. The nurse left with her papers.

"Calogero." He said it with rolling Rs and lilting Ls.

"I like it. Can I call you Cal?"

"Detective is fine." He dragged a chair over with a loud scraping noise. "We don't know exactly what you saw yet. We have some people in custody, and some are talking, but we can't hold anyone because there wasn't nothing illegal going on. We got a lotta girls and guys doing it, no laws against that. As far as Rolf goes, he's got some lawyer and ain't talking. Can't arrest him neither."

"What about trespassing?"

"He rented the unit. Legally. You guys were the ones trespassing."

"And the girls? Were they maybe prostitutes you've arrested before?"

He leaned forward, putting his elbows on his knees and acting like there was some crossword question he really couldn't guess for the life of him. "See, this is the thing we can't figure out. They were all here on legal green cards, and we got three of them working for you."

"For who?"

"You."

"What?"

He took a tiny envelope out of his breast pocket and slid out wallet-sized photos. "You hire this girl in April?" He showed her a photo of a blonde of about twenty.

"No. Are you serious? We're on a total shoestring."

He flipped to another picture, a girl with light brown hair and green eyes. "This one? Around mid-June?"

"No. Do you think I'd be working nights and weekends if we could afford to hire people?"

"Yes, I do." He held up a picture of Meatball Eyes. Her lips were closed straight across her face as if she was afraid to beam too hard for the camera. "How about this one?"

She felt a pang of regret, sorrow even, for a girl she'd met once in an annoying circumstance. "I kind of know her."

"And she worked for you when?"

"You know goddamn well she worked for Ivanah Schmiller before she was beaten and stabbed out in East New York. In an abandoned strip mall? Hello? Don't you people talk to each other?" She choked back a sob that must have been left over from earlier in the day. "I mean, and for Chrissakes, a room full of prostitutes and you're going to sit there and tell me you can't pin any of them for anything? You can't arrest anyone?"

"I arrested your boyfriend."

"He's not my boyfriend."

"Irregardless..."

"That's not even a word." She paused because she didn't care that much about Cangemi's vocabulary. "Why did you arrest him?"

"Assault. And once we had him on that, he took all the blame for the trespass, which we can choose to ignore or not. But he's a real nice guy. Are you sure you're not dating?"

She wanted to cross her arms but couldn't, so she just curled her lips so tightly she felt the texture of her teeth.

He leaned back and crossed his arms and ankles. "It's late. So I'm going to ask nicely instead of getting all subpoena on you. What were you doing up there?"

"I was—"

"Don't leave anything out."

"Can I talk?" He answered by taking out his pad, and Laura continued, "I'm worried that you think Ruby killed Thomasina, which she didn't. Okay, I want to get that out of the way. She didn't do it, but when I found out she and Thomasina were... you know... I know how you guys think. And I know the poison was in her house, but I don't care. Ruby's no chemist. And I don't know if you know that, and I don't know what you're doing. You could be working day and night to find reasons to put her away instead of trying to find out what really happened."

He looked up from his pad with a raised eyebrow.

She knew she'd said something wrong and began backpedaling almost immediately. "I'm not saying you're dishonest. I'm just saying you have a job to do, and you're going to do it. And your job is to put people away and get stuff off your desk is all."

"One day we're going to talk about my job and your job, okay? But not now."

Grateful for the reprieve, she said, "We found this brochure in Ruby's stuff that we'd forgotten about. For the White Rose Foundation. Thomasina was the founder, or Sabine, who is her brother, but whatever. It's a thing where they get orphaned and in trouble girls in Eastern Europe and help them out of the life of prostitution or whatever it is that happens." She felt her cheeks get warm. Would she always be so weird about sex? Her embarrassment was... well, embarrassing.

"Okay, so this girl on the White Rose cover here, she was also in the Pandora catalog you showed me, and she was also with Rolf at Baxter City. So we went looking for her, and I found out she's Ivanah's assistant, which is weird, but you can put two and two together. I wanted to talk to her, and when I went to see her in East New York..."

"Most people go their whole lives without seeing a murder."

"Well, yes, and it was really upsetting. So I figured we should go and see the address on the brochure. I mean she was right on the cover. And it just happened to be nighttime. I wasn't looking for what I found."

Cangemi rubbed his eyes. "I got a life, you know. I got this girlfriend who, we're breaking up, then we're not, and then I get home, and she's leaving me notes about what a dick I am. See, I'm always working because it's life or death, every time. If I don't go meet the crazy fashion girl in the hospital, and the next day she's dead, that's on my head. But then I get here, and guess what? You're crazy. *Botz*, okay? I know you think you broke the Pomerantz case. And I let you think that because you're cute and you have an honest heart. But I gotta tell you, we had him, and we were going to get him. I mean, we were on the way. And we got him because we have the tools to do the job, and we don't sit around cooking up crazy ideas."

"You were still liking Jeremy for it."

"When you walked into that office, who did you think done it?"

They spent a good thirty seconds staring at the middle distance between each other. Laura had walked into the office after Jeremy's show with no little nervousness. She'd just had a limousine ride with Sheldon Pomerantz, the widower whom she'd revealed as a perjurer and purveyor of paid fellatio, and was ready to meet Jeremy upstairs in the office that had been the scene of their friendship. After talking to Sheldon and stepping out of that limo, convinced he hadn't murdered his wife, and having every fact at her fingertips, who *did* she think had done it?

"Jeremy," she said. "I thought Jeremy killed her."

"Well, I didn't. I knew André did it. You were two days behind me. How far behind me are you this time?"

Laura shrugged. "Thomasina died Tuesday, so... can't be more than a day and a half. Kind of an improvement, right?" She tried to smile meekly, but probably looked like the crazy fashion girl of Detective Cangemi's worst nightmares.

Ruby came at ten thirty. Laura had just signed herself out with her left hand. She had work to do for Jeremy, and she hadn't seen the inside of her own showroom in a day and a half. She was sure not a sale had been missed because she wasn't there. She was a little concerned about Debbie Hayworth, who undoubtedly would react less kindly to Ruby-boyfriend-stealer's sales tactics. She had texted Stu four times and heard nothing back.

"Oh, that's attractive," Ruby said of the plastered arm. "Really. It doesn't come in another color?"

"Feel free to sew me a new one. Oh, but never mind."

Ruby stuck her tongue out at her. Of course she couldn't sew.

Laura felt guilty. "How's the showroom?"

"There's no air conditioning vent. It smells like bodies."

"Speaking of bodies..." Laura knew it was a tacky segue, but couldn't help herself. "I have some new developments. Should we take a cab?"

"You have money?"

"I'm broke. How about the train?" She indicated her arm, which looked ridiculous and wouldn't get its sleek waterproof cast for three days. "I think I can make it if I don't walk on my hands. And if the train's not too crowded."

Laura recited the story as they walked east on 14th Street. She wanted to tell everything in order so she wouldn't miss anything. That meant she didn't mention their army of employees until the end.

"They work for who? For us?" Ruby's brow knitted, and she got a faraway look, as if she was trying to remember hiring someone. "I don't think so."

"It's all jumbled, and I don't feel like we're any closer to figuring it out."

"Uncle Graham says he thinks they're going to arrest me. I don't think I could stand it."

They arrived at the train station. Ruby slid Laura's card through the reader and pushed her through the turnstile. The subway car was crowded for late night, and Laura's arm took up way too much space. Even clubbers who wanted to be polite and give her a wide berth couldn't, and she refused a seat because she'd end up jabbing the person next to her, a scraggly woman in her twenties with a laundry bag between her legs. With a look, the girl let Laura know there wasn't any room for her and her cast.

"You won't get convicted," Laura said.

"Convicted?" Ruby asked as if she'd never considered the word, as though the word was so much more powerful than the idea of going to jail. *Convicted*. It did seem awfully strong.

"They have a bunch of circumstantial stuff, and if it was worth a dime, they would have arrested you already. I mean, it's a celebrity poisoning. Every day that goes by without an arrest looks bad for them." Laura realized what she'd said as the last word left her mouth. "Don't worry, Ruby. We'll figure it out."

"We don't have time. I wish I could just run away."

They got off at Union Station and walked underground to the R train, a trek that was beginning to exhaust Laura completely. The girl with the laundry bag who had no room next to her for a girl with a broken arm went by at a good clip, the bag knocking against her leg and bumping Laura into Ruby. Laura sent a choice word at Laundry Lady's back, but was ignored.

Laura missed Manhattan. The space in the house was nice, but the commute was killing her. Her life seemed to be getting harder instead of easier. "Did you ever give Thomasina any information about our business, like the EIN or anything like that?"

"No."

"You swear?"

"We were doing other things."

"Okay, never mind. Listen. It's all pretty clear." She pulled Ruby to a bench designed as a piece of art. She was tired, and she didn't want to explain and get knocked around at the same time. "They were laundering girls through Sartorial. Like money."

"What do you know about money laundering?"

"What's the difference? They had these girls in deep trouble. Thomasina wanted to help them by giving them jobs and a new life." Laura was sure her timeline was all messed up, but she couldn't stop talking. "Rolf gets wind of it, and he's in trouble with the law for being a skinhead, so he needs to get out of the country. But he can't just partner with Thomasina. I don't know why; I guess it was just too tempting to sell them into prostitution. I mean, how much of a stretch, right? So maybe that's what Bob found out when he went to Germany. Maybe he didn't like that. And one of two things happened. Either Ivanah was in it with Rolf and took on Susannah as an assistant to shut Bob up, or she wasn't in on it and she hired Susannah because she wanted to be the first to make the right move."

Laura shrugged. "In any case, who else had access to Sartorial's information? And the power to utilize it? Enough to secretly sponsor foreign women? Ivanah and Bob, and we already know Bob didn't like what he saw when he went out there. This leaves us with what?"

Ruby bent over and pressed her forehead between her knees. "Too much."

"To me, the fact that all this was going on and you had nothing to do with it should be enough to keep you out of trouble."

"I just want my life back."

"I can get it for you. I mean, I can try. Tomorrow, Ivanah's coming into the design room. I'll see what I can get out of her. But tonight, I have to go apologize to Jeremy."

Jeremy's office was buzzing, even at eleven at night. The show was the next day, and no one was sleeping. Emira ran through the racks like a machine, moving garments and checking against a list that put the right giraffe with the right pair of pants. She was the designer who had replaced Carmella, the faux Italian countess, and was an organized workhorse short on innovation, but long on late hours and responsible partying. Tiffany was next to her, having survived the transition after the Pomerantz murder. Jeremy stood over Carlos, the cutter, who had a brown cowhide flat on the table.

"But I told you," Jeremy said with the bite of a pit bull in his voice. "I told you in yesterday's meeting, and I told you three hours ago. If the skin has hair, you cut with a razor."

"It's too short," Carlos protested.

"If you want to spend the rest of your career cutting cotton poplin, Tollridge & Cherry is across the street, except their sample cutters live in China. How would that work out for you?"

Carlos just stared at the stretch of cowhide on the table.

Jeremy held up a trapezoid-shaped blade as if explaining the buttons on a remote control to an interplanetary alien. "This is the handle. This is the sharp part. This is tape to keep you from cutting yourself. Carlos, you ruin this skin because you're afraid of getting cut, and I'm firing you. I know five guys more than happy to take your place."

Jeremy glanced up at her and placed the blade in Carlos's hand, turning his back on his cutter of seven years. He pointed at her broken arm. "What happened?"

"Lost a fight with a fire alarm." His quizzical look forced her to elaborate. "I was chasing a pimp."

He pulled her into the break room with a gravity she hadn't seen from him in a long time. He was playing boss, even though he really wasn't her boss but in the most casual way. He closed the door behind them and sat her in one of the red modernist chairs, helping with the busted arm.

"This is not the week to do this," he said. "Not for me. I had to get Tony to cover the Yasmine pants."

"I'm sorry, I—"

"I'm not ready to move the technical stuff to Asia. They're home patternmakers with a paycheck. I interview people in here to grow a tech department, and they need to manage people, a factory floor, and a pattern. I'm only getting two out of three." He was deep in his own troubles.

"You're trying to do too much."

He didn't even seem to hear her. "Have you seen your sister?"

"Yeah, I—"

"She's been running in here every hour. She's in a panic. Your salesperson looks like a zombie. He doesn't know who's coming or going out of that showroom."

"She didn't say anything." Laura got a sinking feeling, as though she'd missed an opportunity to do something right, and the failure couldn't be undone.

"Yoni's been calling me like a banshee. You have approvals pending and projections you need to organize. And if you want to tack onto my wool crepe, you're going to need to get on it."

"The past couple of days have been really hard. I saw another dead body. This time—"

"Stop." He held up his hand, then covered her left with it. "I don't want Ruby to go to jail."

"I don't care."

"What's that supposed to mean?" She was ready to get offended, because offense was the opposite of defense, and she hated being on the defensive.

"You're qualified to do one thing. Make clothes. That's what you do."

"I can still make clothes."

"No, Laura, you can't. You are running a business, and that business hangs on you. You are the life support. In a couple of seasons, you're going to have employees whose jobs depend on you and how you act and how committed you are to what you're doing. What you're doing now is bailing. You worked too hard, and now you're getting involved in something else because you're burned out."

"I don't burn out." She felt petulant and scolded. Obviously, he didn't know her at all.

"No, you do burn out, just like everyone else. But you don't collapse like everyone else. You don't take a vacation or get drunk. You pour all that energy into something else you're convincing yourself is important. But it's not."

"How is a murder and my sister getting accused of it not important?"

"Ivanah got Greyson?"

"They're making it worse."

"Your sister has a lawyer?"

"So?"

"And the NYPD?"

"I don't understand how that—"

"If you're doing their jobs, who's making the clothes, Laura? Who's running your business? You don't have other priorities right now. You don't have hobbies, and you don't have responsibilities. You don't have a life. *This* is your life. There's not a kid coming out of Parsons right now who wouldn't take what you have right out from under you. And none of them are going to look at the dead body on the side of the road. Not one."

She couldn't look at him, but kept her gaze on her lap, where his hand rested with her left hand. She became conscious of her right arm, stuck in the sling and weighing forty pounds, and she thought, *How is this happening? How are we holding hands in my lap like it's normal?* She wondered if her hand would smell of his salt water, and if she'd fall asleep with her palm over her nose.

He continued, "Ivanah's been strolling in and out, asking questions about where you are. You don't have their backing yet is what Pierre tells me. Until there's money in the bank, you have to prove you're worth it, and when the checks clear, you can take half a day off. But you're going to have to order fabric, and you're going to be cleaned out because you're going to have to sew the garments six months before a store is obligated to send you a check, and you're going to have to prove you're worth more money. You have to prove it every delivery, every season, every year."

"This doesn't sound anything like working for myself."

"That's a myth. We all work for someone."

She looked up into his espresso eyes and thought of his history, his life, and wondered where he had gotten such an idea. "Who do you work for? You're your own financing. You make your own decisions."

"My boss is time."

She immediately knew what he meant, haunted as he was by the specter of his fibrosis and a prognosis that didn't stretch past his fortieth year. "Let me get some sleep, and I'll come in tomorrow ready to go."

"Ivanah's coming with an assistant, so you need to be sharp and cheerful. She's going to want to go to 40th Street, and my show's tomorrow, so I can't come and smooth things over. But you bring everyone tickets, and you show up to my show like you own it. Okay?"

"Okay."

"Ruby, too. She has to be available and sharp all day. She's going to be fine if you let everyone do their jobs. If you aren't on top of it this week, you're failing her."

"Okay."

"Have fabric ready for Fall. And you can steal some of the magazines from my office for swipes."

"Okay."

"And don't be scared."

It was just one demand too many, even if it was for her own good. "Can you stop now, please? You don't get to make out with me in the afternoon and then lecture me at night. You're not my boss anymore, and it's not like I know what you are anyway, but you don't know everything about what I need."

"What if I made out with you right now? Could I lecture you then?"

"No. First, you need to tell me what you want from me because it can't be all business sometimes and... something else... other times."

He let her hands go, and she felt the loss of his touch deeply. "What do I want from you? It hasn't been obvious since the day we met? I treated you different from anyone else from the minute you walked in the door. We hung out for how many hours in the mornings? Do you think I *wanted* to show up at seven thirty every day? Hell, no. But you were there, so I was there. Jesus, I'm expanding all over the place, but I found a way to cut you a piece of my showroom. We're tacking orders and sharing staff. What the fuck, Laura? You want something stupid like a card or flowers?"

"But it's always business."

"If I'm letting you into my business, I'm letting you into my life. You know that."

There was a moment when they looked at each other and an understanding passed between them. This was who he was, and she could love him or leave him, but she knew what she was getting into.

Emira walked in before Laura had a chance to wiggle out of her predicament. "JJ, Carlos cut himself." Seeing them so close seemed to catch her up short. "Oh. Ah, never mind? It's not serious. He just wanted you to see it."

Jeremy stood and helped Laura up so her cast wouldn't catch her off balance. Then he took her left hand, knotting their fingers together. She squeezed with everything she had. He pulled her into the hallway with their hands knitted together for everyone in the design room to see.

As they stood waiting for the elevator, she said, "You don't get to yell at me. I don't like it."

"I know."

"You're a real asshole. You've been toying with me for years."

"What was I supposed to do? I took you any way I could

have you." The elevator doors slid open, and they stepped in.

"I can't stand the sight of you," she said.

When the doors shut, he put his arms around her, and he kissed her and said, "Sorry, sorry, sorry," until she kissed him back.

CHAPTER 20.

The cab was clean. Probably the cleanest she'd seen in years. But wasn't it just like Jeremy to stroll outside with a shaking girl and barely have his arm up before the cleanest cab in the city appeared for him? He was a magical person, but did she love him?

Her face burned from the fifteen minutes of kissing lips surrounded by stubble, fifteen minutes of pure thoughtless heaven, where *it* all went away. She defined "it" as the murder she'd seen that morning, or would have seen if she'd shown up ten minutes earlier. "It" was her sister in trouble and not allowed to go back to her own apartment without pulling up a closet floor. "It" was losing her business. "It" was Stu and his nobody-seems-to-mind-that-I'm-named-after-a-grocery-item-but-you girlfriend.

For fifteen minutes, all that mattered was his lips, his smell, and his hands on her neck and back.

He never joked about her broken "humorous" or pressed for any more information about why she'd broken it. He considered it a distraction from what she should be doing and didn't want to encourage her by asking questions. Or so he said. In the back of her mind, she feared he really didn't care.

Or maybe he was right. How could she be great at anything if she kept spreading her energy around? Maybe she should leave the investigating to the lawyers and cops, who knew what they were doing.

"Drop me at the corner," she said. She could walk a block to the house. For some reason, getting out of a cab with a cast on her arm and with a news van right there felt embarrassing.

She could see the van in the dark, a hulking white and blue thing with a satellite dish on top. As she made her way to the house, she found the big vehicle had a gravitational pull. She thought briefly about her deal with Stu and promised herself she would honor his exclusive right to the story, but she knew that the only people with more information, besides lawyers and cops, who were sworn to silence, were reporters.

Jeremy had told her to forget about it and go to bed, and she would, as soon as she did one thing. Then she was going to drop it like a bar of soap in the bathtub. She knocked on the back door of the news van.

Roscoe Knutt answered in a windowpane cotton shirt unbuttoned to his belly, revealing a marginally clean crewneck T-shirt. He was chewing a green sweet pea crispy salty thing when he said, "You're making it too easy for me."

"I aim to please."

"What happened to your arm? Don't tell me. Something to do with that kerfuffle on Park and 48th."

"I don't remember a kerfuffle."

"Smoking too much pot, I'll wager. Rots the short-term memory. Reduces your RAM." He tapped his head so hard with his second finger she feared he'd make a hole. "Come on in if you're coming in."

The van was not what she expected. Sure, there were

short circuit monitors and the requisite complete lack of space and dials and knobs all over the place. What she didn't expect was the big screen propped up high with multiple Twitter feeds and flashing social media windows.

"Hanging out on Facebook?" she asked.

"They don't let me. Honesty is not the best policy in journalism, apparently. It landed me here in a box in the middle of the night."

"What do they have you looking for?"

"You."

"You should get a promotion now."

"Not if you came knocking looking for Snap Peas." He held out a bag of green crunchies.

She was starving.

"Who you been kissing?" he asked.

Her hand shot to her mouth, but she ended up getting green snack dust all over her cheek.

"Raw lips." He chuckled. "Big tell. We know you don't have a boyfriend besides that kid who writes for the *New Yorker.* You know he's sleeping with the Caston Bleach heiress, right?"

Oh, Tofu was an heiress. That was just freaking rich.

"Yeah. He's not my boyfriend."

"Huh. If you say so."

She could almost see him making a note in a little book in his head. "So, what made you think I was involved in the Park Avenue kerfuffle?"

"Your boyfriend's name came up in the arrest records. We get all that on the ticker." He pointed at something on the screen that looked like a Twitter feed. "He's been arrested before. Never misses a 'nonviolent' protest neither. His commie lawyer'll have him out in the morning. Don't worry."

"I'm not worried."

He tilted his head like she must be lying or crazy or both. But in the world of people she knew or had ever met, Stu was the person she was least likely to worry about. He brought self-sufficiency and practicality to new levels daily.

"Stu really got Rolf Wente good," she continued. "Even

though he's a size or two bigger. Rolf, I mean."

"That's the only lick you're ever gonna get. That guy's got some lawyers, and they ain't pinkos. They're barracudas." He rubbed his fingers together to indicate that they were the most expensive predatory fish in the city. "Family, you know. They kicked him out, but funnel him cash. My kid did what he done, I woulda thrown a nickel at him, then kicked him to the curb. Possibly I'd've killed him myself if no one held me back."

"What did he do?"

"You could look it up yourself. It ain't no secret. Least not in East Germany. East*ern* Germany."

"I've never been."

"Want a soda? I got Manhattan Special and Manhattan Special."

"No, thanks."

He pulled a bottle of chocolate soda from the mini fridge and bent the cap back with a little metal opener he had attached to his wrist with a plastic spiral. "Nasty business, it was. And dumb. Just unnecessary. Skinhead gang breaks into a family house, ties the father down, and makes him watch as they rape the wife and daughters. Which is ugly enough. Then they're about to kill the lot when they realize there was a brother, who had gone and got the police. So, that didn't go well for them. Whole country wants to string them up. And they did. You look a little green, there. You all right?"

She had been considering her broken arm and how meaningless and stupid it was, and how little it hurt. She'd forget it in a couple of months. "Rolf was one of them?"

"Well, no. But the father, who was Jewish, so you know it all looked like regular skinhead nonsense, had some business with Rolf. And Rolf, who was all skinhead, had this habit of beating girls near to death as it was. Got off not once, but twice. He happened to be in charge of those guys, more or less. Now Rolf denies he put in the order to kill or rape anyone, but the prosecutor's just uncovering more and more connections with the Jewish dad."

"Wait. What kind of business?"

"That was the funny thing. It was flowers out of The Netherlands. But not the flowers. The whaddya call it?" He made a fist.

"Bulbs?"

"Supposedly. The prosecutor's getting his suit on for a big press conference because he says he's got him. The cops are outside the mansion waiting for him to say they got Rolf on murder and the business, which is so bad, by the way, the Jewish dad is talking about dropping charges against the skinheads. Then, dontcha know?"

"The prosecutor is dead."

"Found him in a pool of vomit."

Laura gasped.

Roscoe continued, "But it was ruled an accident because they found his dinner from the night before, and the onions in it were chopped up bulbs. Accident. Supposedly happens all the time."

Laura suddenly remembered the boxes of bulbs in her backyard. The last time she had seen them, she was beating up Cangemi for not respecting a woman's right to starve herself. "Narcissus bulbs are poisonous."

"Right. But before you go pulling a rabbit out of your ass, there's not enough to kill a person in what he had there. The Wente family pulled strings to get it ruled an accident, then they disowned Rolf with a few mil' in a bank account. He blew through it already. We don't know how he's surviving."

Laura sat stock-still, staring into the distance.

Roscoe leaned forward. "Now, you wanna tell me what you was doin' on Park Avenue at ten at night when you'd usually be at work?"

She felt she owed him something for unabashedly giving so much information she did not have the brains or resources to find for herself. "Rolf and the Jewish dad weren't trading bulbs. The flowers were girls. Women. People. Look into the Pandora Agency. I have to go."

Laura tore into the house. Ruby was sleeping on the couch in her clothes, and Mom was nowhere to be seen. She went into the broom closet and took things out with one arm, dropping brooms, throwing catalogs, flinging a metal pail, pushing too many bottles of cleaning products out of the way at once. She made so much racket, Ruby woke up.

"Finally," Laura said. "I thought you were dead in there. Help me with the floor."

"What are you looking for?"

"You made Thomasina breakfast the morning she died?"

"Yeah?"

"You made her a Momlette?"

"Yeah?" Ruby said. "She puts this stuff called Maggi on them. Put. In the past."

"And you ate some?"

"Yeah?"

"Which is why you were sick. You've got a basket of shallots in the pantry. Could one of them be one of Mom's bulbs? The ones she was planting? Because if you accidentally cut one up and put it in the Momlette, there would be poison on your counter."

"Wait. Okay. I have leftovers in my fridge. They'll be there tomorrow. So stop."

Laura froze, realizing she was trying to satisfy her own curiosity instead of taking the best care of her sister.

Ruby helped put everything back as it was, then closed the closet door with a final snap. "Go to bed," she said. "Your eyes have big black circles under them, and your skin is green. And you have a broken arm. Go."

"Let me call Cangemi first."

"I'll do it. Go. You make me crazy. Please." Ruby pushed her up the stairs, to the bedroom.

Laura didn't have the energy to resist.

CHAPTER 21,

Laura was awakened at 8:11 by the squawk of radios downstairs.

For reasons she couldn't quite pin down, she didn't want to go down in her pajama pants and yesterday's shirt. She got out some fresh clothes. That made her realize how much she needed a shower after yesterday, which had gone on forever. But she couldn't bathe because her waterproof cast was days away.

She sponged herself off and dressed in something sleeveless, knowing the reason she didn't want to look like a slob was because Detective Cangemi was probably down there, and the more wisecracks she could avoid, the better. That was the story she told herself, and she was sticking to it.

By the time she got downstairs, the squawking had ended, and any extra personnel in the house were gone. Laura knocked on Ruby's door. The keys were in the lock, and the police tape was gone.

The smell of cleaning fluids pinched the inside of her nose. Ruby was still scrubbing the counter in abrasive chemicals, her four-inch stilettos giving her that extra angle she needed to really take the finish off the countertop.

"Here are your keys," Laura said.

"Thanks."

"You're in full makeup and a Halston jacket. Why are you cleaning?"

"I was out the door, and I just had to give it one more pass." She stepped back from her work. "Do you think it's gone?"

"I think you should just get Jimmy to replace the counter."

"He is. But I can't even stand having it in here." She tossed the sponge, and Laura wondered at what point in the previous eight hours Ruby had spoken to their landlord.

"I think Rolf killed his sister," Laura said. "He was using her organization to traffic girls since the Jewish guy wasn't doing it anymore, and she was going to stop him."

"What Jewish guy?"

Laura explained as Ruby put her cleaning products away, leaving out the parts that made her nauseous.

Ruby snapped up her keys. "He would have needed to see her in the morning, and he didn't. She would have mentioned it because she couldn't stand him and bitched about it all the day before. I mean, she loved him." She turned to the door. "Can we go to the station together? Are you ready to go? Do you need help with your bag?" She took Laura's bag, teetered, then slung it over her shoulder. "What the hell do you have in here?"

"Fall inspiration. I'm meeting with Ivanah."

"Good luck. I really have to be in the showroom today. We're having Barneys Co-op again, and I need to be totally, like, early and present. Did you know Debbie Hayworth is their buyer? I'm selling her some clothes; I promise you. Today is the day."

She seemed to have forgotten there was ever a hip little creep named Darren in her past. Laura wanted to tell her that the way to get on Debbie Hayworth's good side wasn't to wear four-inch stilettos and full makeup. Wearing super-slimming Marni pants and having a pile of hair that dropped in place like an obedient child wasn't the way to Debbie's heart, nor was the marble skin or flat stomach. If Ruby could have put on twenty pounds, failed to wash her hair for a week, and knocked out a tooth, she may have had a chance of Debbie's order-writing pen. But as it was, she was walking into disaster, and Laura had neither the heart nor means to tell her why. The information would have done nothing but make her sister nervous. So instead, she built a case around Rolf on the walk to the train station.

"He did it," Laura said, staring down the stairs, which would be a huge pain with her arm in a sling. She wasn't interested in falling down the stairs because she couldn't hold onto the rail with her right hand, but traveling a crowded staircase on the left was the depth of ignorant slum behavior. "Whoever was in that cab with her killed her, and Rolf was in that cab."

Since they were raised by the same mother, with the same life lessons, Ruby offered her arm and helped with Laura's MetroCard, then slipped her own with a sleek push at the turnstile with her hip.

"He hijacked White Rose, and Thomasina got mad," Laura said.

"Yeah."

"Yeah."

"I don't think so," Ruby said.

"Huh?"

"He loved her." Ruby helped Laura down the second flight of stairs. "He was a beast, but he was this total big brother. Always protecting her."

"So?" Laura was getting a tight feeling in her chest, which meant she felt threatened. "If she was so willing to pay your rent without a fuss, she was probably doing the same for him and thought nothing of it. So she probably let him get deeply involved in her stuff to give him something to do and a paycheck, and he screwed her. And maybe she only found out, like, the day before, so she didn't mention it to you."

"She would have said something."

"You can't prove that."

"Why should I have to?" Ruby sighed. "Look, pretending she wouldn't have told me about that *or* about meeting him before she went to the Ghetto, well, to me, it's just unlikely. We talked a lot."

When they got to the platform, Ruby flung herself onto a bench, flipping her hair as if Laura didn't know she'd been having a nervous breakdown the day before.

Laura stood over her. "Corky saw Rolf that morning in the park. I bet he was in the cab with her. He had opportunity."

"So did every model and agent and piece of eurotrash hanging out at Marlene X, which you have no proof Thomasina even went to anyway. Yesterday, you were convinced she was meeting Roquelle Rik, and she was the killer. Today, what?"

Laura plopped her bag onto Ruby's lap and pulled it open as if she wanted to split it in two, except she only had one good arm, so it kind of opened and kind of flopped over. She didn't know why she was so angry. Was it because she was being lambasted for changing her mind? Or because she'd spent all that time away from work and she'd been wrong? Or because she'd gotten Ruby out of danger without finding the killer? Or was it the ugliest reason of all... that when Ruby came up with ideas, Laura stopped feeling superior?

Laura pulled the rolled-up roll of receipt copies from her bag and tore through them with her teeth and the tips of the fingers on her right hand as if she had three seconds to answer a question with one arm. She finally found the one she was searching for and handed it to Ruby. "The receipt for Marlene X. Skinny latte with soymilk and a pump of something it doesn't say. And a drip coffee, which I have no idea who it was for."

Ruby just handed it back. "It doesn't say her brother was with her. I'm not saying he didn't do it. I'm saying you don't have enough to back it up, and you won't. And also, it's not important. Laura, listen." Ruby took her by the wrists even though one was fully encased. "I am so grateful you helped me. I was in such trouble, and I was so depressed. And you pulled me out. You did things no other sister would do. I love you. I appreciate you. Can you please not be mad at me?"

"I'm not mad."

But she was. A little. Maybe a lot. And her anger didn't stem from anything she could explain. She wanted to be the hero and had succeeded in execution, but failed in scope. She stuck the papers in her right fingertips, and Ruby helped her open the bag. As she transferred the paper from right to left hand, a whipping breeze came from the tunnel. It was a strong breeze, the kind that came before the rumbling of the arriving train, and it came without warning, grabbing the receipt copies and blowing them all over the station.

Ten pages fluttered like paper bags. Laura caught one that flattened itself against the side of a baby stroller. She smiled at the mother, then eyed the situation. The platform was crowded. The papers were everywhere, and few passengers even noticed that the flying pages weren't garbage. Ruby bent to scoop up two, then chased another one as it scuttled along the platform, grabbing it by the edge. Laura tried to catch one in midair, but her right arm was unwilling to follow her brain's instructions by snapping her cast, so she reached with her left hand and missed. The woman with the baby stroller must have had warm feelings from Laura's unsolicited smile because she plucked it out of the air and handed it over.

"Thanks!" Laura said.

Mother pointed. "There are two over there."

Laura nodded and went for them, but everyone was in her way and the arrival of the eastbound train increased the breeze. Her busted arm wasn't helping either. It threw her off balance and disabled her ability to grab anything on her right side. As a result, she lost three pages to the tracks and another to the ceiling.

Ruby appeared, lipstick barely smudged, but panting nonetheless. "I got four."

"I got two," Laura replied as the doors slid open. "Thanks."

The page with Penelope Sidewinder's number was present, but the page with the Marlene X receipt was gone.

"You still have everything from that morning," Ruby said, shuffling through the pages.

"No, Marlene X is missing. They were all on the same page."

"What's this, then?"

She handed Laura a paper. It had a taxi receipt from that morning, but it had been so deep in the wee hours, she'd put it with the receipts from the day before.

"There's a twenty-four dollar surcharge," Laura said.

"LaGuardia," Ruby offered. "They started charging two dollars more for LaGuardia last month."

"It has the last four digits of the credit card." Laura scrambled for the copy of the cards. It had been rescued. She scanned it. The digits matched the Amex Black. "Rolf is Sabine Fosh. That's why he wanted her wallet. She took his cards when they met at the Ghetto. And that message on her phone, I don't remember the time, he was saying *wecken ick eeber eer.* Which means, I don't know, what?"

Ruby, ever useful, pulled out her phone. "She used to freak me out with the German, so I got this translator."

A hot breeze blew in from the Manhattan-bound tunnel. The commuters packed up their things and drifted toward the edge of the platform, where they'd get too close, daring the train to take their faces off. Laura needed another minute of delay while Ruby said, "*Wecken ick eeber eer*" into the phone.

As the train sped into the station, Ruby held up the phone, the screen glowing with the words, *Wake up! I got her!*

But who was *her?*

Ruby went to Broadway, and Laura walked west to the 40th Street office, where Ivanah would be waiting in fifteen minutes. She was unprepared at best and out of her depth at worst. She tried to keep her mind on the task at hand. In a couple of hours, she could find out more about Rolf, or the poison, or something. All she had to do was think about line, color, and shape until ten thirty, latest. Then she'd break with them before she was forced to have lunch. Ruby and Corky would call, but she'd pretend she was busy helping Jeremy with his show.

What she intended to do was try and put this thing to bed by the end of the day. She had a feeling of power and competence in murder-solving that she hadn't felt since she quit working full time at Jeremy St. James, and she needed to keep that fire burning. She hadn't realized how depressed she'd been.

She could smell Rolf's guilt. He was a man rotten to the core, selling young girls into prostitution, laundering them through her company, probably with info stolen from Bob and Ivanah through their involvement with White Rose. He would pick them up at LaGuardia Airport and take them God-knew-where.

Laura hurled herself up the stairs, her heavy bag ten pounds lighter in her mind, broken arm tap-tapping against the banister as she ran, too impatient for the elevator. Spring was easy. Update last season and shorten the skirts, lighten the fabric, and brighten the colors. Short sleeves became sleeveless, and long sleeves went half sleeve. Switch pockets and collars until they looked new. Let Ivanah design something outrageous in every group, choose sparkly buttons, and trim with silly fabrics. Tell her she's brilliant, and they're done. Backing secured. Line perfect. Branding protected. Everyone happy.

In the middle of all that, she was going to ask pointed questions about Ivanah's relationship with White Rose and Pandora Modeling. About Meatball Eyes. About how Rolf could have gotten his hands on their EIN and the corporate paperwork needed to sponsor foreign workers without her knowledge. It was going to be a super-productive morning.

She was sure the sun shone right out of her ass when she stepped into the little studio. Her pattern table was clear because she was done with everything, and Ruby's drafting table was the usual orderly clutter. Ivanah and the new Eastern European assistant she expected were nowhere to be found. Two men stood in the middle of the room, talking softly about something she didn't have a chance to hear because they shut up as soon as she entered.

"Pierre?"

"My dear." He gave her the double kiss. "My goodness, what happened?"

"You should see the other guy."

Pierre indicated the man standing beside her cutting table. "Do you know Mister Stern?"

Buck nodded and sat down in her chair.

"Hi, Buck," she said, using the first name as if she didn't hear the formality Pierre had suggested with his introduction. "What's up? Is Ivanah okay?"

"She is attending to other business," Buck said. Laura imagined her getting a manicure, but business took many forms.

Pierre cleared his throat. "Mister Stern wanted to let us know that Sartorial Sandwich will have to proceed without the backing of the Schmillers."

"What?"

"All present contractual agreements are still in force, of course," Buck said, "including payment with whatever profit sharing we previously agreed upon. Nothing new should be required. The Schmillers just wanted you to be told in person, rather than through your agent." He nodded to Pierre, and Pierre nodded back, like two old boys sucking each other off.

"But I agreed she could work on the line with us!"

"Mrs. Schmiller will be pursuing other opportunities in the fashion world."

Laura looked at Pierre for an answer, or a way out, but there was nothing. He just shrugged. Just another line losing its money midstream.

"I can work harder," Laura said, and almost immediately

regretted it. She sounded every bit as desperate as she was. "And I can get Ruby in more often. She was distracted last season. We're selling. Barneys Co-op is in the showroom right now, writing an order. We just need enough for fabric. I'll sew the whole damn line myself to save money."

She could have gone on, but Pierre put one hand on her shoulder while holding the other out to Buck. "Thank you for coming," he said. "Tell the Schmillers we appreciate the courtesy."

"My pleasure."

They shook hands, and Laura knew she was expected to show the same kind of professionalism. She didn't know if she had it in her. Luckily, her right hand wasn't available for shaking because either she would have refused, or he would have felt the sweat on her palms, or she would have tried to break his fingers.

Buck saw her inability to shake his hand and, not understanding what a blessing it was for everyone involved, took her by the shoulders in a brotherly grip. "It was nice to work with you. I hope to see you again sometime."

"Sure," was the best she could offer.

He nodded to Pierre and left.

"What the hell just happened?" she asked.

Pierre sat halfway on Ruby's chair, one tasseled oxblood loafer swinging and the other pressed to the cement floor. "It would help going forward if you spoke more as a businesswoman and less like a teenager."

"What the heck just happened?"

"You're closed. You cannot make your orders."

She fell into her chair before she lost the support of her knees. "But it's not fair." She heard the ridiculous whine in her voice. She must have sounded like a child. When she and Ruby were eleven and twelve, Mom had sent them to a two-week sleep-away camp that had gotten some state-funded grants for poor kids. If there was a scholarship to be had, Mom found out about it and applied. Laura had no idea how many application rejections Mom slogged through, but the benefits of her tenacity always fell on the girls. The camp was a wooded ten acres on Long Island's gold coast, and as usual, Laura and Ruby were the freaks of the camp with their secondhand designer clothes and worn out shoes, before secondhand designer was a thing. When the bus dropped them at the outdoor amphitheater for orientation, she saw a sign draped over the stage. It read, "Camp Is Not Fair."

And it wasn't. The sign was meant to warn the kids that things wouldn't always go their way, and they'd have to be okay with it, because the type of kids at the camp always got their way. But camp was going to be a change for them. It was going to be like the real world. Sometimes you got away with stuff, and sometimes you got nailed for standing up to a mean girl who made fun of your shoes, and sometimes you pulled her Calvin Klein socks off and held her down while your sister shoved them down her throat. And when Mom came to get them a week and a half early because they were kicked out, maybe the fair thing would be for them to get in trouble, but maybe she'd laugh and get them vanilla ice cream for not taking any flak from a senator's daughter. But she wouldn't actually say that. She didn't advocate violence. She wouldn't actually say her daughters had made things fair by doing what they'd done. She'd say maybe the sisters were better off urban hiking, chain-link fence climbing, and camping out in the living room.

Even though an adult definition of fairness had been a mystery before camp, but after camp, Laura still felt she knew it when she saw it, and she was not looking at it. She'd worked hard up until recently. Really hard. Day-and-night hard.

As if he could read her mind, Pierre said, "I think they decided this before the show."

"Then what was the whole dinner at Isosceles about?"

"Feeling out their options is my guess. Who can say? At the end of the day, your destiny is not yours to write."

"Destiny? Are you serious?"

"How else do you explain? You work very hard for this line and have it taken from you, and them? They don't work so hard and have the power to take it. It is not equitable. It's this type of thing that makes me miss France. At least there, we try, and we take not so much glee when we succeed at the expense of others." She felt an odd kinship to him until he said, "Well, onward and upward! My guess is you have the weekend to clean out. You may be able to sell some of this to pay your debts, if you choose to remove the Schmillers from your life. Or you may wisely wish to elongate a bankruptcy process to keep them close. We can discuss further on Monday. I have a client show in fifteen minutes."

He kissed both of her cheeks. "Trust me. I'm not abandoning you. There are things in the works." Before she could ask him what he meant, he left. Another day in the life of super ninja fashion agent, Pierre Sevion, who couldn't protect them from a flame-out.

She thought one thing might go right. There was one place where she could show a little competence and dignity. She sat alone in an office that wasn't hers, with sewing machines silent just on the other side of the door. Owning nothing, in charge of nothing, with little to call her own, she called Cangemi.

"Carnegie, what now? Leg caught in a thresher?"

"Rolf did it!" She told him the whole story in a single breath.

"You copied the receipts before handing them over? Claiming her expenses on your taxes is illegal, far as I know. Dunno what else you thought you were doing with them." She was cowed into silence. "But I appreciate you calling me to tell me what I know. Except the part you don't know, which is Rolf was in a meeting all morning, and it checks out."

"Was he at LaGuardia? Maybe picking up a girl from a German airline?"

She was sure that if he just told her, the pieces of the puzzle would fit together with an audible click. But her optimism did not meet reality.

"Ask him the next time you're chasing him down a stairwell, okay?"

"Please?"

"Go get a coffee, Carnegie."
He hung up on her.

CHAPTER 22.

She wanted Jeremy. She wanted to tell him everything through a veil of tears. She wanted him to tell her everything was going to be totally cool, that he'd hire her back and she shone with a brilliance only matched by his own spectacular light. But his show was in eight hours, and there was a pretty good chance of blood on the walls, burned-out sewing machine motors, overflowing steamers, and frayed nerves and seams.

Then she thought of Ruby, sitting in a tight little room with Debbie Hayworth, being nice to her to the point of supplication. Debbie would be making her grovel, Corky not understanding any of it. Even if she didn't feel like she could make a success of the day, Laura figured at least she could keep it from being the very worst day on record, and she could get some nibble of satisfaction. So she ran down to 38th and across town to Broadway, until her veins and lungs constricted and her arm ached from holding up that goddamn, inconvenient stinker of a cast.

The elevator took forever even though it was right there. Jeremy's reception area was full of racks on the way to the freight elevator, but she didn't care. She wanted to get to Ruby. She wanted to rescue her sister from past foibles with other people's boyfriends and dalliances with supermodels, because if she couldn't save herself and her company, goddamn it, her sister was the next best thing. Maybe even the next *better* thing.

Debbie sat at the table, alone, writing on what looked like an order sheet. There wasn't a Binder Girl in sight. Corky had the look of a man who'd just gotten beaten with a tired stick. He smiled because that was his default setting, but his eyes said something else was going on.

"Hi," Laura said, slipping into a chair. "Where's Ruby?" The tension in the room was as thick as a blizzard. Why was no one talking?

"Oh, my God," Debbie squeaked. "I thought you weren't even coming."

"I'm sorry." Laura glanced at Corky because Debbie appeared to be actually writing an order. In ink.

Corky looked diffident where he should have been bursting at the seams. "Co-op wants a wool crepe dress. Like this one, but—"

Debbie finished writing and chimed in, "No belt. No pocket. Take off the sleeves and get it to a four-fifty retail, and we can put it on the floor." She ripped the P.O. out of the pad and slid the paper to Laura. She had crossed off the company name and written "Laura Carnegie."

Laura looked at the number at the bottom. "This is a big order for us," Laura said.

"We can do it," Corky said. "I'm sure we can figure it out."

"There's nothing to figure out." Debbie smiled. "We need this immediately to fill a space where someone can't deliver. It's an all-door buy. I'll bring you our colors."

"This is private label?" Laura asked. "Or does it have a Sartorial label?"

"Barneys," Debbie said.

"And you want us to take the belt off, make it sleeveless, and do it in your colors for a four-fifty retail? I think we can." She knew they could. It was Jeremy's tack on fabric, and it was coming early, undyed. So it could be put in Barneys colors using a dye house in North Carolina that Yoni liked. She couldn't have asked for anything more perfect. Outstanding news. There were enough dresses on that order form to keep them in business another season. It was a private label deal, which meant a Barneys label, Barneys rules, and Barneys colors. But that was fine. Better than fine. It was a godsend.

"Great! Wow, I don't know if we can still do this dress for our line since it'll be so close, but we'll figure it out. Thanks, Debbie. We're not going to let you down."

"So it's okay that it's just you and not Ruby?"

"What do you mean? How can it not be Ruby? She designed it."

"If you say so," Debbie said, slipping a binder in her bag. "Except that we're changing the colors, the belt, and the sleeves. I mean, if she has a lock on every sleeveless wool crepe dress in the world, well, that's one for the record books." She wrinkled her nose. "I know I can count on you to execute. Okay? You just figure it out, and thanks!" She tiptoed out of the room as if she knew how much of a mess she'd just made.

Laura and Corky stood in silence, looking at each other and wondering what the hell had just happened.

"Did you offer this? Did you tell her we could cut out Ruby?"

"It was her idea from the beginning." Corky started hanging garments. "She came in with an attitude problem about how she only needed you because you were the one who knew how to do things. And asking then about how Ruby liked it in jail, and how involved she'd be, and blah, blah, blah. Ruby tried to make the best of it, but girl, it was ugly. Real ugly."

"Where is she?"

"I think she went next door."

Laura found Ruby in Jeremy's office, looking through his swatches as if there was a Fall line to develop for. The design room was dead, and reception had been cleared, so she had the place to herself. It had been repainted and re-floored since Gracie Pomerantz's body had been found there. The owner of the office was not one to fall on ceremony or sentiment. He did not believe Gracie's spirit lingered, and though the incident had upset him enough to earn a month off for everyone, once it was over, as far as he was concerned, it was over.

"Does Jeremy know you're here?"

Ruby stacked the fabric samples by color, which Jeremy would never do. He could make orders big enough to dye his own colors, and thus he organized everything by concept. And he was going to be unhappy to see everything reorganized. Ruby, who knew Jeremy well enough to know that, but apparently didn't care, continued messing around while she spoke. "He sent me in here like he was sending me to my room. I was crying, and I think it embarrassed him. How did you ever work for him?"

Laura wanted to get the conversation off Jeremy's rigid social demeanor and onto the reason Ruby was in his office in the first place. "I heard about Barneys Co-op."

"I let her write the order because Corky chased me out, but we can't do it. I know you think I didn't work hard for all this, but I did, and she can't decide to kick me out. She doesn't know what a favor I did her. That guy, whatever his name was—"

"Darren."

"He kissed like he wore a neck brace. I mean, do you know how hard it is to kiss someone who refuses to tilt his head?" She held up a burgundy voile, as if she didn't know if it went with the reds or the purples or the browns.

"We need to figure this out," Laura said.

"Figure what out?"

"How to take that order."

Ruby's face melted like a ball of wax in the sun. She gripped the cardboard at the top of the header, bending it.

Laura jumped in. "I went to meet Ivanah this morning, and she wasn't even there. They pulled our backing. Everything. Even the seven hundred dollars we had left over. Pierre has nothing else lined up. We don't have a business at all, period. But if we take this order, it's for winter, and we can deliver it and have enough money to start small again without a backer. I mean real small."

"You mean *you* can start again."

"No, I'd pick it up again with you."

"Do you think she's going to let that happen? She's always going to have more orders for you. As long as I'm anywhere near, she's going to come to you for the Laura exclusive, and it's always going to be easy, and it's always going to be just enough to keep you going. Maybe a little more each season, so you think, 'Oh, next season we'll start Sartorial together again.' I'm sorry, but you can't see that?"

"What if I promised you, just this once? Then you're back. Scout's honor." Laura used her left hand to hold up the cast a little, so Ruby would see two fingers twisted together, even if it was impossible to get them up to her forehead. That may or may not have been a scout salute, but it was all they ever had.

Ruby folded her arms, the burgundy voile draping from her armpit. "You can do what you want, but she'll have control of you."

"There's always someone in control, isn't there? Either it's the boss, or the buyer, or freaking MAAB with their rules. Who's not controlled by someone else?"

"Thomasina wasn't. She just did what she wanted. I admired that."

"Tough luck being rich and beautiful."

"It got her murdered."

But Laura was already lost in thought. "Everyone's controlled by somebody, Ruby. Everyone's afraid of something someone else will do. Who was she afraid of?"

"Oh, God, are you doing this again?"

"She wasn't afraid of her sociopath brother?"

"He was a kitten with her."

"What about MAAB?"

"In her pocket."

"Roquelle Rik?"

"Give me a break."

"Younger models?"

"Never."

"Old age?"

"You're being an idiot now."

"Bobcat Schmiller?"

Ruby paused. "I don't think so."

"I think we need to find out exactly what Bob found out in Germany. Ten bucks says it's going to nail Rolf to the wall. Or Sabine. Whatever."

"I don't care."

"And the girl at the airport that Rolf 'got'? Don't you care?"

"Nope."

"You have something better to do than find out who killed Thomasina?"

She didn't, and Laura happily took whatever motivation she could to get some company up to Central Park West.

Midmorning was busy at the Schmiller's building. A truck was parked outside, making it difficult for the tenants to get a cab without taking a few steps out of their way. Apparently, that was an absolutely unacceptable inconvenience, so unacceptable that the doorman was occupied with stammering excuses to a particularly entitled gentleman carrying an alligator briefcase.

So occupied was he that Laura and Ruby slipped right by him, into the elevator.

"Bob was the only one," Laura said. "No one else had the power over our company or enough information to sponsor people for a green card. Just him and his people."

"He was out of the country when she was killed," Ruby said.

"I didn't say he killed her, but he has something to do with this whole mess."

The doors slid open. As Laura raised her hand to knock on the door to the penthouse, it creaked open.

The first thing Laura noticed was the brown paper rolled across the rug in paths leading between doorways. It was stuck down at the edges with wide blue tape and crinkled with boot prints. She was about to toss out a profanity, but then saw that most of the furniture was draped with moving cloths. The zebra throw was twisted on the marble floor, and the Persian rug with the gold tassels was rolled up against the wall. The big stuff, china closet, sideboard, dining room table, were all present, but the shelves were empty, and the drawers were taped closed.

"I guess they're moving," Ruby said.

Laura didn't answer, but headed right for the emotional center of the house—the kitchen. The pots and pans were gone. The drawers were pulled out and empty. Laura opened the fridge. Just some condiments and Whole Foods containers.

"You should grab the Taiwanese mustard," a voice said from behind her. "It's a hundred twenty a jar."

She spun around.

"Hi, Bob," Ruby said as if she belonged in the abandoned kitchen. "I like your shirt." She spoke of a tattered grey sack of crap with the Penn State logo on the front.

As if they'd been there with an engraved invitation, he smiled and showed it off. "Got it when I was a freshman. Still fits."

"Nice. Where are you going?" Ruby twisted her hips a little. She was flirting. Laura could hardly believe her ears.

"My wife," he started, but switched gears entirely. "Can you get me that orange juice?"

Laura handed him the container. "I think the glasses are gone."

He shrugged and took a swig from the carton. He didn't look like a hedge fund manager in that moment, but a freshman varsity football player standing in front of his mother's fridge.

"You came to talk about the backing thing. Sorry about that. Business."

Laura latched onto the excuse. "I just wanted to ask if there was anything we could have done differently."

"You were always a sweet kid." Obviously, he knew a different person from everyone else. "But no. Nothing you coulda done. Sometimes you get lucky and live in a penthouse, and sometimes not so much. It's not personal." Bob sounded more like a football player and less like a corporate wonk once you got him outside the business milieu. She wasn't sure which personality she liked less.

"Was it Thomasina dying during our show?"

"That sucked, but no. Yes, actually, but no." He pointed at Ruby. "By the way, I'm sorry about that. I know you guys were, you know."

He winked, and Laura wanted to punch him in the face with her broken arm.

He slid the OJ back into the door. "Here's what I told my wife, and this is gonzo advice for anyone. Stick to stuff that only exists on paper. No one gets hurt that way. Low stakes, high returns. I buy a company, and they're just rows of numbers. I break it apart, sell the pieces, and I never have to hear anyone badgering me because see, the whole thing was a piece of paper. I sell some stock here, hedge an option there, it doesn't have a face. But does my wife listen? No. Wants to be in fashion, with models and glamour. Freaking waste. No offense."

Together, she and Ruby said, "None taken."

He gestured toward Laura. "The second you started talking about ordering fabric, she was checked out."

"So," Ruby said, "I'm wondering, your trip, earlier this week?" If they were sitting at dinner, Laura would have kicked her under the table.

Laura broke in, "We have a problem."

"I probably can't help you." He glanced at the door, which enraged Laura because what did he think she was, a piece of paper? Was she nothing but a row of red numbers? Or another kind of liability? Even though she was trespassing and possibly breaking and entering, Laura wasn't about to take any of it.

"We have three immigrants from Eastern Europe, two Romanians and a Hungarian, officially employed by Sartorial. And I didn't hire them, I promise you, but they came here on our sponsorship. The only person with the wherewithal to pull that kind of trick is you."

"I don't know anything about that." His smarmy look and the speed of his denial, coupled with the lack of pointed questions, told her he knew all about it.

"I'll bet it's a federal offense, whoever was doing it," she said.

"Better get your lawyers right on that," he responded dismissively, which really meant he had a legal team and could take on the federal government on a whim. It also meant that, for whatever reason, the "employees" had somehow all been a hundred, or at least 89 percent, legitimate.

"But why?" Laura asked. "Why bring them in like that? I mean, I'm not saying you did it, but if you did, why would you?"

"Maybe whoever it was had to move them right away or they were getting shipped out to service jobs, if you know what I mean. You don't know what happens to girls in some of these places."

"I never said they were girls."

Possibly, she should have held back that little zinger for later, but she'd never had that kind of foresight or mental fortitude. If she had someone, she had them.

He was pretty pissed. She could tell by the way he pushed the toaster back against the wall. "You could shut up long enough to help them before they get deported back to where they're going to get hurt."

Laura took a stab in the dark, "Rolf has them. We think he snagged one at the airport the morning Thomasina was killed. He killed another one already. Ivanah's assistant."

Bob rubbed his eyes. "I shoulda locked the door."

Ruby put her hand on Laura's shoulder. "We should go."

"Where is he?" Laura asked. "Do you know?"

"Are you kidding? He's got more names, more money, and more passports than we know how to track. And what he's doing? With the women? It's the only thing he enjoys. If I were you, I'd stay out of his way. He's crazy. Over and out. You know where the door is."

They found the door, which was still open. Two moving guys carried a love seat into the hall, and Laura wondered if Rolf was scary enough to scare the Schmillers out of their house.

CHAPTER 23,

"I'm sorry, Yoni. The contract says you'll be paid, but it's over. They pulled everything." Laura stood in their empty showroom, talking on the phone and listening to the hubbub next door as Jeremy's team prepped for his show that night. She kept trying to rub her eyes with her right hand, but her arm was set and wouldn't bend that way. Ruby snapped the samples away and did the job of folding. She was the only one who was going to fit into them anyway.

"Yes, even the tack on. And I know he's going to be pissed," Laura said. Yoni was in the process of a breakdown. She did not manage change or failure well. "I'll tell him. No problem. Just try to rest okay?" She hung up before Yoni could argue further.

She held up Debbie Hayworth's wool crepe dress. It looked fantastic on a hanger, which was mandatory. If it looked bad on a hanger, the customer would never try it on. And if she didn't try it on, she wouldn't buy it. The store buyers who came into the showroom knew it, and so the samples were made to look good on a hanger to appease the buyers. The smaller the size, the better the hanger appeal, but that meant the girls on the runway had to be no more than hangers to wear the samples, hence the issue over skinny models.

"Was Thomasina taking them? The pills?" Laura asked. "Because there's no way someone could have injected her with anything unless she expected it."

"On and off." Ruby lovingly folded samples and boxed them. "I talked her out of them when we started, you know, and then she had to stop eating because her boobs got too big. I tried to feed her, but…"

"You were interfering with her job," Laura said. "You don't get to do that. And *you* lose weight when you eat cookies."

"Not my fault."

Laura sat down, feeling defeated. "You know who I feel worst for? Corky. He came on, gave us everything he had, and we failed him."

"You want to do the crepe dress for Debbie, don't you?"

"We'd be able to pay him. He's the only one not covered."

"Can I think about it?"

"No. I can't do it. You're right. She'd have me trapped and I'd be her private label whore."

Ruby snapped all the wool crepe dresses off the racks, sending hangers flying with the crack of wood hitting wood. She balled up the dresses and stuffed them in a plastic bag. "Done. You are not a whore."

"Do you think Rolf is really crazy?" Laura wasn't ready to accept or reject Debbie's order with any finality. "Like crazy enough to scare Bob Schmiller out of his own house?"

"If that's the case, I don't want anything to do with any of it. Let the police take care of it. We're out."

Laura pressed her face to the cool wood of the table and saw the showroom sideways. Her phone blooped, and she looked at it without picking up her head. "Pierre wants us to meet him at Marlene X. God, I hate it there." She looked at the clock. Barely noon, and Marlene X closed at one. The morning had been days long already.

Ruby dropped the bag of samples as if it were full of body parts and reached for her jacket. "Let's get out of here."

"He's going to jerk us off about some crap. Don't tell him about Debbie. He'll make me take the job, and we need to decide for ourselves."

Laura had a great view at Marlene X. At five-foot-four, she was eye level with boobs, pierced bellybuttons, and the occasional clavicle. None of the giraffes paid her any mind, as usual, not the ones who were there looking for an agent or the ones Roquelle had already scooped up. They glanced at Ruby. Some even smiled because they were taught to keep their enemies close. More than one bumped her a little because she was a squat five-seven, but still beautiful enough to be a threat.

The line was ten miles long, and they were cut more than once by giraffes with friends ahead of them, but giraffes don't have friends, just competition. She elbowed one hipbone with her cast, but it yielded nothing but a smile, or maybe a snarl. She couldn't tell the difference.

Laura was aware Marlene X was bringing out the surly worst in her, but it was awful, the single most despicable place in the world. Mirrors were everywhere, along with some wildly expensive greyish black wood. Green drapes with big metallic embroidered Xs on the borders hung over the windows. Chintz cups lay next to modernist silverware, which shouldn't work. None of it should work, but it did, and it awed and infuriated her because a place with that kind of bad vibe should look as bad as it felt. There were pitiful few tables, all booths around the perimeter, and they were all taken up by important people. The rest of the patrons stood. And if someone sat where they shouldn't, they were told politely to get the hell up. The problem was that one was never told who was important enough to sit, people just knew or they didn't.

Despite the floor's dense population of giraffes, the tables were near empty. Everyone who was important enough to sit at the tables was at the bandshell and surrounding tents. The models were either getting primped for the first round of shows or managing the primped. The hangers-on and second-rate beauties were left.

Pierre had a corner booth and tapped something into his phone while some gorgeous thing of about fifteen summers sat up straight and moved her lips. Laura thought underage models shouldn't be allowed to talk. It polluted the space around them terribly. Marlene X was notorious for poor bussing because it was hard to move, so Pierre's table was cluttered with dirty cups and plates.

When they sat, Fifteen Summers glared at Ruby and didn't even acknowledge Laura's existence. Laura wished she had the opportunity to not hire the girl, but her spite wouldn't be satisfied that season, or the next. Or possibly ever.

A glance from Pierre sent Fifteen Summers scuttling away. "You're not thinking of repping models now, are you?" Laura asked.

"And cross Roquelle?" he answered, putting down his phone. "I'd start writing my suicide note now."

Ruby pushed away the dirty cups. "You need to find us something. My sister is going to break down. Look at her."

Pierre looked at her, which was incredibly uncomfortable.

"I'm fine," she said.

He cleared his throat and watched the door as it opened, but it was apparently no one he wanted to speak to. "I may have something of interest. Tomorrow morning. Saturday. You need to be here. At this table."

Ruby clapped, but Laura held her own as the jaded one of the pair. "Who is it?"

"I can't say."

"You're just popping them on us? How can we prepare?" Ruby asked.

"You can start by making sure you both look presentable and have something to talk about. Besides the bodies falling all around you, of course. The news already has too much to say about that. You'd think Greyson was pulling strings. Bring nothing for design. They don't want to see it. They know what you do. Do something stylish with that sling. My God, did it come in another color?"

"You mean we'll keep getting to do what we like without rhinestone buttons?" Laura asked, hoping against hope that her life would be restored.

The busboy rushed over and picked saucers and teacups off the table. Laura caught a glimpse of something on a saucer that didn't belong there.

"No promises," he replied, sipping from his little chintz teacup. He pointed at Laura. "You need to just make sure there's no more chasing around after murders unless that murder is your own. No?"

"I understand." But when the busboy turned to leave, Laura said, "Excuse me?" and picked the foreign object off the saucer. It was an eyedropper. "Is this Penelope's?" she asked, remembering the vitamin boost at Baxter City.

"Ah." Pierre held out his hand. "She was here. Give it to me; I'll return it."

"No, I'll do it. Come on, Rubes. We have to go." She shoved Ruby out of the booth and out the door.

"What?" Ruby shouted once they were on Third Avenue. "Why are you pushing?"

Laura held up the eyedropper. "It doesn't matter who was in the cab with her because that's not where it happened. It was in Marlene X." Laura filled in the blanks for Ruby. "Penelope had a really tough time when she became a model. Like really tough. Like rape tough. That's why she's hell-bent on protecting models from themselves. So what do you think happens when she finds out Thomasina's importing sex toys and telling them they're going to model? And then finding out she can't do anything about it because Rolf's covering his tracks?"

"She's not crazy."

"Oh, yes, she is. And she droppers her tea with vitamin D

and sat at the same table with Thomasina that morning because they all sit in that corner. So how hard would it be just to put something else in it? Something that's the same as what she knows Thomasina's already taking, but strong enough to kill her?"

"So, what do you want to do? Because I know you're not calling that detective."

"Let's go return this dropper."

On the way to Central Park, she realized that Stu had gotten into a brawl with a psychopath dangerous enough to frighten a hedge fund manager out of his ivory tower. She called him.

"I wanted to tell you what I found out about Rolf."

"You mean Sabine?"

"He's scary."

"You have no idea. Where are you?"

"On the way to the shows in the park."

"I'll meet you there."

Laura had a plan for their trip to Garmento Ghetto, naturally, and it involved going to the MAAB table in the administration tent. All the models had to register there, get weighed in, and have a good talk if they were new or a pat on a bony shoulder if they were old hands. If Penelope wasn't present, there should be more than a few acolytes to direct her to the correct show, interview, or weigh-in.

The street running through the park was closed off and well-populated with coffee-holding buyers and fashionistas with cellphones and damp hair. There were the usual altercations between joggers and cyclists and the oblivious ditzes with zero situational awareness who walked in front of their well-scored paths. Collisions, altercations, elbowings, and fistfights were reported daily. Rather than move the shows, yet again, to a different venue, the city sprayed Central Park with police.

Laura kept her wits about her when she crossed the road, guiding Ruby by the elbow because her sister was texting. They'd been lectured by Stu numerous times on how hard it was to be a cyclist anywhere in the city, and Laura didn't want to be a part of the problem.

The Garmento Ghetto had been moderately crowded on Tuesday, when she'd been there for Sartorial's show, and the volume had increased steadily for the three days following, culminating in a balls-out fashion blowout Friday night. The last show was the monster, as it led directly to parties, and there were no showroom meetings after. That had traditionally been Jeremy's spot. But since he'd taken a season off after Gracie's death, he'd lost his treasured place. He had bought the second to last spot, and the two before it, which pissed off any number of designers, and used the time to rebuild the runway.

Barry Tilden had partnered on the change. On Seventh, that might have been seen as a sign of weakness, because if you weren't cutting someone's throat, you were a weakling, but surprisingly, it had strengthened both of them. They actually seemed to like each other, and as two designers with lifestyle brands, Barry having done it already and Jeremy striving for it, they developed a runway design they could sink their teeth into.

They tore down the bandshell's center runway and replaced it with a design that splayed out like petals on a daisy. The center was a lazy Susan that spun the models onto one of the petals as they came out from the back. Each petal was meant for a buying category. So a model would come out with a special bag or shoes, and the lazy Susan would stop on the petal with seats for accessory buyers and photographers for accessory trade magazines. If she also had on an outfit meant for sportswear, outerwear, makeup, or textile buyers, she would return to the center and get spun onto that petal.

Easier said than done, of course. The choreography was positively mathematical. Jeremy and Barry had spent weeks planning how it would work. Even though their shows weren't combined, they found their efforts were more valuable when they worked together.

Ruby drifted over to a klatch of garmentos she wanted to stroke. Laura beelined past the construction teams hastily building Jeremy and Barry's stage, to the admin tent, which was half information desk meant to turn tourists away, and half actual administration. The MAAB desk was hidden way in the back.

She walked in as if she owned the place, which if she counted the dues she paid to the CFDA, plus her taxes, she kind of did. "What do you mean I can't come in?" she asked the guard at the front.

He wore a tight T-shirt and sprayed on black jeans. He looked at his clipboard, then held it up for her to see. "Right there." He cracked gum when he spoke, leaning on one foot as if he were planting bulbs and his boots were better than shovels. "It says, and I quote, 'Admin tent for show day: patrons only.' So, no tickee. No shirtee. Having a show Tuesday means you can't come in on Friday. Do you want the MAAB office number? It's right on 40th Street. They'll be back on Monday."

"Penelope said I should come." Lying was bound to go poorly, and it did.

"Did she write you a yellow ticket?"

"She must have forgotten."

"Call her and get one, and I can let you in."

Laura scanned the crowd for her sister and found her outside the biggest tent for the Ricardo Ofenhelb show. She stood with a fashion writer from *Bazaar*, the editorial director of *Black Book*, a reviewer from *Apparel News*, and a klatch of buyers from the juggernaut of Federated. They were laughing at something the VP of sales from Brandywine Girl said.

That was why she needed Ruby, and why she resented her. That was why taking Debbie's order seemed so right and so wrong. Because doing that sort of business meant Ruby's skills were unnecessary, but *cultivating* as a business required exactly what Ruby had that Laura lacked.

"Can you stop?" Laura whispered. "I just got turned away at the admin tent and don't want to stand outside by myself like a loser."

Ruby said quick goodbyes.

Stu showed up in front of the admin tent soon after.

Laura thought that by the time she saw him, she'd at least know where Penelope was sitting for the next show, but she had nothing, and she felt crummy about that until she got a look at him. He wore his grey mis-buttoned cardigan, but it didn't look intentional. It looked like the product of a disheveled mind.

"You okay?" Laura asked. "They didn't give you a hard time in jail or anything, did they?" He waved the notion away, but didn't say anything. "What? It's something."

He gave her a slight shrug. It wasn't like him to avoid telling her anything, even if he were mad at her. So when he shrugged off a simple question, Laura worried.

"Leave him alone," Ruby said.

"Tell me what you have since last night," Stu said in a flat voice.

She didn't like it. Not one bit, and though she had let their romance slip through the cracks, she would not let their friendship. "No, you have to at least tell me the general area of what's bothering you."

"Tofu," he said, pronouncing it exactly the way it was spelled, and with relish, as though he wanted to insult.

"She didn't like you getting arrested?"

"Not when I was out gallivanting with you, she didn't."

Laura couldn't tell if he was angry at Tofu or himself.

Ruby, not content to sit in a mystery for too long, interjected, "You set her straight, right?"

"Yeah," he said, "and she went straight for the door. Anything else you want to choke out of me? Because you can see how much I want to talk about this."

It was out of character for Stu to behave that way. Typically, nothing was too painful for him to admit, and she was torn between being happy he was free of the catty bitch and angry at Tofu for treating him so shoddily. She also thought for a second that it might be the perfect time for her to slip in. He was free. Technically, she was free. Except for Jeremy. She knew she didn't have it in her to juggle two men.

She changed the subject. "So, why did you get arrested yesterday and not me?"

"I told them I told you I had access to the office."

"And they believed that? Even Cangemi believed it?"

"We believe what we already have in our heads. Isn't that what you say?"

"Did he tell you about my team of female Eastern European staffers, running around, doing my bidding?"

While they dodged crowds and circled tents all over the Garmento Ghetto, she explained the immigration laundering at White Rose, the origins of the purple pills, the social strata at Marlene X, the eyedropper, and Bob's exit from his overdesigned penthouse.

"He's right to leave," Stu said. "Rolf, Sabine, he's both. He's wiggled out of at least four murders in his home country. Brutal, all of them." He pointed at Laura and dropped his voice half an octave. "You need to stay away from him. I have never been so serious in my life."

"I get it."

"I wanted to tell you in person. The next time we meet this guy, you're not pissing him off, and you're running into a crowded place, and then you're changing your name and moving out of state."

"Jesus, Stu." She didn't appreciate the drama, not when they had so much else going on, nor did she appreciate hearing the message again from yet another person who wanted her to sit and sew.

As they made their way across the park to a food court, the schedule began, and the tent city that had been so full of bodies emptied like a crowded highway after a popular off ramp.

They stopped at the tent marked "Café Couture" and ordered three four-dollar coffees.

"Okay," Stu said, "what I'm hearing is that Thomasina was given the poison sometime between when she saw Ruby in the morning, and when she got to the tent to do your show."

"Right," Laura answered.

"And what you've put together, so far, is that she left home and then what?"

Since Ruby didn't correct Thomasina's point of exit, Laura decided not to either. "Marlene X, then the tents. Poisoned somewhere in there. She saw all her high-end buddies at Marlene X, and I think she was in the cab with Rolf."

"And from the cab to the dressing area? Something could have happened then."

"Ruby walked her in; I saw them."

Ruby interjected, "I saw her outside the MAAB offices, and we walked back together." Laura noticed her sister's cheeks redden.

"Right back all the way?" Laura asked.

Her sister reddened further, and Laura realized it was because Stu was there. "No," Ruby said, "we made a pit stop. Uhm, there's this corner behind the generator for the makeup tent, and ah, we…"

Stu's face was blank. Either he had no idea or he had on his journalist face. Laura wanted to fill him in, without awkwardness, and knew she'd failed in her mission before the words even left her lips. "You guys had a make out session or something?"

"Little bit," Ruby said into her cup.

"Wow," Stu said with his face still emotionless. "Big wows."

Ruby tightened like a drum. "ShutupStuIhateyou!"

He leaned back. "No, come on. She was hot. Nice going."

"Stu! Are you baiting her on purpose?"

He looked incredulous. "She was *not* hot? Am I supposed to say that? Or like I should pretend it's not a big deal?"

Ruby balled up a napkin and threw it at him. "I can *see* your freaking imagination. Stop it."

Stu turned to Laura, completely unflustered, and spoke as if delivering the weather report. "I had the most incredible sex with Jeremy St. James last night."

She spit out her coffee. Ruby cried out an exclamation that was lost in the white noise of the wind.

"Wipe the pictures from your mind, the two of you." He leaned back and sipped his coffee. "Pots and kettles, ladies. All black, all the time."

Ruby snapped a used *WWD* from an adjacent table, as if in a huff.

Laura turned to Stu. "We need to find Penelope. I want to return the dropper and see what she says, but she could be anywhere here. I think Ruby should ask around."

"You're going to openly accuse her of poisoning Thomasina Wente?"

"Maybe it was an accident. I don't know."

"You're—"

Ruby interrupted by reading, "'A kiss-off to the overtly commercial dreck meant to attract Target business that designers are trotting down the runway this season, Sartorial Sandwich is refreshing, spirited, wholly sophisticated, and just the right side of wearable.' And look! Your origami failure!"

Laura snapped the paper from Ruby. Sidewinder's review, which Ruby had read in its entirety, was jammed in the side with a picture of the trapezoid dress. "This is excellent!" She pulled out the full weight of her sarcasm skills, to say cheerfully and loudly, "Too bad we don't have a company anymore!"

"We're getting this backer tomorrow." Ruby snatched at the paper, but Laura held it away with her one good hand. "He's mine. Or she. Whatever."

"Gonna be hard to accuse her of murder after a review like that," Stu said, which was exactly what Laura was thinking as she stared at her own little rectangle on page seven.

Ruby cried, "We earned that review."

As if somewhere there was a cue, or a bell, people started drifting out of the tents and making their way to the coffee tent and the bathroom. They gathered in clusters and klatches, and laughed or spoke in hushed voices, gossiping and kvetching, sometimes comparing notes about what would sell and what was going to be on clearance a month after delivery.

Ruby snapped her paper shut. "Barry's on after this. You going to see the lazy Susan?"

"I'll just go to Jeremy's. There's like half an hour between, so we have an hour and some."

"Okay," Ruby said. "It's fifteen minutes until the next session. I'll be back before Barry even starts." She took off into the crowd, all smiles and pleasantness, with sunshine and rainbows coming right out of her ass.

CHAPTER 24.

L aura sat across from Stu, hogging a table when there were people more important and entitled than them waiting to sit. She glanced at him, he glanced back, and they moved their chairs from the coveted table, which was descended upon and covered with papers and phones before they'd even settled the chairs three feet away.

"Maybe you should take the dropper to someone who can detect what's in there," Stu said.

"It's vitamin D. I'm sure she's not poisoning someone every day."

"Do you ever think how crazy you have to be to kill someone? How many times a day do you want to commit murder, or how many times a month? And think about how few people actually do it. We're actually doing all right, as a species."

She had a hundred comments, all involving a question about his actual identity, because the man sitting next to her, saying that, was not the Stu she knew. Stu complained about horrible injustice and accused CEOs and media magnates of murder by proxy.

The crowd thinned again as the next show began, and they knew Penelope would be at Jeremy's in half an hour, but there was still no sign of Ruby. Laura's phone blooped. Chase's top ten pictures came in. Even though it was pointless and she'd have to cancel the editorial in *Black Book*, she wanted to see how the shots from the rooftop looked.

"Should we go look for her?" Stu asked.

"Why?" She shook her phone as if that would get the pictures to load faster.

"I don't know. Maybe she's chasing around a murderer?"

"What's Sidewinder going to do? Drag her behind a tent and poison her?"

"Don't forget Rolf. I don't think he's in custody for that girl behind the strip mall."

The pictures loaded. She didn't look at them because Ruby ran out from between two tents, her heels digging in the grass and forcing her to tiptoes, which would have been funny if her expression hadn't been so serious. Laura and Stu stood up and grabbed their bags and jackets.

"What?" Laura cried.

"Penelope's gone," Ruby panted, chest heaving from the run. "No one knows where she is. She wasn't at the Champagne & Trash show, and now everyone's talking about it." She jerked her thumb toward the bandshell. "Jeremy's seating now, and her chair's empty."

Laura pursed her lips and thought for a minute.

"What's on your mind?" Stu asked.

"If she killed Thomasina for abetting a prostitution ring, don't you think she might go after someone feeding models diet pills? Like Roquelle Rik?"

"You're grasping," Stu said.

"You didn't hear the story she told."

Ruby scraped the dirt off her shoes. "I saw Roquelle going into Jeremy's show. Everyone's there."

"We can get in through the back," Laura said. "He'll let me in. Come on."

It wasn't a far walk, especially since the crowds were all seated. The back entrance to the bandshell structure was around a corner and past a fence. She walked with purpose until she heard a siren, then saw flashing lights.

Laura turned and saw a trail of police cars speeding from road to grass to asphalt and stopping at the bandshell. In the other direction, an unmarked car parked in front of them.

Ruby grabbed her hand. "What did you do?"

"Nothing!"

Car doors opened and were left that way as cops armed to the teeth got out and ran into the big tent, fanning out in a formation only they could see. Cangemi exited another unmarked car and ran toward them. She waved, but his intensity made her feel ridiculous.

"You!" he shouted, pointing at her. "Get down!"

She froze, but Stu pulled her and Ruby down to crouch on the grass. When Cangemi reached them, he grabbed Stu and Laura by the collars and pulled them into a black and white car.

"What the heck?" she shouted as he stuffed Ruby in after her.

"Stay here. Just sit and stay. Don't move."

Not wanting to allow Cangemi to tell her the killer without getting in the first shot, she yelled, "It was Penelope!"

"If Penelope had three women tied to a broken boiler in Washington Heights, I'm about to get fired."

"Rolf," Stu said.

"We think he's after Ivanah Schmiller, so if you see her, give a shout." Cangemi ran to the bandshell with the rest of the cops, jacket vents flying behind him like a comic book hero.

Stu sat sideways on the seat, feet dangling outside. Ruby looked out the window and sighed. Laura, who felt trapped and infantilized by everyone around her, took out her phone to look at Chase's selects. Ruby leaned over to see.

"Oooh, that's incredible," she said when Laura flipped to Rowena in the sewn-shut dress, arms raised, looking for all the world as though she were about to drop from a rooftop into Manhattan. "Wait, I can see the wires."

"They're not retouched yet."

Laura flipped to the next one: Rowena in the trapezoid failure, jumping on the roof's shed. She looked as though she was flying. It was unbelievable. Breathtaking.

The police shouted and ran, and more sirens came from some unidentified part of the park. Laura flipped to the next picture, trying not to catalog all the ways she might have pissed off Rolf, and came to a close up of Rowena's face. She was monstrous, powerful, even without retouching. She was a beauty who could eat up an audience and spit out the bones.

When Laura zoomed in, she saw a little flaw that seemed unusual. Then she knew that the subtext of Rowena's gaze was the force of an unstoppable ambition because the flaw was not just a flaw. It was a little scratch on the eyeball, made in the death throes of someone who had stood in her way.

She explained the scenario to Ruby and Stu. She related her conversations with Roscoe Knutt, when he had told her of the little bit of membrane under Thomasina's fingernail. She told them how Rowena had inserted herself in the rooftop shoot almost immediately, and that Roquelle was at the corner table at Marlene X that morning. Rowena had gotten herself into the Hudson gown as if she knew she had the same measurements as Thomasina, and she had left the shoes in the bathroom because her feet were a size too big.

"I told Penelope I thought Rowena was too young," Laura said. "I was just making conversation. And now we can't find her, so I'm wondering, and I'm only wondering…"

"You think she's doing it to the next in line," said Stu.

"I know Penelope was at Marlene X this morning, but I don't know about Rowena. If Penelope started asking too many questions or trying to get her pulled off this season's roster because she's too young, that's a career-killer."

"Call Pierre," Ruby injected. "See if she was there this

morning."

"He won't pick up if he's at a show," Laura said. "Come on. Let's get out. Rolf's not going to do anything with all these cops around."

Stu didn't budge, blocking the way. "Roscoe Knutt's one of the greatest investigative journalists of all time, and you're handing him this story?"

Ruby pulled the opposite door handle, but it snapped back with a clack. "I can't open this side."

"What is it, Carnegie?" Stu asked, still not moving.

"Would you stop? It's you, okay. All you. He cornered me. Can we go find Penelope before she chokes on her own vomit please? Because there's not a cop in this city right now who would a, believe me, and b, give a crap."

She pushed him with her cast, and he got out of the car.

They decided to stick together by dint of the fact that there was a psychopath around, and both Laura and Stu had pissed him off in the recent past.

"Everyone saw her last at Ricardo Ofenhelb," Ruby said. "It was in the same tent as we had ours."

The tent was close by, and they stood outside, hearing the music thumpity-thump inside and seeing the security guard who was done checking tickets, but not done keeping people out.

They collectively decided, without speaking about it, to go around to the back.

Voices came from behind the fence. A woman said, "You don't cross me, and you don't threaten me. You don't get in my goddamn way."

Stu opened the gate, and the voice stopped. Just as she was about to head in, Laura rammed face first into Rowena, who was running like a bat out of hell in one of Jeremy's calf-length dresses for Fall.

"Sorry, I have to go!" Rowena tried to move toward the bandshell, but Ruby got in her way. After they slammed together, they paused and seemed to wonder what the other knew about their intentions. Rowena snapped out of it first, trying to get around Ruby.

"No, you don't," Ruby said and tackled the model with blunt force from her shoulder.

Rowena fell into the mud. Laura cringed at the soiling of Jeremy's seventy-seven dollar a yard (plus duty) fabric. "You killed her." Rowena was apparently not concerned with the fabric or with the accusation because she grabbed Ruby's ankle and twisted, sending her flying, then scrambled to her feet while her opponent was still stunned in shock at being felled so easily.

Laura was about to jump in when she heard Stu call her name from behind the gate.

She glanced at Ruby, who had Rowena down again and was using all the fighting skills she'd learned in the back alleys of Hell's Kitchen to keep the model down. Laura knew her cast made her useless, so she ran to check on Stu, who was picking Penelope Sidewinder up from a grassless patch behind the generator.

"She's not good," he said.

Laura ran back to Ruby, who had wrestled Rowena to the ground, belly down, and had one arm at the small of her back. "Why? Why did you kill her?" Ruby cried for her lost lover, twisting Rowena's elbow until she screamed.

The model saw Laura and said, "Get her off me. Jeremy starts in seven minutes. Come on. I was calling the cops when I saw Penelope was sick."

"Why?" Ruby twisted again.

"I didn't."

"You did," Laura said. "She was just one peg above you and the same measurements, and when Penelope came after you for being underage, you had to take her out, too. You're just too ambitious, Rowena."

"Like you're one to talk," Rowena said.

Laura swung her cast around and clocked the model in the head.

CHAPTER 25.

Laura didn't put any distance between herself and the police until midnight. Apparently, the fact that Rowena "allegedly" killed Thomasina and "allegedly" almost killed Penelope Sidewinder didn't play into Laura's favor, nor did the fact that Rowena was sixteen, meaning she'd assaulted a child. Cangemi read her her rights with no little relish. Then Uncle Graham had slowly (to her) and methodically (to him) secured her release.

She was approaching the train station and so very tired when Jeremy called.

"You didn't come," he said. She heard noise and music on his end. Must be a party. Must be swell.

"I was keeping Rowena Churchill from your show. I'm sorry."

"She was in a secondary set anyway. Where are you?"

"Outside the Times Square Station."

"Meet me at my place, would you?"

Twenty-Fourth Street and Second Avenue used to be a haven for drug addicts and prostitutes until the artists moved in during the 1970s with their plants and their handy habits and their eyes for making things pretty and nice. Jeremy had told her all about the place over five years of early-morning coffee. The building had been a chair factory until it went out of business for all the usual reasons and had been sold for fixture fees floor-by-floor over the next seven years. Jeremy moved in after Catherine Cayhill had departed, leaving paint blobs on the wood floor, a loft contraption that had to be dismantled, and windows so lovingly kept that light streamed in unfettered.

The lobby harkened back to the industrial roots of the building with exposed brick and aesthetically chipping paint, big lights hanging from the thirty-foot ceiling, and exposed vent work. The elevator was an automatic job, but the brass fixtures from the days of elevator men stayed, as well as the exposed wood frame of the freight lift. She thought it amazing that a perfectly functioning elevator could still be scary in the twenty-first century, but there it was, creaking as if the co-op board had paid more for that extra bit of tension in the ride, which Laura didn't need at all. Not even a little. Because she was going to see Jeremy St. James on a social call, which was enough to give her a heart attack. No one was ever invited to Jeremy's place. Business associates who had known him for years complained they'd never seen his fabulous loft.

She looked down at her outfit: striped maxi, black blouse, and a cast in a dark pink sling. It had been a long day.

The hall was short and had only two doors. She went to the one with the welcome mat. She stood at the door and waited. Breathed. Put her fist up to knock. Dropped it. Touched the red door. She steeled herself to knock, and Jeremy opened the door before her knuckles even touched it.

The top three buttons of his shirt were undone, revealing a little black hair on his chest. He pressed a phone between his ear and shoulder, and the fact that he was distracted, yet still had his eyes on her rendered her speechless. He motioned her in, and she tried to smile when she walked past him because she thought she was going to stop breathing.

She saw immediately why she'd never known anyone who'd been to the loft. Yes, it was gorgeous in all the usual ways. It had a huge open space with perfectly managed furniture, fat, full-color art books in the bookcases, and a fully functional kitchen that looked out into the bigger room. Just-right drapes in an inconsequential color because of the beauty of the texture hung over factory-sized windows. Exactly-as-they-should-be area rugs in the right plums and mosses lay on the cement floor. Not-too-warm-or-cool lighting illuminated the right knickknacks everywhere. Everything was so perfect that the thing that was *wrong* stuck out like a mutton chop sleeve on a dropped shoulder. Vents in ugly, flat white vinyl, horrible louvered things blasting white noise, marred the walls, so many she couldn't count them. Two were cut into the floors that she could see below, and above, she saw big vents ducting on the ceiling. By a doorway, she spotted a control panel with blinking lights and approached it cautiously.

"Look," Jeremy said into the phone, "every season you treat me right, and I'm grateful, but I think this way it would help both of us. It's where we can test new technologies. It fills out the high end side of the brand."

Laura glanced back at him, and he held up a wine glass, giving her a quizzical look. He was asking her if she wanted wine. God, it was too much. She was going to hurl herself out the window, but she nodded instead.

The blinking control panel was about the size of a sheet of paper and had a label that read Aire-pur 2100. There were buttons, dials, and little gauges with numbers she didn't understand.

"Yes, that's what I want. You let me know if you need any more information. I'm always here for you." He clicked the phone and dropped it on the counter. "Sorry about that. I couldn't be at the party another second. Too many people."

She drifted over to the kitchen area, where he was rummaging around under the counters, wondering if he had to be there to be with her, or if it was the Aire-pur 2100 he needed.

"I don't have anything decent," he said. "I had no time this week." He held out two bottles by the necks. The labels were a color, and they had words on them. And the humming of the machines drilled her brain and the salted smell of him was so close she wanted to close her eyes so she could breathe it in just a little deeper.

But she had to choose. Light label or dark. Smooth curve at the neck or not. Both blackened red. She looked at his hands on them and noticed the callous inside his right thumb where scissors rested as he cut thousands of yards of fabric. Before he was anyone. Before the shows. Before Gracie, probably. She reached out and touched his hand, looking for the place on his index finger where pins were pushed to cut, to drape, to sew, to bring dimension to flat fabric. And he let her. He let her touch his hand.

He put the bottles down, because who cared, really, which wine she wanted? And she didn't want wine. She wanted to look at his hands and touch the rough spots, and she did something that surprised her because one, she never imagined she'd be actually doing it. Two, she never made a conscious decision to lift his hand to her lips and kiss the cutting callous inside his thumb. But she did.

It was wildly forward for her, and it opened a floodgate. As her lips touched his hand, he grazed his face against her neck. Her knees went from under her, and he put his arm around her waist to hold her up. Was that why she had come? Yes, she knew it right away. It was what she came for and what he invited her for. It didn't feel ugly, but like the natural culmination of their friendship, finally.

They banged into furniture that had seemed so sparse a minute ago, with him steering her toward a room behind a closed door. My God, she thought, the bedroom. It was happening. With Jeremy. Happening. She doubted she could stop, pause, or slow it, but she had to.

"Jeremy?"

"Don't worry."

"No, Jeremy, really."

He had her pressed up against the doorjamb with her legs around his waist and his face buried in her neck, when he whispered, "I can't have kids, from the CF. Don't worry."

She wasn't thinking about that at all, though she knew she should have been.

He must have felt her stiffen. "Speak," he said, though she barely could.

"I'm sorry."

"Don't start that way."

"I have to tell you something."

"I don't care about the cast."

"Not that."

"Tell. Quickly. You're mine today, no matter what you say." His hands ran up her thigh and under her skirt.

Somehow, she made words. "I've never... you know..."

He actually stopped kissing her long enough to ask, "Really?"

She felt things cooling a half a degree and spoke quickly so they could get back to it. "My sister stole all my boyfriends, so I gave up and then... then there was you."

"You want to wait."

"No! I just don't want you to be surprised."

"Noted."

The bedroom door made a whooshing sound when he opened it.

He was nice. Very nice. Nice in a way that was not saccharine or cynical or fake. Just nice, even with her cast totally in the way. So nice, in fact, that she wondered who the hell she was dealing with. She wondered how that nice person had developed the cutting professional demeanor that was his trademark. In the next hours, he demonstrated a hundred little kindnesses. He got her water. He covered her when she was cold. He made sure her pillow was fluffed. He laughed a lot. In the six years she'd known him, she'd never seen him laugh as much as he did in those first hours of intimacy.

Jeremy, she thought, *I never knew you.*

"I shoulda just clonked you on the head and dragged you in here years ago, after this one day," he said. "It was seven thirty in the morning, and you were already in. I brought you coffee. I was pissed about something. Probably Gracie putting limits on me. We fought about that all the time. More than anything else. And there you were with the Harmony blouse on the form."

"The little stand ruffle collar."

"Yeah, you were working on the muslin because the collar wouldn't do anything."

"You wanted the impossible. It couldn't stand up and sit down at the same time."

"You were frustrated as hell. And I wanted to show you how to do it."

"Oh, God, I remember that! I thought you were going to fire me."

"I never had an employee slap my hand before."

"And I yelled." She buried her face in the pillow. "I'm sorry."

"You said something like, 'If I wanted the Shell answer man, I'd go work in a goddamn gas station.'"

"You just left the coffee there. I thought I was finished."

"I went back to my office, and I thought, my God, she cares. She really cares. And I started thinking of ways to keep you. I gave you that raise."

"Thank you."

He waved her off. "It wasn't what I really wanted to do, but when I saw Gracie again, I thought, if Laura were with me, she wouldn't keep me down. And by the way, you're beautiful. I always knew it, but after the hand slapping? You were it. You were the one. But it was impossible. For one, Gracie made sure everyone thought I was gay."

"Are you?"

"Shut up." He kissed her. "And for two, Gracie. And for three, do you have somewhere to be tonight? I don't want to keep you. But I'm not going in to the office for a couple of days."

"I'm going to have to call my sister at some point. We have a meeting with a backer in the morning."

"Ah, a magic backer. Someone to hold you down while lifting you up."

"I'm okay with it. I decided."

CHAPTER 26.

They didn't sleep. The sun came up, and he pulled some old samples from his closet. She fit into a sleeveless thing and a pair of cotton twill trousers that were only a little out of style. He helped her get her cast through the armhole, and he walked her to the street in sweatpants. He took off for his daily run, and she went to Marlene X.

She made an effort not to think too hard about Jeremy or the previous night. She kept her hopes high and her expectations low. She tried not to worry about the assault and battery charge against her. Or that Rolf Wente was still at large. She only wanted to think about how much money they needed to continue, whether or not she could get Yoni and Corky back online, and how much damage had been done with the Thomasina Wente affair.

There was the matter of time as well. The women who

had been found in Washington Heights all officially worked for her, and though she could cut them loose, she intended to give them jobs. But she needed a company, and she needed it to happen fast, before they got deported or picked up by someone else who wanted to hurt them.

Ruby was already waiting in line. The other girls looked as though they'd been partying all night, while Ruby looked as if she'd just stepped out of an editorial spread.

"Where were you last night?" Ruby asked.

Laura must have blushed fifteen shades of red because her sister raised her eyebrows. "Tell me about your night first."

"I was out at a few parties. No one knows who our potential backer could be. They're all saying there's no money for fashion anymore. They're all going into movie production to take a loss."

"I feel totally unprepared."

"Do you feel like you haven't slept? Because that's how you look."

"Can we talk about something else?"

"Where did you get those pants?"

They found Pierre already at the superstar corner table, tapping on his phone. He looked Laura up and down, then waved them to their seats. "Good morning," he said, "nice to see you." That was a completely ridiculous opener, and Laura was about to say something about it when he continued, "Your job is to be charming, as usual. But today, Laura will speak, and Ruby, dear, try to watch and not say anything too forward. There will be no flirting. Yes?"

"Yes," Laura said, gratified.

"Why?" Ruby asked.

"This individual is concerned with how things are made. Quality. I am sure commerciality will be important, but this person has been in the business a long time and knows the difference between something made beautifully and something made with expediency. This is why Laura should do most of the talking. Okay?"

They nodded.

"You're still wearing that absurd color on your arm."

"Sorry, I was busy."

"What on Earth is more important?"

The door behind her opened, and she was saved from having to answer. Pierre smiled and waved, and Laura clenched her fists and unclenched them, trying to release the tension before she looked at him or her, so she could be her most charming, sharp, erudite, and professional self.

She caught Ruby's smile and looked around. Jeremy stood behind her, wearing a jogging suit and a wide grin. She wondered what he was doing there, when she'd told him she'd be there and why, then she realized. Jeremy was her new backer.

She stood up so abruptly her chair almost fell. She looked at Jeremy and said, "Outside."

"Laura, really?" Ruby said.

Laura indicated Pierre and Ruby. "Stay here."

When she got onto Third Avenue, she found Jeremy at her heels, smiling, which enraged her further.

"Not acceptable," she said. "Not acceptable."

Jeremy shifted his feet in the morning chill. "What's the big deal?" he asked. "You need money, I have money. I believe in you. Look, I knew the Schmillers would bag for some reason or another. I stepped in months ago."

"Not acceptable."

"Why?"

"Were you *there* last night?" She lowered her voice. There were too many people around, and she was already ashamed to be having a lover's quarrel in the middle of the street. "Because what we were doing precludes us from being business partners, and it especially precludes me from accepting money from you."

"Oh, really?"

"This is exactly what happened with Gracie. You slept with her, and then she backed you, and she controlled you for your whole relationship. You're just redoing the whole thing again, except backward. Now you're the one with the cash, and what am I?"

"A pain in the ass?"

"You're not helping at all."

"I need you. I need you to mind the store with me. I can't do it all, and I trust you. You can do Sartorial any way you want. You guys did a fantastic line. I don't want to see it go under. You take my staff. Use my factories. But stand beside me. I bit off more than I could chew when I made my line bigger, and I can't make this happen alone."

"Are you my lover because you want to be in business with me, or are you in business with me because you want me to be your lover?"

"Why does it have to be a choice?"

"I can't see how both things won't go bad."

"Do you trust me?" he asked.

"I don't know."

That shut him up. He looked up at the buildings and closed his eyes halfway. She watched the curve of his jaw as he bit back whatever it was he was going to say.

Then he coughed twice, big phlegmy things that seemed only a prologue to more. "I have to get back. You have a week to think about the business part. The lover part is non-negotiable. You're mine." He kissed her quickly on the lips and jogged off.

She watched him weave through the crowd and turn left onto Twenty-Fifth Street with the grace of a cat and the confidence of a much bolder creature. It wouldn't matter to him in the end if she took his backing. He would push himself and get sick, and she would step in and run whatever part of his business she needed to, because as much as she wanted to choke the life out of him at that moment, she loved him. His death was non-negotiable, even if it meant an uncomfortable merger of sex and money.

He was right. She was his, and she knew it.

THE END

Acknowledgements

This book was written once without models. Three quarters through, I tossed it and started over. Lots of whining and puling ensued, and I have to thank my family for tolerating me, especially my husband, who is a superhero. He was totally behind me for NaNoWriMo, where I wrote those first 68 thousand trashed words, and thereafter, where I wrote what you see here.

I hate research. I hate it so much, I wrote a series of books about something I know so well, I'm the person people come to when they want to do research in the first place.

But, damn you imagination, new stuff keeps popping up.

So, I'd like to thank Art Van Hecke and the folks at leatherworker.net for help with a NaNoWriMo plot twist that got moved to a future story. Look for something about rare animal skins in *The Case of the Jealous Lover*. Or not. I have a way of deleting entire books.

Toward the editing phase of this book, I enlisted the help of Emily Schaller, an adult living with cystic fibrosis. This was way too late. Any errors within are completely mine, but I'll be making her crazy throughout the rest of the series.

My beta, Alisa Tangredi, knows more about my characters than I do. Thank you, Alisa, for letting my badly punctuated parade of damaged, insecure, acerbic garmentos into your mind.

Speaking of poor punctuation, thanks, Lynn, for trying so hard to teach me where the commas go (and don't) and for pointing out my tics and bad habits. I promise at least half of it gets into my long-term memory. Also, I'd like to shout out to Jim, one of my proofreaders who kept me from looking like a complete ass in *Dead Is the New Black* and has undoubtedly done so here as well. However, if I do look like an ass, it's probably my own fault.

The fashion industry is no joke. Life-choking dedication is not only encouraged, it is expected. Like working 60 hours a week, Skyping China at 9 p.m. from the office, and being so committed there's no time for family or... I don't know... novel writing. I have the only fashion job in Los Angeles where the most important thing is getting the job done. For this attitude I have to thank Anne, my boss, without whom I'd have a job at this other life-sucking company I won't name.

Renee Barratt of *The Cover Counts* helped with the cover and with overall partnership and friendship in my graphic design business. I won't tell you what she did, but doesn't it look great?

It would be a little peculiar to have an ugly book about designers. So my formatter is Heather Adkins. The fact that you're reading this right now, without little weird tags and oddball justifications, and the fact that it's so pretty in general, is due to her expertise.

The indie author community is lousy with whackjobs, narcissists, and psychopaths, which is what makes the sane communities I have found so precious. For the cream at the top of IWU, and that other little klatch who shall remain ever nameless, thank you for just being there. Sausage for everyone!

Christine DeMaio-Rice, Los Angeles, California.

Word-of-mouth is crucial for an author to succeed. If you enjoyed *Death of A Supermodel*, please consider leaving a review where you purchased it. It would be much appreciated.

About the Author

Christine DeMaio-Rice lives with her family in Los Angeles. She has been in the fashion industry for over twenty years, but would rather not talk about it.

Find Christine online at fashionismurder.com

Email her at sartorial.sandwich@gmail.com

Praise for

Dead Is the New Black:

The book was first-rate in terms of humor, characters, and plot. *Dead Is the New Black* is a witty, entertaining book you won't want to miss.

—*Silver's Reviews*

Dead Is the New Black is a complex novel, woven with delicate finesse by the author. At it's core is a heroine that underestimates herself on many different levels. But she's smart, talented, and takes it upon herself to get to the bottom of everything. Which gets her into trouble. I will say that I really enjoyed this book. It's been polished to perfection by the author and that really shows. The careful crafting and layering of details made me feel like a part of the novel, and not just a reader.

—*Quirky Gurl Media*

You are wholly ensconced into the mystery with Laura as she works to remove the suspicion off of herself, tries to find missing buttons, investigates her co-workers, breaks up a fashion counterfeiting ring, and we can't forget the fashion show!

—*Books-n-Beans*